The New Man

For Maude

JEFFREY WELKER

THE NEW MAN

Edited by Greg Dent
Cover by Lauren Grosskopf

Epidemic Books
Seattle

THE NEW MAN

An Epidemic Book
Published by Epidemic Books, Co. Ltd.
Seattle, WA

www.epidemicbooks.com

ISBN 978-0-9844417-7-8

Printed in the United States of America

Editor's Note: The following collection constitutes the accumulated personal writings and documents of the Duke Siemowit II of Masovia, scribed during the first half of the fourteenth century. The bulk of the pages were discovered embedded in the wall of a ruined tower in Wiskitki, Poland during recent (2014) renovations. While the history of the documents up until this point is lost to time, their modern journey is rather less complicated. The papers were graciously donated by the construction company to the local university, where they were cataloged, and through some fortunate familiar connections, Epidemic Books was able to acquire the originals on long-term loan for translation. The result now rests in your hands.

Most of the collected writings appear to be notes and reports made by the Duke during the course of his scientific experiments and other endeavors. Included with the scattered notes is a longer document that, by all appearances, can only be described as the manuscript of a memoir; there are a great many missing pages, and what remains has been somewhat edited and rewritten. Handwriting analysis does indicate that whoever wrote the original lines was almost certainly the same person who edited, crossed-out, and rewrote. This is mentioned here only for the sake of historical interest. Whether or not the memoir was abandoned during the Duke's lifetime, or its missing pieces lost over the course of centuries, we may never know. For those more interested in the scientific and historical aspects of the Duke's papers, the Editor has appended footnotes giving greater information on certain points. It should perhaps also here be noted that the Editor, despite his title, has merely served as an aggregator and compiler; the papers of the Duke have not been altered by any hand but his own. The Editor's only task has been to arrange them in an order that would make contextual and historical sense, and to add notes that would enlighten the reader, and in this endeavor, he hopes he has presented a complete and seamless work.

Translator's Note: Here at the onset, the Translator wishes to acknowledge the difficulty and hardship involved in his receivership of the succeeding documents. Medieval Polish is a language ungraced by simplicity, and in the course of this work, through diligent and persistent research and interviews, I have noted and corrected numerous defects in the translations and dictionaries prepared by others over the years. While the work of the Translator, as an abstract, is generally unsung, it is fervently hoped that in this case in specific, it will be noted how finely the instruments have been tuned to accompany the music of the language. If I have any regrets, it is only that, at the publisher's request, I have anglicized many of the beautiful names of the medieval people and places so as to make the work more accessible to the modern reader. I only hope, by addressing the larger audience, that I can draw greater attention to a much-neglected era of speech. May my endeavor show, blessed by the spirit of the Elbow-High, that it is not the size of the man that counts, but the size of the wake that his works leave upon the world.

Publisher's Note: While it is the publisher's hope that you, the reader, do enjoy this unique body of work, we regret to inform that this may sadly be our last publication. Through unforeseen circumstances, the original documents are now again lost, and the expiry date of the loan is rapidly approaching. It is hoped that perhaps sales of this book can fund a large enough grant to the school to assuage any ill will generated by this mishandling.

ŻYCIE SIEMOWITA PIASTÓW, JEST RELACJA Z CZASÓW I PRACY[1]

---

1   Translated as, "The Life of Siemowit of Piast, being an account of his days and work". Piast is the noble house to which Siemowit and his family belonged. The original document was written in contemporary fourteenth century Polish. A copy was then subsequently translated to Latin by either the Duke himself or someone in his employ, and a copy of the Latin work converted into cypher. All three copies were found in the same location. All three documents were weathered, and unreadable in passages. Each also contained some passages not found in the others. The original was used for the translation wherever possible.

1

By all accounts, the day of my birth was marked by storms and lightning crashes. Several of the horses of my father's stables were killed when a bolt struck the place and it crumbled around them. Naturally, this was taken as an omen by some of the peasants of the village and the servants of the castle. It is perhaps this singular fact that shaped my mind at that young age. The weather on the day of my birth resolved into legendary status in the castle, amongst the servants and pageboys who attended me all through my youth. Hardly a blustery day could pass before some old crone would mutter, with a kindly smile upon her face, that it reminded her "of the day of his lordship's nativity." To hear them tell it, it was a veritable Flood that washed over the Polish frontier that October day; the sky rent itself from horizon to horizon, and the thunderous racket was enough to shake the stones from the walls of the granary tower in the courtyard[2]. I have even heard some of them tell that the lake and the river froze over in the night and birds were seen to fall from the sky, their blood frozen solid in their veins. In the morning, a thick layer of snow had fallen, reaching almost to the tip of the gateposts, and a thick coat of ice had grown upon the castle walls.

My mother, of sainted memory, was confined for some time after my birth, the delivery having been uncommonly difficult.[3] My wet-nurse was a peasant woman called Gudmunda, who had nursed several of the babes of the castle, my cousins and my subsequent siblings—even some

---

2   Archaeological surveys conducted at the ruins of Siemowit's childhood home do seem to confirm severe damage to the walls of the granary tower, but whether this occurred at the time of his birth cannot be ascertained with any degree of certainty. The methods used to repair such damage would have remained the same for some decades prior to and after the Duke's birth.

3   The Duke's mother, the Princess Sophie, was the daughter of the Grand Duke of Lithuania, a family connection that would serve the Duke well in his later life, and not so well.

of the babes of servant-women. She was handsomely paid and made her living with her teats. I have fond memories of her, for even into my boyhood, she was still in the castle, as there always seemed to be a new babe to be suckled amongst the many relations who came to live there in the early days of my life. Later, I was to find that most of these "cousins" were the illegitimate children of my father[4].

From an early age, I learned my letters and sums. My tutor was a Russian count called Tetchkov, exiled to Masovia for some reason I did not know at the time[5]. He had, of course, heard the tales of my birth day, and so to start me on my lessons in sums, he would instruct me in the making of scientific devices to measure the speed and direction of the

---

4   While unconfirmed, contemporary sources indicate that the Duke's father, Bolesław II, was indeed quite the ladies' man, and rumors were rampant in the area for decades after his death that the old duke had fathered upwards of fifty children out of wedlock, mostly upon peasant or servant women. A description as given by a guest of Bolesław and Sophie at a banquet given sometime before the birth of the Duke: "The Duke (Bolesław) is gregarious and loud, tall and sturdy like an ox and so besotted with every serving wench to lay a platter before him, the girl-folk titter amongst themselves when they see it is their turn to serve him, and only the least comely is spared his groping hand."

5   Dmitri Alexandrovich Tetchkov (1263-1313), Count of Tetchkovoye. Son of a Russian nobleman and himself educated in Constantinople, where he had been taken as prisoner during one of the innumerable wars between the Russians and the Turks, he escaped by garroting his jailer with a cord made of his own hair and swimming the Bosphorus to safety in Greece, where he sold his services as a translator and scribe to pay his passage north. Upon reaching Masovia, he was hired as the tutor of the Duke's children, but this position lasted only as long as Siemowit needed him. He left the service of the Duke and attempted to return to Russia but was waylaid on his journey and press-ganged by the Teutonic Knights, for whom he fought in several battles before assassinating his superior officer and attempting to escape to Sweden on a lumber ship. His body was found in an abandoned prison on an island off Lithuania in 1315, where it was estimated he had died two years before. His life remains a mystery from his escape to Sweden to his death, a period of some ten years, and it is indeed tempting to think of this Russian count as worthy of a picaresque tale of his own.

wind. He would have me trace and plot the flight of birds that passed my window upon a grid. The first blossoming of the cherry trees in the yard, or the first spring flower he would have me chart, and over the months a great catalogue of data was compiled under his guidance, so that even today I am able to go back and with some small effort discover the weather on a date when I was but a boy of six, when the first crocus popped up from the earth in the spring of 1287, which direction the wind was blowing at bedtime on Saint John's Day of the same year. It was and remains a great source of comfort and indeed of power to me, this totaling up of the natural world. It has remained a lifelong pursuit, one that I cannot imagine going one single day without. Even today, upon waking, the first thing I do is to peer out my window with a pen in hand, and note down the time, the speed and direction of the wind, the shape of the clouds and their temperaments[6], the first bird I see or hear singing[7]. The world is merely a vast compendium of data waiting to be accumulated and studied, and once it has been compiled, then the serious work of making sense of life and creation can begin. This is, of course, my only aim in life.

To those ends, under the guidance of my tutor, I

---

6   In his minor work, *Vivum Aeri*, or *The Living Sky*, Siemowit classifies the clouds based upon their shapes and how they travel across the sky, assigning them aspects, or "temperaments", as he calls them. There are "jagged" clouds, "wispy and uneven at their edges, who scuttle across the sky like slow beetles, and putting into the hearts of them below a vague sense of jitteriness, a sense of forgetting something." There are "lumbering" clouds, "vast mountains of white froth, sailing slowly through the heavens, bringing with them a peaceful sense of quiet, of completeness, but tinged with a faint restlessness, almost as though saying 'The hard labor is now done, allow yourself to wander a moment.'" The only known copy of this work resides in the Vatican Library.

7   Siemowit also developed a system which attempted to predict how one's day would transpire based upon the first bird seen or heard in the morning. Larks portended a "musical" day, one filled with joy and sparkling with life. Robins meant a day of "happy labor", while ravens, surprisingly, foretold an "industrious day filled with rude chatter".

engaged in the rudiments of scientific experimentation. My first dissection was under his watchful and educating eye; it was of a sparrow that had landed upon the casement of my window. I had caught it with quick reflexes and the aid of a sturdy overturned flagon. The first part of the experiment was to time how long it would take the little bird to suffocate within its confine, and once the little fellow had expired, my tutor showed me how to spread it upon a makeshift dissecting table, pinning the wings and feet just so, and I watched as he carefully made the incisions and catalogued for me the innards and mysterious pathways of the sparrow's inmost cavities.

As the months went on, we graduated upward, from rats and other vermin that lurk in the darkness of even the most well-kept castle, to stray cats that I caught while out walking in the village of Płock, which was near the castle.[8] From the time of my first initiation into the mysteries of science until the departure of my tutor when I was ten years old, I must have dismembered several hundred animals, mostly birds and cats, but on some very fortunate occasions, even a dog, a fox, or a stoat found its way onto our table.

I learned to measure the volume of each creature's blood, to identify its humours, weigh and sum up its organs. I calculated the length of time it would take various species to expire from loss of blood, or exposure to cold or heat. I created a chart to classify the types of sounds each animal made as it died. In short, there was no aspect of these creatures' lives, or rather deaths, that I could not, and did not, quantify.

Eventually, our experiments focused more closely upon the brains of these beings, and we spent hours and countless efforts attempting to extract that clear fluid from the brains

---

8   A civil proclamation on display in the Płock City Museum and dating from 1288 warns the townsfolk that "the possibility exists of some large wolf or bear stalking the streets at night, for innumerable cats have gone missing of late."

of them that my tutor called "ichor" but which I learned to call by a different name, that he had learned from the Turks, who in turn had learned from the Egyptians, who had been instructed by the ancient Greeks, and this was the essence of life itself. But, our search was fruitless; we found no such ichor in our subjects. My tutor was convinced that ichor, then, did not exist, whereas I developed the theory, later in my life and after much further investigation, that ichor merely was not present in animals.

The Monastery of the Blessed Virgin Mary was located nearby in Płock, and from the monks there, my father had commissioned several fine Books of Hours and a very large illuminated Bible. I learned my letters on these, and thus also became intimately familiar with the religion of my native country. My father and mother were not overtly religious, but the Catholic faith was and is strong in Poland. I grew up with a fear of God and of Hellfire, but as my scientific studies went on, I found myself more and more amazed at the intricate workings of the living machine, and so my respect for the Creator grew boundlessly, and I was constantly, it seemed, filled with awe at the things He had created and how He had brought them into being and how they worked.[9]

When I was five years old, my mother the Princess Sophie died. My brother Trojden was but a year younger than I, and our sister Anna was a babe, still at the tit of Gudmunda. Our father remarried three years later, a woman called Kunigunde, daughter of the King of Bohemia.[10] In time, they would give me three new siblings, two sisters and

---

9   At this place, the line "But it would not be long before I rejected the God of my father and turned to the golden light of science and knowledge." has been crossed out.

10   And thus Siemowit became a cousin by marriage to his great enemy John of Luxembourg, who would marry the daughter of his father's new wife's brother.

a brother.[11]

The three years of my father's widower-hood was a time I remember fondly of collecting insects and closely examining them with my tutor, or catching fish in one of the lakes on the castle grounds, eating it in the privacy of my rooms and then examining the skeleton, drawing it faithfully and carefully in one of my notebooks. In short, it was a time not all that different from the rest of my childhood, although I remember vividly a steady stream of various servants coming and going from the employ of the castle; it seemed every week brought a new, pretty, fresh-faced girl to work in my father's house, and just as often as they were set up, off they would go to be replaced by another girl, still prettier and fresher-faced.

As we grew, my brother Trojden and I often were at odds, fighting and sparring with one another. But with the arrival of our new siblings, we, almost as though by consent, drew closer, as though we saw the new children as a threat to us. My tutor attempted to teach Trojden some of same lessons I had mastered, but once my brother had the rudiments of his letters and numbers down, he wanted no more of education. This seemed to be very disheartening to my tutor, and it was not long after this that he left the employ of my father and went on his way. I am not sorry to say that still I miss him very much.

I continued my scientific experiments just as my tutor had taught me, and even endeavored to develop new methods and investigations. With my own hands, I invented new instruments. I went often to the observatory at the Monastery and spent many nights with a quill in one hand and vellum across my lap, charting the positions of the stars and planets and the moving objects of the upper air. And often, I was joined in my nocturnal studies by a young monk

---

11   It is the brother Wenceslaus who figures most prominently in Siemowit's life.

called Adelbert.

Adelbert was a German, from Braunschweig, who had come to Poland as a youth and joined the order. He was, I suppose, barely out of his youth. Many nights I spent with him in the observing tower, the both of us silent and intent on our work. And often, as the sky would begin to pinken with morning light, he would lead me down the stairs and through the grounds of the monastery, through the gardens, and I would ask him what plant was this and what flower was that and what herb was what. From him, I began the rudiments of my learning of apothecary, which I took to as a lark to springtime.

I would return to the castle and spend hours scouring the grounds, searching for flowers and buds and herbs that grew wild, or in the kitchen gardens. I would collect them, and bring them to the monk, who would instruct me as to their properties and uses. And of course, all this knowledge I would write down and embellish as more and more information was given to me. These, too, I would draw flawlessly in my notebooks, and soon the collection of herbalism I had amassed was envied even by the monk, though surely this was one of his Deadly Sins.[12]

I learned through experimentation to make tinctures and powders from the seeds and leaves and flowers I had collected, and likewise through experiments I ascertained their uses. Once, I burnt my forearm with a candle quite badly, for the sole purpose of testing whether a poultice I had made of chickweed and comfrey would aid in healing. To satisfy the curiosity of posterity: the poultice worked like

---

12   True enough, one of Siemowit's herbological treatises, *Usus ac natura plantarum Masovia*, or *On the Nature and Uses of the Plants of Masovia*, is held in the collection of the Polish National Library.

a very miracle.[13]

In the autumn of my eleventh year, my uncle, my father's brother Konrad Duke of Czersk, died, and through this death my father was elevated to power over all of Masovia. My father grew confident with his new title and the next year went to war to claim the Crown of Poland. I went with him. I was not a fearsome soldier, but I knew how to handle a horse and a sword. It was a brief war and I saw little action, but it was there on the battlefield of Krzywiń that I killed my first man. My father saw the whole thing, and praised me as a natural fighter, which I knew I was not, and held me up to the other soldiers proudly as a model. I was profoundly embarrassed, but comported myself as a Duke's son should in front of his vassals. As long as I live, I will never forget that sensation of my sword entering the man's body, the slight resistance when the tip met his skin, followed by the almost imperceptible rush as the mounting pressure is no longer able to be combated and the sharpness bites into the flesh, digging deeper and deeper into the muscle and tissue of the human organism. I remember the man's blood splashing onto my greave, and it was all I could do not to clamber down from my horse and run off to find some way of preserving it, so that I could have it and keep it and study it whenever I so desired.

He fell from his horse, a deep and jagged wound in his shoulder and neck. His eyes lolled and bulged, like a spooked horse. I looked down at him and he up at me, and I realized that to him, he was seeing the last thing he would ever see, and it was the man who had killed him. I was very moved by this, and I suddenly and without forethought knelt beside him, watching intently as his life's blood spilled

---

13   Or perhaps not. In one of his more charitable moments, John of Luxembourg remarked to one of his generals that Siemowit "was fearsome to look upon from the standpoint of handsomeness. One can only imagine the improvement that would have been made had he let that candle consume his face rather than merely his arm."

from the gaping tear in his neck and drenched the grass and dirt beneath us. I watched it spurt in time with his fading pulse, the bursts coming less and less frequently, less and less strongly as the animating fluid leaked out of him. An idea came to me, and I removed the kerchief I wore around my own neck to keep the sweat and grime from my skin. I clamped it onto his wound, not to stop his blood but to soak it up. When it was drenched as a sheep in a rainstorm, I tucked it sopping into my boot. I thanked the man and stood, feeling the warmth of his blood trickling down my shin and onto my foot.

When I returned to my rooms in the castle, the bloody rag was stiff and dried. Using a knife, I scraped what I could from the kerchief into a small glass phial. I had no way of reconstituting it, but I was pleased enough that I was able to save even this small sum, which amounted to hardly more than a few flecks of what looked like crimson crystal. I still have and cherish this small phial; it sits before me now, on my desk, a constant reminder of my beginnings, and of the humble and human thoughts I had at that moment.

Though my father made peace and did not attain the Crown, he was stronger than ever before in Masovia. Partly as a result of this, more and more peasants began arriving at the castle, seeking some sort of work, of which there was now a great deal more, since my father had inherited vast amounts of territory and merchandise upon his accession. There were hundreds more horses to be cared for, dozens more nobles and their retainers to cater to. New buildings had to be built, storehouses, stables, barracks. In short, there was an influx of people into Płock and into the castle.

One of these influxes was made my new page. He was of an age with me, or perhaps one or two years younger. He was called Kazimir, and he would become my first true helper. He had previously been the serving-boy to a great Saxon lord who had brought him along on a journey to the Holy Land, but had died en route, in Płock, as chance happened. His Saxon master had been a great scholar of some note, and had imparted much of his knowledge to the young man, and he was more than willing...[14]

[pages missing]

---

14 At this point, the manuscript is missing several pages. As the Duke did not number his pages, it can only be estimated how many are lost from this first section. When the tale resumes, the Duke is in his middle-teens, and the boy Kazimir does not appear again by name. His identity remains unknown, as does the "great Saxon lord" who was his first master. A veritable cottage industry has developed over the years in scholarly circles in determining the identity of this Saxon. The Duke makes several oblique references to him later in this work, and from the references it can be inferred that the Duke, at least, felt he owed the mysterious Saxon a debt of knowledge and expertise.

2

[pages missing]

...a great delivery of the Knights' gold.[15] As the Duke's eldest son, I was entitled to a share, which I duly withdrew from the Treasury. Some of it I banked away, but some I set aside for my scientific purposes.[16] The gold allowed my father to strengthen his army, which had again seen war the previous year.

On my eighteenth birthday, I received from my father the village of Wiskitki, which I cherished in my heart from the time of my childhood summers there. It is from my lodge here that I write this record of my life, and I have spent parts of many years of my reign here. It has fitted the purposes of my life almost as though it was created specifically for me, and for any whim that might fire upon the convoluted, brilliant workshop of my brain. It is from here that I have made my most significant advances in the sciences of the natural and hidden world.

Wiskitki is a small and rural village, surrounded by forest, and the winding, slow-moving Pisia Gągolina River wends through its farms and flatlands. Wheat and potatoes

---

15   The manuscript resumes at this point, in the midst of relating the arrival of a modest sum of gold paid to Siemowit's father by the Teutonic Knights. The historical record of this transaction, which is housed in the State Museum in Vilnius, Lithuania, shows that the Knights paid the sum of "50,000 florins" to Bolesław II in 1301, likely to pay for his allegiance in various border disputes with Bohemia and Lithuania.

16   By this time, it is apparent that Siemowit has developed an interest in the uses of gold in his scientific exploration. Whether at this time he had learned the rudiments of alchemy, and from whom, is open to speculation, as this section of the manuscript ends prior to the actual experiment is conducted. At the very least, Siemowit has some idea that gold can be used as a medium of some sort, whether it simply be smelting, or something more elaborate. This passing reference to banking is most likely to one of the Jewish houses of the city of Płock; the local nobility often put a percentage of their monies into these primitive banks.

were grown on my father's lands here, and in the springtime the river was a sparkling blue ribbon snaking through a green, blooming patchwork of fields. There was only one road leading in and out of the village, and from the stone outcrop where my lodge was later built, one could look from west to east and see the road threading itself into the misty distance, like some long slithering brown worm slowly making its way across the land.

It was along this road, also in springtime, that the Gypsies would travel in their caravan. Their arrival was an annual event, and occurred usually in the first weeks of April. The villagers begrudged the wanderers a place in their fields and a fair-like atmosphere ruled for a week or so while the olive-skinned pedlars went about, staying aloof from, yet also preying upon, the simple folk of Wiskitki.

In the first April of my overlordship of Wiskitki, I purposely traveled to the village for the arrival of the Gypsy caravan. I had seen Gypsies in Płock on a few occasions, and had always been struck by their colorful garb, their vast array of trinkets and tools, and their seemingly bottomless well of expertise at the making and fashioning of nearly any kind of article. I had seen a Polish lord, in sport, demand from a Gypsy artisan a halter made of birch, sea-grass, and ostrich feathers, and in mock-magnanimity, offer to return in two days to retrieve it. With no expression whatever that would betray his inner thought, the Gypsy replied only to this pompous lord that six hours only would be needed. I myself made a point of returning to his stall later in the evening, around the time the Gypsy had specified, and had seen the delivery of what was undoubtedly a beautiful, delicately made halter to the Polish lord, who stood with jaw agape, and who readily parted with a large sum of gold florins for the small masterwork he had so jokingly ordered.

But, more than all that, it was the air of otherworldliness that surrounded the Gypsy folk that intrigued and, to some degree, frightened me. They seemed to me the original people of the world, that the rest of humanity was some bastardized descendant of theirs. I do not mean to imply that God created the Gypsies first, or that Adam was a Gypsy. I am referring more to the natural order of things, that is outside the bounds of Rome and the Holy Father, the knowledge that is subsumed by religion and the Bible. The Gypsies are a mysterious people, insular and loyal only to themselves, and it seems to me that they possess a knowledge of the world that surpasses our greatest scholars, that even the wormiest grandmother of them could debate the origins of the universe with our sainted clerics and likely score a point or two. I found myself, in those times in Płock, lingering to overheard their conversations, and though their language was almost like mine, it was different enough that I could make out very little, and the similarity was enough that I could almost believe that they were speaking the real version of my own tongue, and the reason I could not understand them was that I had learned the wrong way of speaking. Everything about them, their skin, their eyes, their hair, the beauty of their children and the vibrancy in the colors of their cloth, the litheness of their movement, the restless nature and their seeming innate ability to know and utilize the earth, all of this made a great impact upon me as a young man, and so that first April in Wiskitki, I arrived in high anticipation, eager again to immerse myself in this foreign, and yet so utterly strangely familiar, group of wanderers.

That April was cold, and a dust of snow still sprinkled the ruts of the road and lay in dirty rills in the ditches beside the path. I was dressed still in furs when I rode into town, and my breath made little clouds that dispersed before my face. I came to the dwelling of the village hetman, who made a great show of his obeisance to his new lord, and gave me a place to sleep in his home, sending his older sons to sleep in the hayloft.

The Gypsies had arrived the previous morning and had set up their camp in a field that banked the river. There were about a dozen of them, of all ages, but there were four or five youths in the caravan, one of whom was a talented minstrel. He sang the songs, he told me, of Greece and Thrace, where he and his sister were from. From him I learned a few phrases of Greek, and how to carve a pipe from the soft wood of the sapling of a spruce, on which I also learned a delightful air.

I delighted, each morning, in seeing their brightly painted wagons standing in a circle on the frosty field. The swatches of bright, gay fabric overpowered the gloom of the overcast sky: a flutter of crimson splashed with saffron wafted in the light breeze, alongside gonfalons of aquamarine and tyrian. The wagons were rickety and well-traveled, and each had surely seen enough births and deaths within its thick oak walls to warrant a Domesday Book for each wagon. I would come down from the hetman's cottage to the circle of wagons and watch them lay out their wares on vibrant, woven blankets. Sometimes, the morning clouds would splinter for just a moment, and the rays of the golden sun would shine down on the trinkets of silver and worked metal, making them sparkle like rude gems. I admit that once, it was simply this trick of the light that led me to purchase a filament of spun wire.

On the last day of the Gypsy fair, I spent the morning with their barber, who had a collection of herbs and metal shavings and some of the tools of my methods of science. Camphor, which I had attempted to distill from the oil of evergreen, he had in no small quantity. I have used it before in culinary experiment, but I was attempting, at the time, a balm for snakebite, and the major ingredient I was still missing was camphor. I bartered a small amount from him, and also a good quantity of his silver flake and phial of mercury. The Gypsies are notorious, of course, for never divulging the sources of their merchandise, but from half-hints, I gathered that this fellow had traveled through Heidelberg within the last year.[17] From him as well, I obtained a worn vellum manuscript in the Arab tongue, which I spent several years attempting to decipher.

In the evening, before the Gypsies began to pack up, for they always left in the night, I sat with their crone, their seer-woman. I had met charlatans before, men who had come to my father's castle purporting to know the future and costing him richly in their deceit, but never before in my life had I ever met someone who so exuded the truth of farseeing as this old woman. To sit beside her, even without speaking, was to feel pulsing from her body wave upon wave of future time, your own and all mankind's. Her eyes were milky but alert, and I knew that she had locked them onto me long before I had picked her out of the bustle of the crowd.

I settled beside her wordlessly. She was expansive on her colorful woven blanket, though her frame was brittle and small, like a withered stalk that had been overlooked in the reaping, still holding its roots fast to the living soil. I nodded to her, as it was apparent we shared no tongue. She grinned at me, friendly but predatory all at once. To this day, I can still recall the scent of her, wafting to my nostrils on the light evening air: onions, sweat, cut grass. Overhead, the sky was clouding up, great rolling gray pillows swimming high above, interlacing and making a thick cover.

She sat, looking at me expectantly. I had never sat with a true seer before, I had no idea of the protocol, but I had the distinct sense that she was waiting for me to observe some unspoken, unwritten set of rules that all who come to her seeking assistance were required to perform. I erred on the side of a sacrifice. With a groping hand, I found a modest sized stone in the patchy grass beside us, and taking it up, I searched above us, my eyes darting, searching the pale gauze

17   A notable comment, for even Siemowit would have known of the renown of the University there, and the "science" practices in some of the circles there would have been very familiar to him.

of the sky for anything that moved. I locked upon a passing raven. With only a half-conscious awareness of the wind and distance, I loosed the stone, flinging my arm in a sharp arc. She and I together watched as the stone shrank from us, higher and further than I had intended, and yet some fluke of the wind or some other providential event drew the stone like a magnet to an ingot of metal, striking the raven and knocking it out of the sky. We watched it fall, landing with an audible sound some small distance from us. I sent one of my servant boys to fetch it, and when he returned with it, I saw the stone had split the skull of the bird in half. The shattered skull was not as messy as I had assumed it would be; perhaps the gore had dispersed in the air as it fell.

Solemnly, I held the bird in my upturned palms, and offered it to the Gypsy seeress. She nodded, still smiling. Taking the bird from me, she rummaged with one hand in a pocket of her worn cassock-like dress, and drew out a filthy square of silk. At first glance I assumed it was her nose linen, but upon closer inspection, I saw the stains upon the silk were more like blood and bile. The smile faded from her face and she held the spilt skull of the raven over the square, letting whatever fluids remained there drip like a viscous rain onto the silk.

The breeze, the slight tremor of the woman's hand, the jagged crack in the raven's skull, all of these helped to create the pattern that sprinkled onto the little square, and when the skull was drained, she tucked the carcass under her arm and closed her eyes, muttering in some far-off tongue that I strained to remember the sounds of, so I could later go back and catalogue them, perhaps someday to discover her incant.

Her eyes suddenly flew open and she grabbed and took my right hand in both of hers, palm up. She spit onto it, a phlegm-y glob, a grey oyster of her throat, and with her left fingers swirled it in a spiral to the edges of my palm. Then, she angled my fingers so the sputum ran down and dripped off, meeting with the raven's fluids on the silk. She released my hand and leaned over, her nose nearly touching the vile mixture she had just created.

She sat there, hunched over her work, for some long time before she finally sat up; I could hear her backbone creaking as she righted herself. It was sunset now, and the clouds overhead had looked as though a great inferno had exploded in the heavens, burning savagely just behind this merciful shielding layer of gray. I was surprised to find my heart racing, pounding in my chest; it was a wonder that she did not hear it, or if she did, it was a thing that had ceased to be remarkable to her. She yawned widely, her mouth seeming to expand and drink up all the nearby air, so that I myself felt a tightness in my chest, as though I was not inhaling deeply enough.

Shutting her mouth, she gleefully laughed and nodded at me, urging me on. I was at a loss as to what more she could want. Instead, she began to speak in her language, rapidly, as though in tongues, without pausing, without breath. She spoke for some long time like this, until it seemed she was an inexhaustible cavern of the winds, given the power of speech. I let this wash of words spill over me, insensible to a thing she was saying. My heart was breaking as I sat, still and dumb, that I would never know the majesty of whatever was pouring forth from this woman, whose eyes saw not only this world but who knew how many others.

Suddenly she stopped, and tumbled over, exhausted. At that same moment, beside me my serving boy slumped over against me too, and from his lap fell a vellum covered with tiny writing; a quill was still clutched in his fingers, and the words he had somehow written were not in ink, but rather in the gore of the raven's skull that had poured onto the silk. I can attest to my dying day that the boy knew not his letters before that moment, and had never had cause or opportunity before to take quill to vellum. I peered down at the miraculous writing, the whole leaf covered in a neat, though quickly-written, hand. And the greatest shock of all revealed itself to me as I latched my eyes onto what the boy had written, for although the woman had spoken in her unknown Gypsy speech, my boy had written her words in perfect Latin, which I could decipher as easily as my own tongue.

The seer-woman was still on her side, now asleep. I rose and tossed several gold florins onto her blanket. Taking up my boy in my arms, I carried him back to the hetman's lodging and gave him over to one of the servants there. I went up to my rooms and pored over the Gypsy woman's long-winded ramble. A chill set itself in my bowels and spread throughout me, slowly creeping up my spine to my skull then down again, leeching out of my toes and into the stone floor. The room itself seem to grow colder as I read her words. The more I read, the more my heart struggled to take its next beat.[18]

The ecstasy into which I fell when my eyes read the last words cannot be described. I felt at once drained of all my vital energies, and yet overfilled with purpose and confidence. I left Wiskitki that evening, my servant boy now riding at my side in a place of honor, full of ideas and already composing in my head the experimental treatises that would result from the massive and holy work I was formulating on the road home to Płock.

---

18 No transcript of the Gypsy woman's prophecy has survived the centuries. The Duke, however, writing in retrospect, seems well-pleased with what he read. As a side-note, the Gypsy caravans stopped at Wiskitki until just before the First World War.

[pages missing][19]

---

19   There is here another large gap in the memoir of Duke Siemowit. In 1915, however, a fragment was discovered in a copy of the *Oxford English Dictionary* at the National Library of Wales, probably used as a place-marker. It was forwarded to the preeminent Polish history scholar then working in Europe, David Proctor-Hedges, who conclusively placed the fragment within the canon of the Duke's papers. Through extensive research and investigation, the fragment has been placed chronologically here and is presented without comment. Professor Proctor-Hedges, sadly, was killed at the Battle of Ypres just five weeks after his work on this fragment.

3

[pages missing]

...[Hi]s body was scarred and twisted, and some of the men were afraid to approach it. I, however, was not, and boldly I strode through the ranks of the cowards to where the stricken boy lay. He appeared to me as a youth of some years fewer than I, perhaps still a boy. He could barely speak, but I managed to draw from him that he was the house-boy of the innkeeper called Ignacz. His skin was roasting hot, and I began to sweat somewhat kneeling beside him, even though the night was cold. The boy was burning alive, in addition to the rest of the horrors visited upon his form.

I collected him up, careful to wrap him tightly in a horse blanket, and tied him to my saddle. I paid off the men I had brought, though the cowards received less than I had promised them before, but enough to keep them silent. I rode with my gruesome prize back to the castle, where I brought the boy straightaway to the lowest cellar of the keep, where even the cook and kitchen-boys rarely went, for there was always a shin-deep layer of stinking green water down there. I placed the boy gently on a stone counter and arranged him on his back, as comfortably as I could make him. I settled in to wait for him to awaken.

It must have been past midmorning when he finally began to stir. One thin, malformed leg stretched slowly out from under the blanket, like some new-grown shoot pushing up from the dirt into the sunshine for the first time. Instantly, I was on my feet, ignoring the sloshing fetid water that overtopped my boots and chilled my feet. I pulled the blanket off him and peered down at him, searching for any sign of improvement or decline in the night. He appeared, however, the same as before.

His agony, however, must have lessened, or perhaps his capacity to experience it had diminished somehow. He no longer squirmed and sputtered. Instead, he merely lolled his head from side to side, in slow arcs. The heat no longer rose from his body as from a cauldron, and so I placed my hand upon his chest, to feel the pace of his heart. It beat steadily, and without distress.

I went up to the kitchens and fetched him a hunk of bread and a flagon of water. I also threw my sabretache over my shoulder, for it contained some of my tools. I helped the boy to sit up and poured a small quantity of water down his parched throat. He lay back down and docilely allowed me to measure him up. With calipers and woven string, I tallied the length of his arms and legs, twisted though they were, and the circumference of his skull and trunk, amongst many other measurements. I noted the color and shade of his eyes and skin, his hair and I scraped into a glass phial the dirt from under his fingernails.

I opened one of the sores on his chest and let it dry in the air, to see how long it would take. I opened another, and collected the vile humor within. He made no indication that he had felt either of these incisions. I began to wonder if indeed this boy had lost his ability to feel pain, or rather was his mind merely overtaxed by his illness? I began to contemplate opening his skull to examine the human brain for the first time.

Once, he turned his head to the side and vomited a long stream of black bile. I dabbed at the rivulets of it that trickled from his lips. Eventually, he regained his faculty of speech. He was called Jaromir, and he did not know his birthday. He became my first human subject.[20]

For several days I left him there in the cellar, visiting him often and making new measurements and calculations. Eventually, I learned all I could from his living body, and

---

20 The Duke made meticulous notes on all his human and animal experiments, in a cipher which the endeavors of the Publisher and its agents have been unable to decode.

decided that his death would open a new door to knowledge for me, and so one evening I visited him with a bowl of broth into which I had crushed a large amount of datura seeds. He grew sleepy rather quickly after drinking the broth, and in short span of time fell asleep and did not awaken.

I quickly went to work, once I had established that his heart had indeed ceased its regular work. From my tools, I withdr[ew]....

[pages missing]

4

[pages missing][21]

...But for this, I felt more and more sure that I would need to begin with a human in the full bloom and vigor of life. There was no shortage of potential specimens at the castle, but my own sense of ownership made me shy from using them. For several weeks running, I made regular forays into Płock and surrounding villages, eyes always searching for the strong, the healthy and hale, yet the ones who would not be missed. Stable-boys, blacksmith apprentices, masons. Folk like that ran off frequently and were never hunted with much alacrity. By the time a runaway apprentice could be tracked down, a master could have taken on two or three others, and garnered from their parents the fees that went along with apprenticeship.

The Monastery of the Blessed Virgin Mary, where I had had my celestial tutelage under the monk Adelbert, kept an orphanage, and often bonded out children to tradesmen as well, and I even once went to the place and looked over a roomful of pale, sickly, worn children, none of whom I could imagine undergoing the rigors of what science would do to them in my hands.

One evening, just as the clouds had faded from slate to coral, I was riding past a farm on my way to Żuromin, a small village on my father's lands. I was planning to stay the night there and meet with some of the village elders next day about the price they were demanding for their wheat crop. My father's treasurer had sent me; I did not relish the prospect of the task, but it got me out into the country,

---

21 The memoir resumes again at a point which has been determined wherein the Duke is approximately in his early-twenties. Around this time his father founded the city of Warsaw, which would later become the seat of the duchy. Siemowit, however, now spends most of his time in his rooms at Płock Castle, which have been converted by him into a rudimentary laboratory. The work picks up again in the midst of recounting another foray into the world of science.

which I always enjoyed. Riding, walking, hunting: all these filled my heart and mind with such clarity, such peace. I felt I was partaking in the rich pageant of the created world, that the vast and incomprehensible machine of the earth was unfolding a secret corner of itself for me alone to examine.

It had been a chill winter day. I piled furs and pelts about me, and still the cold cut through every seam and tear of my clothing to prick my skin with little icy blades. The first snow of the winter had not fallen, but the farms I passed were covered in a thick rime of frost that had slid over the land in the night, and the day had not warmed sufficiently to melt it. The sun, giving up, was now merely a hand's breadth above the horizon as I rode steadily along the rutted path. Out in the field, which was fallow, long trenches in the soil stretching far into the beech forest at the farthest edge of my sight, I saw a man leading a draft horse in my direction.

He was some way off, but coming at a steady pace. I slowed my own horse to wait for him, for I had a sudden sense of import, in that meeting him would alter my very destiny. The nearer he got, the faster my heart began to race, the louder its beat would sound in my ears. He looked up and saw that I had stopped; I could make out his form now. He was tall and young and strapping, though wrapped, like I, from head to boots in furs and coats. As he came closer, he resolved into an individual, a ruddy-faced youth with a hank of dark yellow hair poking from beneath his cap. The body of the horse, a sturdy animal, was of a height with him, and only the neck and head of the beast towered over him.

The farm, which I took to be his family's, bordered the road I was traveling, and so he halted as he came near, looking up at me still mounted. I did not expect him to know me as my lord, for I wore no markings or sigils of my house; I had packed them away in my bag to be worn during the meeting. Still, something of my presence must have alerted him, perhaps my noble carriage or personage, or perhaps he had seen me before, but as he recognized me, he bowed and kept his face pointed to the ground as he spoke his greeting and his name.

I dismounted and went to him, bidding him to rise. He straightened and I looked him in the face. He had a harelip, but otherwise he was untarnished. His eyes were green like forest moss and his nose was small and round like a girl's. He was called, he said, Kristjan; he and his family were Livonian refugees who had come to Poland to seek work in the fields after an unproductive harvest season in their homeland. His mother and sister were washerwomen to the Archbishop of Poznan, far to the west, while he and his brother worked this farm in exchange for food and board. His father, he said, had died on the journey to Poland.

At my urging, he led me along to road to where his master's farmhouse was. It was a modest stone building, with a thatched roof and tall chimney, from which grey smoke unfurled into the darkening evening. He led my horse and his, and I waited while he set them in order, then led me to the house. Upon entering, he called out to the master of the house, telling who I was. The master came quickly, a robust and earth-stained man with few teeth and a holy cross about his neck on a leather cord. He, too, bowed and told his name, which I have since forgotten.

The master's woman came and set before me a wooden plate piled with cheese and hunks of roasted meat. I thanked her and she went out. A boy came in then, so alike to the one Kristjan that I took them to be twins. The other boy lingered in the room until the master shooed him out, and Kristjan went with him. It was then, alone with the master, that I took my first step on the road that has led me to where I am today, on the verge of a great and terrible discovery.

With the master, I bargained for the two boys, giving him a price that would doubly compensate him, and allow him, if he were so inclined, to purchase the services of four boys to replace them. We sealed the agreement over a cup of homemade wine, and I took my rest in the farmhouse that night.

In the morning, I took Kristjan and his brother, who was called Jonas, with me to the village. Kristjan seemed to speak for both of them, whether due to the bond shared by them as twins or whether because of some defect in the other boy I was not sure at that time. The brothers were, by Kristjan's estimation, somewhere between seventeen and twenty years old. They had been in the service of their master for three years and in that time they had never traveled further than the market town, some half-morning's ride.

As important as it had seemed to my father and his treasurer, I cannot now recall a single moment of the meeting I had with the village elders regarding their wormy wheat. I raced back to Płock, eager to inaugurate a new chapter in the unfolding text my life had become. I was transfixed by the rhythmic clatter of the horses' hooves, and in my waking dreams, the potential of what I now possessed blossomed in my mind.

Twins. The bond and connection between twins was a mystery and source of wonder to science, and the more I lingered on the thought, the more I became convinced that there was something in the very foundations of these boys' spirits, their humors even, that could unlock some great secret of the universe. Perhaps they were one soul dwelling in two bodies? Or perhaps twins had stronger, more powerful soul energies that did the single-born? Could the one endure the pain for the other? Could they endure pain differently than each other? Than single-born? Were their very consciousnesses linked in some way? I could not stop the scientific explosion of questions in my mind. I was desperate to return to my laboratory at Płock Castle.

We reached the gates of Płock Castle well into the office of Matins. It was dark and very cold and I had to rouse the gateman from his brazier so he could unfetter the gate. A wind carried up from the Vistula, and I could scent on the air the river. It refreshed me to no small degree, and I glanced over at the brothers, who were veritably asleep on their mounts, and felt no heaviness of eye, no sluggishness of mind. I felt I never needed sleep again as we rode through the finally-opened gates and into the courtyard, the hooves of our horses echoing off the stone walls of the keep, coming back to us again like some massive cavalry descending upon us from all sides.

I installed the brothers in my quarters that night and allowed them to sleep until they awoke. I, however, as I had suspected, did not sleep, for my mind raced and plotted experiments until the sun broke from its dark prison and threw its feeble winter light out across the plains of the world. On my vellum, I set down the rudiments of some six or seven experiments which I wanted to commence as quickly as possible.[22]

When they had awakened, I sent for a large breakfast of eggs and ham and bread with wine. They had been well-fed by their former master, who needed them hale and strong for their work, but they dove into this food as though they had not eaten for weeks. After they had finished, I showed them about the laboratory and told them I had secured their services to assist me in my scientific explorations. They both expressed their shortcomings in this field, neither of them having their letters or sums, but I waved away their concerns, telling them I would teach them what they needed to know as we went along the path of science together.

My repeated unconcern for their lack of education seemed to allay any misgivings the brothers had. Each showed a curiosity as he peered at the retorts, phials and books scattered and stacked and strewn about the large

22 Thus begins the lifelong fascination of Siemowit with the hidden power of twins, especially of twin brothers.

room. An odd scent permeated the air, the residue of past experiments I was loathe to explain to them so soon, and so I merely explained that some of the herbs I had collected, when stored together, produced a pungent and non-aromatic odor.

I was reluctant, that first day, to show either of them my store of gold, that I used during my experiments. I had it safely hidden, and none but I knew its location, a stone in the wall that when removed allowed access to a box-like cavern, only an ell deep and three wide, but large enough to hold a vast amount of my experimental materials.

While it was rather primitive and of a smaller scale than the laboratory I constructed at Wiskitki, my scientific room at Płock Castle was still impressive, as can be attested to by the scholar Vermundr Karl[23], who visited me at my invitation several years later and was favorably impressed with the quality and thoroughness of my equipment, much of my own making, and my methods.

That first day, I made my first notations on Kristjan, and later in the day, while his brother recovered, instructed Jonas in the making of ink, so that he could assist me in the recording of my findings, as needed. I debated for some few days the nature of the experimentation I wanted to embark upon. In the end, I elected to begin separately, and then to integrate my investigations, bringing the brothers together for a more intensive series of experiments.

Providence, it seemed, had smiled on me, in the form of Jonas, for not only was he a prime physical specimen, strong and healthy and able to grasp tasks quickly, but he was also a mute, or near enough so that he could only communicate

23   The scholar Vermundr Karl of Zurich factors heavily into the Duke's writings, interacting both as something of a colleague and a rival. While he appears to be a major figure in the learnings of the age (particularly as to research into the occult), he is sadly lost to history, having perished along with most all of his work in a suspicious fire in his lodge just outside of Winterthur in 1345.

through a series of purrs and grunts that his brother could interpret, and over time, I too was able to decipher. I was delighted, for this aspect of research, that of speech and its failures and faculties, had thus far been an area to which I had not given thorough attention, but the more time I spent with him, the more convinced I became that I could return to him his heaven-given powers of speech and communication, if only I could divine the correct process.

The way around the problem, as I saw it, was simply one of unlocking the proper knowledge. Through the years, my methods had allowed me to unearth countless clues into the inner workings of the universe and the hidden mechanisms of creation. I had not seen the whole picture, but merely had glimpses at the vast and intricate canvas of the Great Work. But, with every secret, no matter how seemingly insignificant, that I was able to decipher, I knew I had come one small, imperceptible step closer to realizing the final truth.

It was Christmastide, and the town and castle itself were in a particularly festive mood. I remember that on Christmas Eve, I attended the procession through the streets of Płock that ended at the Cathedral of the Blessed Virgin Mary of Masovia. The Midnight Mass I was obliged to attend, as the son of the Duke, but I resented every moment I was away from my laboratory. As the procession wound its way over the snow-covered cobbles and past the icicle-spiked eaves of the shops and guildhalls, I marveled anew at the great masses of men and women, all of whom seemed an unlocked chasm of potential. It felt as if all around me whirled and danced the very animalcules of a gigantic living being. The men and women solemnly trudged over the crust of snow, making their way to the Cathedral, but I saw instead spinning and sparking pinpoints of light, like fireflies, orbiting around me. Eventually, in this daze, I came to the Cathedral and sat in my father's pew.

The Mass washed over me as if I had been submerged in the Vistula; I heard the Archbishop as from afar, muted, his words empty and formless as the Void that began all things. I paid little heed to the forms of the service; I rose and knelt and sang like some clockwork man. Instead, my mind was expanding, soaring upward through the vaulted ceiling of the mighty fortress of God. I rose up and up, leaving below me the crude and faltering world, and I ascended up into the heaven, and beneath me all Płock, and then all Masovia, all Poland, and all of Europe spread at my feet. Soon, the horizon which bound my sight fell away and I could see the great ocean that crushed the beaches of the earth, and I looked about me and saw the stars in their courses, the planets, the milky curtain of the outer heaven. The Mass went on and on around me but I was far away, my head in the stars, the tallest mountains of Europe merely brushing my ankles. I looked up, above me, and the endless vault of heaven spread overhead and I saw a ladder coming down. I reached up for it, and with that action, I began to shrink and descend again, no matter how I clawed and tore at the air around me. Down, down I fell, it seemed to take a whole summer's day to fall back into my body, seated in sweating rigidity in my father's pew. I came back to myself as the Host was being consecrated and I realized the words of the Gypsy seeress had rang with more truth than I had expected.

For days after that Christmas, I locked myself in my laboratory, with the boy Jonas assisting me in the mixture of tinctures and herbs. His brother Kristjan I kept in a state of sleep for most of the day, hidden away in a secret chamber of the laboratory; I told Jonas his brother was recuperating from a terrible chill he had taken on the previous morning. As the New Year neared, I became more and more restless, and the spark of an idea came to my mind. I could not rid my thoughts of the vision of the ladder that led into the deeps of heaven, to whatever mysteries were gathered and cherished there.

I would go to the monastery of Święty Krzyż on Bald Mountain, several days journey to the southwest. For centuries, going back probably to the times of the legendary peoples, this place had been the subject of countless encounters with witches and other dark spirits. From these, I surmised, I would be able to learn whole new aspects of the Great Art to which I had devoted my life.

The vision I had had in the Cathedral had awakened my mind to the possibilities of all the pathways of science. For without dark, there can be no light. I cast my mind upon all I had learned, and realized it paled in comparison to all I had left to discover, and here I had ignored an entire half of the science to which I was such a devoted slave. Surely, I surmised, the darker arts could be bent into the service of the light; surely from wrong could be forged the tools of right, and I had no doubt that merely because the source of some knowledge was considered forbidden by some, that did not render its usefulness mute. The Benedictines at Święty Krzyż would know of what I sought, and I would go to the mountain and witness for myself the infamy of the Witches' Sabbath there.

The Year of Our Lord 1305 dawned cold and bitter with wind and snow. I had informed my father that I intended to depart for the eastern frontier for some weeks, under the guise that I was inquiring amongst the peoples there as to the levels of support my father could rely upon should he again endeavor to the Crown of Poland, a desire that I knew was close to his heart, but which I admit to hoping fervently he did not attain. Should my father become the undisputed King of Poland, and I the heir, my life would become a stultifying, suffocating one of protocol and policy. I feared nothing more than the success of my father's dream, for it would signal the collapse and abandonment of my own.

For some days I debated whether to embark alone on my journey, or to take the Livonian twins with me. And truly, it was my feat of leaving Kristjan unattended for so long a time that persuaded me to bring them both. We were a small retinue of three; I brought along no other manservants or boys. We traveled lightly, a single wagon for our baggage and an empty one to carry back the volumes and tools and implements of knowledge I expected to find at Bald Mountain.

Our progress was slow, but in five days we had reached the Monastery, where a supposed piece of the True Cross was enshrined. We were given lodgings by the brothers there, and I asked to see the holy relic. The twins were left in the barrack and I was led by the abbot to a chamber directly beneath the altar of the chapel. With delicate, trembling hands, he parted a velvet curtain that was set into the wall, revealing a long narrow box made of pearl and bone and adorned with gold filigree and silverwork. The abbot spoke in a reverent whisper and I bowed my head in accordance with his solemnity as he lifted the lid of the box.

Even a man such as I, steeped in the science of the universe to such a degree that my veins seem to flow not with blood but with the sacred elements themselves, I must admit that at the moment he opened the box, I felt a warmth radiate from it and heat the small stone room, and a faint light did radiate from the box, although it seemed to come from a great distance, as though the box were infinitely deep.

I fell upon my knees and the abbot placed the box before me on the flagstones. I looked into it with misting eyes, though I could not then and still cannot now explain the reason for my emotion. Inside the fragment was barely more than a toothpick, jagged and unlovely in its repose, resting upon a silk of whitest cream. It was the length of a man's finger, and was of cedar, the scent of which now filled the room so strongly we may have been in the heart of a dark forest.

I realized, most suddenly and with a start, that I was muttering under my breath. Though, it was no prayer that escaped my lips and whispered over the fragment. It was an incant, one I had read and memorized from an ancient Arab text brought out of Palestine by the Crusaders during the time of my great-grandsires. Slowly, yet building in intensity and volume, the incant poured from me, and as it did, the abbot's eyes widened and his body froze, unmoving, a statue-man.

I stared at him for some moments, but not a single blink did his eye make, nor did his chest rise and fall in breath. A rush of blood seared my head and I reached out for the fragment. I took it up from its box and withdrew from my cloak a glass phial, a store of which I always kept upon my person. From the fragment, I excised a piece the size of fingernail's crescent and secured in into the phial, then replaced the fragment as I had found it.

It was mine, a piece of Christ's Cross. My hand trembled like a falling leaf as I placed the phial back into my cloak. I glanced again at the abbot; still, he was unmoving. I knelt, sweating, my heart racing, light-headed, for some long moments before I was able to collect myself and apprehend the great significance of the thing I had done and that which I now possessed.

It was some time before the abbot stirred, slowly coming back to himself as a man surfacing from a deep dive. I made a great show of attending to him, saying he had fainted shortly after opening the box, and suggested he had been overcome by the glory of the True Cross, which he allowed was likely and thanked me profusely for my ministrations. So flustered was he by his recovery, he did not notice the tiny missing piece of the fragment, and he led me back to my quarters on shaky feet.[24]

That night, I could not sleep. The twins, when I had returned, were busy cataloguing a bundle of herbological samples I had had brought up from the monastery gardens; Kristjan showed some small signs of lethargy, which I noted in his experimental journal after he had fallen asleep. I assumed they were a subsidiary effect of the forced sleep I had chemically laid upon him. Nevertheless, he did his work competently and well. As the evening wore on, they grew more tired and I allowed them to retire without attending to me. I removed my cloak carefully as soon as they had fallen asleep, and withdrew the glass phial. I held it up to the candle light and marveled at the smallness, and yet the palpable power contained in just that small piece. I could feel a cold fire pulsing into my hand and up my arm to the elbow as I held the phial up. I set the phial down, and the cold fire faded, only to resume again once I took up the phial again. The power inside just this small bit of wood was unimaginable. I felt the entire excursion to Bald Mountain had exceeded even my wildest imaginings.

I lay on my pallet, staring wide-eyed at the stone ceiling, hearing the light snores of the two young men across the room. I was excited beyond all imagining. I had placed the phial beneath my pillow and could feel the cold fire even still coursing through my head, causing the brightest colors to pinwheel across my eyes. I seemed to hear a far-off music, like the singing of many voices several leagues away. I listened as closely as I could, straining to shorten

---

24 The incant referred to is most likely the النوم او الاستيقاظ, or "the waking sleep", a minor stupefaction incant found in the Book of Acre, a 6th-century treatise on magic and alchemy captured during the Siege of Acre in 1191 by the victorious Crusaders. It eventually found its way through Greece and Hungary, through various university libraries, before being sold at auction to the Burgomeister of Zurich in 1339, whereupon its trail runs cold. It is likely that Siemowit had a copy made through his connection and friendship with Vermundr Karl, who lived in nearby Winterthur.

the distance between my ears and the voices, my mind struggling to catch but one syllable, like some tattered shred of a flag that is windblown and becomes caught in the branches of a bramble. Concentration burned through me like scalding water, but it was all for naught; I made out no sound, did not comprehend. The effort exhausted my brain, but still I could not and did not sleep.

The morning seemed to come on fiery wings. I rose and dressed before the others and went down to the hall where the monks took their morning meal. The abbot greeted me warmly, and I inquired after his health, and he stated he had fully recovered from his ecstasy of the day before; I detected a distinct sadness in his voice when he said this, as though wishing he were still in its throes. A wooden plate with Spartan fare: a bread roll, a hunk of cheese and some grapes. As we ate, I asked the abbot about the local legends surrounding the witches of Bald Mountain.

He told me that during his time as abbot, some ten years at that point, he had never had cause to believe that a single Black Mass had been held upon the Mountain, and I realized my mistake in trying to glean information from this man, whose life's work was to combat such things and bring the light of God to such places as the Mountain; after all, the monastery been built there long after the witches had already been a presence. After the meal, I thanked the abbot and later that morning, with the twins, went out on horseback to the villages and solitary farms that were in the land roundabout.

For most of the day we rode, encountering farmers and crones and milkmaids as we went, each of them assuring us that indeed the witches conducted their Sabbaths upon the Mountain several times a year. It was, I admit, no small coincidence that I had decided to embark upon my expedition at this time; the researched I had done on the Witch Sabbath had indicated that the 1st of February was often one of the dates upon which the Sabbath was celebrated, and that day was less than a week hence.

Eventually, we came to a small farm as the sun was going down, and the farmer and his woman took us in and gave a modest repast. They both were elderly and bent with a lifetime of laboring upon the earth. The twins were given their meal and a place to bed down in the stable and I was invited to share the home and hearth of the couple. After the meal, the old woman brought out a stoppered bottle of homemade vodka, and as we sat before their fire, and the fiery liquid scorched our throats and stomachs, I asked them question after question about the Mountain and the witches, and they, who had lived at the foot of the Mountain from the day of their births, were able to cast back their minds and recollect, in tandem, many of the tales they had heard as children, and much else that had passed as they had grown to their present age.

The Mountain, they swore, was afflicted with the strangest weather in all Poland, storm clouds piling up in mere moments on the clearest spring day, thunderstorms that began in the dead of night, crashing loud enough to topple the tombstones of the graveyard, and then dissipating with the morning light. Of course, given my fascination with the weather as a child, this more than piqued my interest. The old woman could describe with ferocious intensity the lightning strikes that scorched the top of the Mountain and the keening wail of the winds that rushed down its flanks to find every chink and crack in their stone walls and then burrow into their half-sleeping ears.

When I asked about the witches, they became more animated, each trying to outdo the other in tales of sorcery and witchcraft they had heard or seen over the years. The old man himself claimed to have stumbled upon the remnants of a Black Mass once, some thirty years before, while hunting on the slopes of the Mountain one spring morning; he told of a great stone slab stained with blood, a silver chalice overflowing with excrement, shreds of some sort of flesh hanging from the branches of the trees. They proceeded the elaborate for me the details of the Black Mass, which they had had from an old washerwoman in the near village, ancient when they themselves were newlywed, and who had claimed to have participated as an acolyte in one of the rites.

The perversion of the rites they described awoke in my heart a revulsion coupled with the even stronger dawning of curiosity. The vodka kept flowing, and although I slowly nursed my cup, the old couple were by now far gone in their intoxication. At length, I asked them where the witches came from, and after some hemming and hawing and false modesty, they admitted that the local parish priest was acquainted with the witches of the area, and even provided the Host for their use in the Black Mass, in exchange for the use of whatever virgin was despoiled during the rite.

I spent another sleepless night at their home, and early in the morning we set off to the parish church. Even before the sun was full up, we came to the church door. Candles flickered inside the small structure, and I knew someone inside was already in prayer. Dismounting, I went through the doors; my eyes adjusted quickly to the low light, and I saw before the altar a man kneeling, his shoulders jumping lightly as though weeping. At the sound of my footsteps, he started and looked over his shoulder.

I ascertained he was the priest the old couple had spoken of, and told him why I was here. He at first denied his part but after promising him the use of a virgin in my employ, he succumbed and admitted all. With force, I extracted from him that the next Sabbath was indeed upon Saint Brigid's Day, February 1st. A mere three days hence.

For the rest of that day, I imposed myself upon his hospitality, and eventually it came to light that the priest fancied himself a minor sorcerer. Inwardly, I laughed, but I used a meager portion of my knowledge to impress him and prove to him my goodwill. Using a cup of sacramental wine and the priest's rosary, I cast an incant that raised green flames over the chalice, simple enough for me to do, but from the look upon his face, far beyond the measure of anything he had ever accomplished.[25]

I allowed him to show me one or two of his tricks, and enthused and praised his technique to the point that I made myself nauseous to continue. In the evening, after he had celebrated the Catholic rites he sought in his soul to corrupt, I imposed myself and the twins upon him for the night; it was my intent not to leave his side until the Witches' Sabbath. I inquired when the witches would arrive, but he was loathe to reveal any of the details of such things so close to the actual event.

The three days passed in a torment of boredom for me and especially for the twins. Each morning I would place into their wine a powdered elixir, which I carried upon me in my traveling cloak, and whose effect was to make their minds more docile and susceptible to the power of suggestion, and as such I kept them occupied with menial tasks, such as copying the priest's chapbook of spells on the off-chance he had unknowingly stumbled upon an incant of great power, or a listing of the names and dates on the gravestones of the graveyard.

The 1st of February came, dawning clear and chill. The priest was in an agitated state, becoming visibly more and more nervous and awkward as the morning wore on. Finally, shortly after the sun was full up, there came a most persistent and fearsome pounding at the door of the church. The priest's face fell ashen as he rose to answer it,

---

25   This incant is likely the "Water of Hades", an illusion referred to in Geoffrey of Monmouth's now-lost chronicle *Historie of Ancient Magick*. It was mostly used in this context, a magical parlor trick to impress a neophyte.

motioning for me to follow just behind. Opening the door with trembling hands, the morning light streamed over the stones of the floor and outlined in the sunshine was a tall, slim figure, hair wild about the head.

In stepped the figure, and the priest closed the door wordlessly. As the dimness again overtook the room, the figure resolved into that of a young and exceptionally beautiful woman, perhaps still in her girlhood, although her eyes held such maturity and knowledge I had no doubt she was far older than she appeared. She was a witch, I could tell the moment I looked upon her. Her hair was golden like flax, and she wore it plaited about her head, and her eyes the green of the moss on a river stone. Her skin was pale and shone faintly like moonlight. She was tall, as I said, almost as tall as I, and a head taller than the priest. She wore a gown embroidered with flowers at the hems and the smell of her filled the entire room. My head swooned and I quickly put myself on my guard; I saw that the priest was already enthralled by her.

She spoke to him in some tongue; her voice far-off, as if she spoke from another room. The priest nodded, and I watched him walk up the center aisle to the altar and retrieve the Host. While he was gone, the witch fixed her eyes upon me, and smiled. Instantly, as soon as our eyes met, the noise of the world was stilled; I could hear not even the beating of my own heart in my ears. I wondered if she had struck me deaf, but suddenly I heard in my head her voice, speaking Polish, telling me I should not be there. She seemed to know my purpose, for next she asked what I was willing to give for the knowledge I sought.

The question had indeed lurked in the cellar of my brain the entire time. Nothing was given without cost, much less such knowledge as could alter the fabric of the world. I knew that whatever I must be prepared to offer must be equal to the value of what was offered me. But what was the equal of such knowledge? I thought the only thing I could grasp at that moment: I offered up my fear, for was not Fear, and its mate Ignorance, the true price of Knowledge? We fear that which we do not know, do not understand. I thought of all the things I feared: wolves, dwarfs, the clubfooted, my own deficits of understanding. It would not be enough, I knew, but the witch's laughter sang in my head like the trickle of a stream.

Suddenly, the priest was there, handing the Host to the witch. The noise of the world erupted again in my ear, and a pain split my head. They spoke again in their unknown tongue, and the witch left. The priest collapsed into a pew, still ashen-faced. He seemed startled that I was still there, but recovered after a moment. He went to the altar again and poured himself wine and drank it from the chalice. He refused to answer any questions I put him about the witch, and so I went and gathered the twins and we went up to the foothills of the Mountain.

We climbed through the thickly-wooded forest, up and up. Our horses were sure-footed over the craggy slope, and even though it was only midday as we made our way up, the sky darkened perceptibly as we went on. We followed a worn track through the woods, perhaps some hunter's trace, that seemingly led to the summit. But eventually, after several hours of riding, in fact long after we should have reached the utmost pinnacle of Bald Mountain, we found ourselves still slogging through the woods, seeming to have made no progress at all.

Of a sudden, a thick fog descended upon the forest, rolling down the slope from the peak. It overcame us almost at the moment we apprehended its coming, and before we could make any sort of preparation for our own safety, we were engulfed in a shroud of mist so thick, I could not see my fingers extended from the outstretch of my arm.

Rather than proceed confounded by the fog, I ordered

the twins to rein up and the three of us stood still, each dismounting and holding tight to the halters of our horses, fearing to stray even a step into the mist. The chill that came over the air with the fog was enough to set our teeth rattling, and though the day had been warm before, now I wished I had thrown my furs over me.

From above, we heard the sudden crash of thunder, as though some great iron cauldron had been cast down from heaven and shattered on the stones of the mountaintop. Lightning flashed overhead, making the fog into a shining curtain of luminescence. The horses began to stamp and throw their heads about, and I feared them breaking free and stranding us up so high. The jags of lightning came with increasing speed, and soon the smell of burnt air was carried down to us, along with the unearthly howlings of some kind of animal.

I wrapped the reins of my horse several times around my arm, as precaution, but just as I had affixed them, a great clap of thunder exploded seemingly just above us, rattling the trees all about and sending dead branches from the upper canopy crashing down all around us; one of these struck Jonas upon the head and felled him over.

The horse spooked and bolted, dragging me behind it. It sped blindly through trees and over great stones, buffeting me like a small boat in a gale. Finally, after what seemed a very long gallop, but what in reality was only some few seconds, the horse stumbled and fell face-first into the trunk of a tree, sending me vaulting over it at some great speed, and myself knocking my head against an outcrop of rock.

I lay stunned, and blackness crept at the edges of my vision, threatening to enclose my sight in darkness. I knew this was the first signal of losing one's faculties, and so I fought as hard as my addled mind would allow, but to no avail. I succumbed and closed my eyes.

I have no way of accounting how much time elapsed until I awoke, but when I did, the fog had lifted and the sun was just coming up. I had at the very least been insensate for the rest of that day and the entire night. My horse was alive, but its head was gashed and bloody. My own was split on the crown and forehead, and dried blood was caked on one whole side of my face.

I struggled to stand, and as I rose to my feet, my vision swam, and in that swirling sight, I perceived a memory of something that had occurred in my unconscious state. I saw myself disembodied, surrounded by wraiths, dancing and cavorting around a bonfire. I heard in my ears, as though they were really there beside me, their chanting and singing, and the words were in some guttural, ancient tongue I knew I had never heard, and yet I fully understood every word. It was the tongue of the witches. They were in the throes of their rite: I saw warlocks and witches rolling atop one another, I saw the virgin tied to an inverted cross, slashes across her breasts and belly. I saw a great book lying open on a stone altar and a man in a black cassock bent over it. I knew every word he read from the grimoire, and I could recall it still as I stood leaning against the tree, coming back to myself, my injured horse snuffling his blood-caked nose in the dirt.

I walked back the way the horse had dragged me, pulling the animal behind me with a gentle tug. There was no sign of Kristjan, but shortly I came upon Jonas, still insensate from the blow he took on his crown. His head, too, was bloody, and as I bent to lift him, I fairly swooned and collapsed myself. Eventually, I raised him and threw his across my horse's back, as there was no sign of his horse about. I led them down the Mountain, down onto the foothills, my head swimming in the growing warmth of the morning, until finally we reached the road that led to the village of the priest.

I carried Jonas from the horse to the church and kicked the doors open. Inside, the church was empty, and I laid the boy on one of the pews and went to search out the false priest. There was no sign of him in the church, and I went out into the graveyard to see if he was there. While I was there, I heard from beneath the church the sounds of metal upon stone, and found a cellar door open at the rear of the building. Going down the step, I found the priest wielding a hammer upon the flags of the floor.

He had opened a great crack in one of the large stones; his face was sheened with sweat and he had stripped himself to the waist. It appeared he had been working for some time. As he was absorbed in his hammering, he did not note my coming down the short flight of steps in to the cellar, and I stood for a moment watching him swing the heavy mallet. Thin shards and razor-sharp chips of stone flew each time the hammer struck, sparks kindled and went out. On the floor several paces from him, held down by a large piece of broken rock, were several leafs of vellum, covered in small writing and diagrams, the ink as carmine as new blood.

I knew in an instant what the leafs were, or at least, their nature. I had to have them, and with a sureness and speed that rivaled the cat, I moved behind the priest and at his upswing of the hammer, I took hold of it and wrenched it from his unsuspecting hands, the unexpected loss of his own momentum startling him so much his hands were unprepared to cling. He whirled and saw me for the first time, and as he recognized me, I drove the hammer into his face, which dissolved in a crunching mist of blood and teeth and bone.

His body collapsed as a marionette whose strings have been cut, and I paid him no more mind, but straight away went to the vellums and took them up. There were five leafs, filled from margin to margin with sigils and signs, words in a language I had never seen before that moment, but knew in my heart was the tongue of the witches, the Vulgara[26], and as my eyes roved over the pages, I comprehended it fully as though it were Latin or Polish; I began to suspect that I had not been completely insensate on the Mountain after my injury, but rather had been translated to the spirit plane in some fashion and allowed some measure of knowledge by the witches.

I secreted the leafs upon my person and left the cellar, closing and fixing the door behind me. I returned to the church to find the witch seated beside the body of Jonas. I approached and her head raised up, her eyes meeting mine. Again, the noise of the world about me was stilled and I heard nothing until her voice cooed in my head. She indicated she knew I had the leafs, that they had been taken by the priest from the Dark Book during the rite the night before. Her amusement at the idea that the fool of a priest would have any comprehension of what he had taken was apparent on her face. I told her the priest was dead and I did not deny having the leafs. Again, she asked me the price I was willing to pay for the knowledge I had been given.

But one price came to my mind and willingly I offered it: the life of the boy Jonas. He was still pure, and knowing the high value placed on unstained males by the witches, without hesitation, I indicated to her the unconscious boy beside her. She smiled, pleased, although she had known all along that this was the bargain I would make.

We held each others' gaze for some small time, as though sealing our bargain with silence. I made a slight bow to her and left through the church doors, leaving the fate of the boy Jonas in her hands. I regretted that I was not able to make further investigations into his condition, and that now it appeared that I had lost for the time being my means

26   Vulgara, a corrupt version of Latin, is the name given by scholars to the language witches and warlocks speak amongst themselves. It is considered one of the Five Forbidden Tongues, but is also considered the least of these.

to inquire further into the nature of twins, but I suspected I now possessed something that would make any such discovery I would have made upon them pale in comparison.

I rode back toward the monastery, careful to skirt the edges of the village so as not to be seen, but most of the folk were by that time hard at work in their own fields or shops and paid no mind to passing horseman. It was coming on the late afternoon, and I rode until the sun was down. Even several hours into the darkness of the night I went on, wanting to put as much distance behind myself and the dead priest and his witch as I was able.

Eventually, I came to a small village, Żarnów. We had passed through it without even giving it mind only days before, but this night was different. The village was a cluster of houses and shops fronting the dirt road; before, there had been nothing to cast one's eye upon with interest. But, as I came down the road in the dead of night, I saw there had been constructed, crudely and obviously with haste, a gibbet, and from it hung a body.

I slowed my horse and stared. The wooden steps the body had stood upon in its last moments were still kicked over onto their side beside the post. I dismounted and righted them, looking about me; the town seemed asleep, not even the dogs were sniffing about. I climbed the seven steps and peered up into the moonlit face of the hanged man. He had been left there as a warning to whomever else thought to commit the crime he had been strung up for. The rope creaked very slightly overhead, and his body swung almost imperceptibly in the night air. He was newly dead, I could see, and was likely hanged in the early hours, for his stink was considerable, and I surmised he had been in the sun and weather for over a day.

His face had been disfigured, but the longer I looked, the more the features of Kristjan revealed themselves. One of his eyes had been cut out and his nose and mouth slashed, but it was surely him. I lifted his head by the chin and turned it from side to side in the moonlight, examining him more closely, and as I brought the dead face to center again, so I could look it in the remaining eye, the mouth opened and the boy's voice spoke.

The sound that came from him sounded like hailstones falling upon a sheet of tin, so distorted and gravelly were his words. I supposed it to be the trauma of being hanged at the neck that had made him sound thus, and I confess some small difficulty in understanding his words, if not his intent. The boy Kristjan, though newly dead, seemed well informed of the events of past day: the witch, the priest, his brother's fate.

I denied none of it, as is always the best course when dealing with such situations. And though it did nothing to lessen the anger and bile that the hanged man spewed forth upon me, it also seemed to serve to tire him out somewhat, for his words became more breathy and the spaces between them became longer and more pronounced.

This was my first conversation with one of the Dead, and although I had innumerable questions to pose, I rightly surmised this was not the creature whom I should ask. Rather, I demanded what the Dead wanted with me, now that the fate of things had been cast and the deeds done. What power he had over me, if any, was unknown but I suspected it was negligible.

The air coming from the cavity of his mouth was fetid and rotten, and I had to turn my head away to keep from becoming ill, and as such, the boy seemed to take my intent to be that he should whisper in my ear. The ability of a dead man hanging from a rope to lean himself towards a stationary object, such as myself, is a thing that I cannot explain through science, but suffice it to say, I heard the creak of the rope and felt the hot, stinking breath on the side of my face an instant later, closer than I had expected. And in my ear, the cracked and swollen lips brushing the lobe, I heard the rasping demand he made, that I felt I could not deny him.

I sawed at the rope and gently lowered his stiff and awkward body to the platform. He made not another sound as I bundled him in blankets and carpets from my horse. I left a wergild on the top step of the gibbet and fastened the boy to my horse. We rode on, through the night, reaching the monastery late in the morning.

Upon arriving, I bundled the body into the empty wagon we had brought and secured it in a wooden chest that I emptied of old linen I had brought for the purposes of wrapping manuscripts, which in the end I had not obtained. I rested in my quarters, telling the abbot I had sent the twins ahead with some important relics I had obtained on the Mountain. I ate with the monks that evening and took my leave of them and of the abbot shortly after the sun had set. I thanked the abbot over and over for allowing me the honor of seeing the True Cross, confident as I felt in my cloak the phial in which my own piece rested that none would ever notice the missing part.

The ride back to Płock was uneventful, although I made it at all speed, for I did not want the presence of a dead body in my wagon to be discovered. It had taken us five days to make the journey outward, but in three days and a half I drove through the main gate of Płock Castle, exhausted and my nerves on edge. I waved off the stable boy and unloaded the wagon myself. I followed closely behind the footmen as they carried the trunk up the stairs and into my quarters, but nothing untoward occurred. I gave instruction that I should not be disturbed until the following evening, and after a short rest and some refreshment, I set about the task I had not intended when I left, but which had come upon me as I returned, one of the Greatest Works that science had given to man: the Resurrection of the Dead.

5

I had never attempted something of this level before. The Resurrection of the Dead was a process for scientists far more experienced than I in the works and methods. As I lay the body of Kristjan on the stone table, arranging him for preparation, I felt my own inadequacies and doubts growing stronger and stronger, threatening to overwhelm my heart and kill whatever ambition I had, and perhaps even to drown in self-loathing and self-reproach all that I had learned in my life so far, which was not inconsiderable, though still I had far to go.

I consulted every work I had in my library concerning this elaborate ritual of science. Several of them contradicted each other, which only compounded my nervousness and doubt. Finally, though, I settled upon the methods of the great Persian sorcerer and scientist Avicenna.[27] His first piece of advice, which closely mirrors that of the prophet Elisha in the Holy Bible, is to place one's mouth upon the dead man's, and breathe into it.

I cleansed the body and face of Kristjan as best I could, using ardent spirits. I laid out before me all the tools and solvents and manuscripts and tinctures and facets I would need. It was such a far cry from the last time I had Kristjan on this same table, during his Examination. I could even still see the faint red slashes across his back from the birch switch. His body was still untainted; whoever had hanged him had not desecrated his body, leading me to believe that whatever he had been hanged for was some earthly offence, perhaps theft, and not on suspicion of sorcery, which I had feared upon first seeing him hanging there.

Laying out the sacred fire in the pit, I placed a silver

---

27 Renowned polymath and father of medicine, Avicenna also dabbled in alchemy. However, there exists no extant records of the manuscript to which Siemowit is referring. None of the existing papers of the great man make any reference to raising the dead.

dish above the flame, heating it in preparation for use in the ritual. The scent of the fire filled the room as the smoke roiled: rosemary, salt, granules of Ruby of Arsenic, a droplet of holy water, golden flaxseed, all these had been piled upon the wood of cedar and yew. I inhaled deeply, letting the smoke fill my head, to inspire me to greater heights of science.

As instructed by Avicenna, I bound the body with cord of silver-adamant at the arms and legs, affixing it to the table at the points of the compass. I took up the jeweled Knife of Solomon and made the Three Incisions: in the forehead, in the breast, in the pubis.[28] As the blood in his dead body had congealed, nothing flowed from his wounds. Once I had done this, I placed my own mouth over his and breathed into him once. I watched his chest rise and fall slowly as my breath went into him. I waited, apprehensive. In some literature, this was enough to reverse the death and bring the man to life again. But, I knew I was not a powerful enough scientist to revive Kristjan with my breath alone. I would have to use the full array of the science I had learned and all that which had come before me.

Into the heated silver dish, I now tossed with my left hand granules of Jerusalem sand, and with my right petals of lily. I spoke the incants and stood back as the heat flared momentarily. Over the dish, I held my right hand, and with my left I cut the palm and allowed the blood to drip, sizzling as it hit the warmed silver. Several droplets of holy water were next, along with no small amount of Kristjan's own blood that I had collected during his Examination. I let the mixture coalesce in the dish, and at another, smaller pit, I built a very hot fire, and from my hidden stores, took a small amount of refined gold, and in this smaller, hotter fire, melted it.

---

28 The Knife of Solomon is the name used for any adorned cutting implement used in alchemical life-experiments, and does not necessarily suggest any provenance to King Solomon.

I poured the molten gold into a stone cup and then admixed it with the solution from the silver dish. Together, they made a thick syrupy liquid, deep burgundy in color. It smelled sweet and metallic. I then turned to Kristjan's body, and upon his chest, I burnt a page from the Illuminated Bible my father had commissioned from the monastery in Płock. I spat upon the ashes and drew the proper runes upon his body, making sure to align the aleph with the northeast.

I peered out my window; the belt of Orion was just visible over the trees. According to the charts, Betelgeuse was the dominant Referant during this rite, the point upon which I must align all I did.

On the floor of my laboratory in Płock, and reproduced in even more detail here in Wiskitki, was a vast map of the sky, as it is seen on the summer solstice. I had long committed to memory the star charts, knowing with the certainty of breathing, the position of each constellation at any point of the year. I took from the floor a long iron rod and affixed to a slot at the top a crystal prism. I dragged the heavy pole across the floor, calculating as I went the position on my map of Betelgeuse this night.

When I reached the proper place, I poured a solution of alkahest onto the floor and a round hole was eaten into the stone. I placed the base of the iron rod into the floor and affixed to my own eye the glass I had created, allowing me to peer through and see that which is small at a much increased size, or rotating to a different lens, one with small numerals etched upon it, to look through this crystal and out the window at the star that was to guide me.

Everything was in preparation. I went to Kristjan's body, waiting for Betelgeuse to swim into proper position. I took up the stone bowl and a withdrawing needle I had invented[29]. The stars aligned, and I drew up into the needle the solution from the bowl. Into the boy's chest, I inserted the fluid, chanting the incant as I did, willing the spirit of life back into his heart. I did the same to his forehead, willing the spirit of knowledge back into his brain, to permeate his skull and soak into the membranes of the mind. And to his pubis, willing the spirit of the eternal back into his loins, that he may perpetuate his line far into the future.

Then, I went to the crystal prism, and took it from the iron rod. It was permeated with the light of the star Betelgeuse. I opened Kristjan's mouth and placed the crystal under his tongue, willing the star to quicken this boy with heavenly light, releasing its captured luminescence into the cavity of his waiting body. From the smaller fire, I took a spadeful of ashes and worked it into the boy's hair, that the memory of fire would kindle his waking. And from the larger fire, I took the silver dish with my bare hands, for it was still but warm, and held it over him, spilling the dregs onto his body, that even the least moments of life, that which we do not account and forget the moment they pass, would not be neglected.

With thread of spun gold, I sewed up the Three Incisions, in the reverse order I had made them. I said over his body the final incants and prayers. Then I sat and waited. Avicenna gave no indication as to how long it would take for the revival to complete. I was exhausted, and the fumes and scents of the laboratory had made my head swim, and feel

---

29 A crude syringe, invented by Siemowit, that allowed, despite its name, the user to extract or inject liquids. The tube was of copper and held approximately the equivalent of 10cc. The needle was reused, although cleansed with solvent of diluted alkahest. The plunger was made of bone. The device was found in wreckage of Wiskitki after it was burned in 1345 and was sent to the Archbishop of Poznan, who forwarded it to the Roman Inquisition, suspecting it of being an "infernal device". In the 1890's, it was donated by the Catholic Church to a medical museum in Ireland, from which it went missing in the 1960's.

heavy. I dozed.

Or rather, I allowed my mind to rest. I was satisfied I had done the work to the best of my ability, and I left the rest to the hands of science. I began to wonder at the boy Kristjan, how I had lost him and then come upon his again, dead. How he had spoken to me in his death, what he had said and the accusations he had made, the guilt he had tried to make me feel. And perhaps he had succeeded, for when he whispered in my ear his morbid request, that I bring him back to the world of the living, I did not blush, did not hesitate. My fortitude did not collapse nor waver. I merely cut him down and brought him home. Did I owe him? I subscribe to the idea that we are responsible solely for our own lives, not for the fates of others. Surely his request instantly seemed a challenge to me, something that I could set myself to accomplish, that if successful would set me in a pantheon of scientists that stretched back to the prophet Elisha himself. Is it only this, the furthering of my own ambition, that brought me to cut the boy down? Over time, I have chosen to believe so.

Betelgeuse had risen to her apex and begun her slow slide down the heavens again by the time I recollected myself. Dawn was still some hours off, and I half-suspected that was when the fruits of my nocturnal work would make themselves known. I had gone almost two days without sleep and a minimum of food. My limbs and mind felt heavy and slow and I poured myself a goblet of wine to fortify myself. I sat down again and recorded the night's work on a parchment of vellum, intricately detailing each aspect of the procedure, far more so than I have here. By the time that was done, the world outside was growing faintly pink in the rising sun. I rose and went to the stone table, watching over the boy.

The first rays of the sun shined through the window of the laboratory some moments after full sunrise, and as they struck Kristjan's body, my heart stopped in my chest and I froze in anticipation. I stared, waiting, for interminable moments that seemed to stretch like ancient eons. I wondered, did Elisha wait as I waited thus? Did Avicenna? Did Christ over Lazarus? Trembling inwardly in fear that they had failed?

I watched the sunlight crawl up his body, from his knees to his chest, neck and face. As the light reached his eye, though, all my waiting was ended, the fear slid from my heart as a melting icicle drops after the evening of winter gives way to the morning of spring. Kristjan's eyes fluttered, his mouth opened slightly, and I heard him intake a breath. I had succeeded. He was alive again.

Every detail of his waking I put down on the vellum: how his head lolled from side to side, how quickly he blinked at the light of his new life, the sequence in which he flexed his fingers. He lifted his head finally and looked about the laboratory, his eye roaming over the room. I wondered if he recognized the place, all the tools and implements he had assisted me with in his recent past, or whether his death had somehow made a tabula rasa of his mind, erasing all that had occurred before?

His neck was still raw and red, the skin shredded and ugly, and his lips and face were still disfigured, his one eye cloudy but undoubtedly seeing. Only a minute had passed since his waking when his eye swam and locked onto me, standing over him, looking down. He held my gaze for a very long time, and finally his mouth began to move, the ruined lips opening and closing in a pantomime of speech, and yet no sound came from him. He tried again and again to force words out, finally succeeding only in making an animal growl from somewhere deep in his throat.

Long ago I had devised an alphabet to catalogue the sounds of the beasts, and it was in this hand that I recorded his growl. Of course, I had no way of translating it into any sort of comprehension, but at least it was not lost in the moment of miracle. The sound he made was akin to a dog wounded in the stomach, coupled with the thrum of a baby lynx's purr when it is contented in its mother's embrace. It was, entirely, an otherworldly, inhuman sound. I spoke his name, repeating it over and over again, but he made no indication that he understood my speech, merely making his low, continuous growl.

Suddenly, like a startled cat, his hand jumped out and gripped my wrist tightly. He lifted his head up off the table, raising up at the waist, a froth of crimson flecks bubbling at the corners of his mouth. His grip was, as I said, firm, but not painful, and had I wanted, I could easily have broken free. But I did not desire it; I allowed him to hold onto me. A smell of flowers, of crushed rose petals, emanated from his mouth, and there was true panic and fear in his eye. I quickly put my hand around his back to support him as he sat up; his flesh was scalding hot in places, ice-cold in others. Avicenna had said nothing about this.

A gurgling rose from the root of his throat. A great gob of thick, gelatinous sputum dripped from his lower lip and ran down his chest. His body began to tremble as from some internal vibration, and I wrapped both arms around him tightly, as the seizure took a greater and greater hold upon him. I did not want him to fall to the floor or otherwise injure himself. With a sudden force, his abdominal muscles contracted and a violent retching overtook him; a thick mist of blood and bile exploded from his mouth, and he gagged and coughed so that no air could enter him.

He shuddered, and I felt something inside him shift, as though his bones or organs were realigning themselves. Another fit of coughing, though not so severe, came upon him. I began to ask him questions about death and the other world, whom he had seen there. But it was akin to speaking to a stone wall, for all he reacted. Not a word could he make, and I do not know if he understood a single sound that came from me.

Finally, as though exhausted, his body slumped and went limp in my arms. I felt his shallow breath on my hand, felt the slow rise and fall of his chest. I placed my fingers on his neck to feel his pulse, but it was very weak, almost imperceptible. I lay him back down on the stone table and tried to clean the mess of his vomit from his body. I watched, silent, as the motion of his breathing slowed almost to stopping. The other world was reclaiming him, and I had learned nothing from him.

At last, the breathing stopped, the muscles relaxed, the eye went glassy. He was dead again. A trickle of viscous black dribbled from his mouth; I had no conception of what it was, but I collected it nonetheless. He had only been alive for some four minutes, but I could only rejoice in my heart, though my success had been short-lived. I recorded every detail on the vellum, and at the end I realized a great truth.

On the top of the vellum, I had begun with the date, 5th of February, 1305, the Year of Our Lord. But now, I realized that a new time had dawned, a new era in mankind. I crossed out the date and in its place I wrote, Day I of the First Year of the New Man.

6

[pages missing] [30]

....[fr]om the Archbishop. The herald delivered his message and I paid him his due and sent him on his way. Ever since my experience with the True Cross at the monastery on Bald Mountain, I had been wary of churchmen, and so soon as the door was shut of the herald, I put out of my mind what he had said, on the behalf of His Holiness though it may have been.

I had more important things on my mind, in any event: the Diacodus. I had learned from my first helper of the uses and benefits of this most rarest of gems. The divination properties of the gem allowed a scientist, throwing the stone into calm water, to summon up a demon or devil and force it to answer any questions that were put to it. My first helper had insisted that his Saxon master had one of these gems, and had foretold the coming years to the King of Scotland on one occasion, and that he had it from the hand of one who claimed to have wrested it from the storehouse of Merlin himself.

Where I was to garner myself a Diacodus was a thorn in my side from the moment the helper had put the idea into my head. In all my travels, I had never come across anything remotely like it, and in my correspondence with other scientists of the age, none could give any information,

---

30   The manuscript at this point is damaged severely, from fire and water. It is possible that this damage occurred in the fire that destroyed the Duke's lodge at Wiskitki on the day of his death. Reconstructive analysis, done in the late 20th Century, indicates that though the thickness of vellum pages from the time period could often vary, it can be safely estimated that approximately ten to fifteen pages of the manuscript are missing and presumed destroyed. The manuscript picks up sometime in what is likely the spring of 1306, or Year II as the Duke refers to it. His human experimentation appears to have continued unabated, although the pressures of his life as his father's heir are bearing upon him as well.

or perhaps chose not to do so, regarding this gem. I knew it was a type of beryl, and I suspected it was related to the emerald, for this gem was especially prized in the Science[31].

I was convinced, through my failure to completely resurrect the Subject Kristjan and subsequent others, that the answers I sought regarding the other world, the world beyond death, could not be won by any other means than through the Luciferic.

An idea, though, had been forming in my head for some time. I took down from my library the atlas of the Ley Lines of Europe, made by my own hand after the original by Gothmard of Gourdon, the court astronomer to Charlemagne. I followed the Line with my finger that intersected Bald Mountain, coming from the southeast and moving toward the Baltic Sea. At the village of Głodowo, far to the north of Płock yet not on the Sea itself, was made a marking on the map, a crude sigil that the mapmaker used to denote places of great supernatural power; interestingly, Bald Mountain was not so denoted.

I had noticed Głodowo several times in my perusal of the map, but now the idea that somehow the Ley Lines could lead me to the Diadocus seemed so probable, so likely even, that I was irate at myself for not having comprehended this before.

Next, I took down the Catalogue of the Churches of Poland. The Catholic chapel in Głodowo was listed as having a relic from the Mount Dol in France, a piece of the menhir that fell from heaven and landed on the mountain where the Archangel Michael fought Lucifer. No doubt existed in my mind that this piece of the menhir was the reason Charlemagne's astronomer had classified the place as he had, and that the menhir was in fact a Diacodus. Perhaps,

---

31   The first book of Alchemy, written by Hermes Trismegistus, was said to have been inscribed upon an emerald that fell from the forehead of Lucifer as he was cast from Heaven.

64

even, a piece of that first Emerald that fell from the Morning Star's forehead.

In the spring I left for the North, traveling alone. I equipped myself with weapon and gold and tools of science. For two days, I rode in the mild weather, and I came to the small village in the late afternoon of the second day. Fewer folk lived here than I had expected, perhaps only two dozen. Dirty children peered at me from under hooded eyes as I passed them on the single dirt road that divided the town. This was a farm village, and the men of the town were still out in their fields; I could hear their work songs filling the warm, golden air. Womenfolk were washing clothes about a trough of milky, murky, stinking water.

I rode to the chapel and found it a ramshackle timber shed, crudely made, with a prominent cross atop the roof. It looked able to hold less than half the town's population. Dismounting, I went to the doors and found them locked. As the breadth of the town was so insubstantial, I tied my horse to a tree near the church and walked some two-hundred paces back to the village, inquiring politely of the first woman I came upon the whereabouts of the village priest.

She told me the priest was a wandering one, that he would ride a circuit of several small village churches during the week, and that he was not due back in Głodowo until three Sundays hence. I expressed my horror for the state of the souls of Głodowo, that they were neglected so by the church, but the woman assured me they were a godly folk, and that even on Sundays when the priest was not there to conduct the service, most of the townsfolk kept their Lord's Day in prayer and thanksgiving, and that a caretaker, a seminary student, lived in the chapel to upkeep it.

The seminarian, as it turned out, also doubled as a farmer, and I waited with the woman, helping her haul up her somewhat-cleaned cloth from the bleaching trough, until she pointed the young man out to me. He was tall and lank, his hair like a thatched roof, thick and unruly. His ears stuck out from the sides of his head, and he was dirty and sweat-sheened from his day in the field. I went to him and made his acquaintance, introducing myself as a pilgrim on my way to a shrine in Lithuania that had been dear to the memory of my sainted mother.

He led me straightaway into the chapel, where he made us small meal of bread and cheese and wine. He offered me a pallet for the night, although I could tell he was loathe to offer such accommodation to one such as I; although I had not mentioned my rank or place, my clothes and bearing gave me away as a noble. We ate, and made meaningless chatter about the harvest and the weather.

I asked him about the chapel; he related that it had been built by the villagers themselves, some seventy years before, when a vision had appeared to a local girl of the Archangel Michael grappling the cast-down Lucifer on the very spot. I made a show of being impressed, although somewhat skeptical, for, as I told him, everyone knew that that particular battle had happened in France.

At this, the seminarian became animated and excited. He nodded his agreement, reassuring me that the girl had merely seen a vision, not the actual battle, but that, should I wish to see something amazing, I should follow him. He rose and I indeed followed him up to the altar of the small chapel. He went to his knees, I thought at first, in prayer, but instead he retrieved from under the altar a fine-worked wooden box. In my mind, I flashed back to the monastery on Bald Mountain, and the True Cross.

The young man opened the lid of the box; a musty smell wafted up. These folk did not know what they had; the piece of the menhir was casually wrapped in a dirty rag, and when he unfolded it, it proved no larger than a man's knuckle. He showed it to me, grinning and pleased, as though he had made it himself solely for my approval. It was a grey stone, veined with bright green tendrils. It looked like any sort of rock that could be found in any stream in Poland.

I felt a great pull from the stone, as though it were a planet itself exerting its force upon me. My head swam and my heart began to quicken. Suddenly, my nose was filled with a scent of rose petal and myrrh, and in my ears I heard the rushing wind, as though I were falling from a great height. In my scientific adventures, I had done enough experiments upon minerals and non-anima creatures to formulate a theory: that even though they may not have a mind as the human does, the mineral or non-anima contains within the animalcules and channels of its inner structure a form of memory, that can be accessed through the study of certain principles. I believed I was experiencing the memory of the Diadocus, as it fell from heaven, where the air was rose and myrrh, and crashed through the vulgar air of earth, slipping from Lucifer's forehead.

The seminarian said the stone was from the Mount Dol, a gift from the local priest there, who claimed it was part of a gem that had fallen from the hilt of the sword of the Archangel Michael on that fated day eons ago. He grinned, obviously unbelieving the story, happy to share it nonetheless, like some educated city man who travels to the country with a friend and spends his days fooling the rubes with tales of modern life that make them sputter in incomprehension.

Promptly, without preamble, I laid on the floor between us a leather pouch filled with gold. I had not a doubt in my mind that the stone was a Diacodus, and there was nothing that would stand in the way of my taking it from this place. The young man's eyes bulged in his head as he opened the bag, and I told him I was a collector of such curios and I was willing to buy the stone from the chapel, or from him, whichever he chose. The bag contained two-hundred gold florins, enough for the young man to leave the seminary and become anything he thereafter chose, were he inclined.

He was. Wordlessly, he exchanged the stone for the gold. I stood and left the chapel, turning and riding home as the first stars of the night were beginning to sparkle overhead. All through the night I rode, sleeping in my saddle only briefly. The next day passed in a blur of wheat fields and blue skies, the nods and bows of passing horsemen or travelers, the singing of birds and the rush of the breeze through the boughs of trees. I rode into Płock Castle, my hand sunk in the pocket of my cloak, wrapped tight around the magical stone.

As badly as I wanted to shut myself up in my laboratory and study the Diacodus, I was unable to do so at the time. For my father the Duke was in the midst of another preparation. My father had grown disillusioned with the machinations of his wife's brother, Wenceslaus of Bohemia, and had sent her home to Prague some years before, effecting a separation that was never reconciled[32]. However, it was another rival of my father's, the Elbow-High as he was called, that had, through force, established himself in the southeast of Poland as a great power. I and others in the nobility of the land saw that my father's power was waning, that any hope he still kept for the Crown of Poland was unfeasible; there were far stronger lords with greater support and more powerful armies than Masovia's. At more than one council, and several times in private, I advised my father to abandon his quest, foolhardy in my eyes, of uniting and ruling Poland.

The months and years since he had sent his wife away, and perhaps the low but insistent chorus of us who wished to protect him and Masovia from ruin, eventually tempered him. It was with intense joy and an unbounded sense of

---

32 Kunigunde was sent back to Prague in 1302, where she joined a convent with her daughter. She died in 1321 at age fifty-six. Her brother, Wenceslaus II, claimed the throne of Poland, as did her nephew, Wenceslaus III, who was assassinated in August 1306.

relief that I accepted my father's charge to ride to the Elbow-High and, for all intents, lay my father's supplication at his knee.

Władysław, also called the Elbow-High, had his court at Krakow, perhaps a two-day's ride to the south of Płock. A wagon laden with gifts followed: gold, bolts of cloth, barrels of wine and casks of potatoes and barley and rye, and two unmarried girls of my father's court. The first was Elisabeth Swantiborde, a distant cousin of mine whose father was a noble in Pomerania; the second was Jadwigę Stolp, also a countess from the north. I knew Elisabeth somewhat and our acquaintance over the course of years made the trip and the fate that awaited her in Krakow somewhat more easy to bear. In the course of the short journey, we found a shared passion and I was truly sorry to leave her in Krakow.[33]

But my embassy to the Elbow-High was the effort to which I devoted most of my energies. We arrived in Krakow and were taken to the Elbow-High's court, a modest keep overlooking the Vistula, the same river that wends through Płock. It was early evening, and a great feast was laid out. We had not arrived alone; several other delegations from smaller and lesser lords had also accompanied us, of whom I befriended the servants of several and offered their masters to buy them from their servitude. They, of course, suspected I had libidinous intent, and I did nothing to dissuade them from this ideation.

Libidinous intent, however, had become as unappealing to me as the fashioning of lace or the comings and goings

---

33   The nature of the passion, of course, can only be speculated at. However, the fate of Elisabeth may shed some light: she spent several years in the court at Krakow, never being suitably matched. When she finally was married off to a Swedish count in 1310, he sued for divorce the next day. The proceedings of the divorce, collected in the Royal Archives in Stockholm, list "gruesome defects of the person and a perverse and unholy delight in evil" as the reason for non-consummation. She died, in Wiskitki of all places, in 1312.

of my father's court. The apathy with which I regarded the carnal aspect of life I endeavored to keep hidden, for I knew it was not a thing to have one's disinterest in such things flaunted. True, I had in my youth several encounters which allowed me to study and perhaps master the rudiments of the physical act, to know the body of another as well as my own. But, as my youth gave way to manhood and the urgings of the physical became more and more distracting, more and more threatening to drive me away from what I perceived as my true mission in life, I was unable to allow myself the luxury, as I saw it, of lowering myself to the basest of my needs. Science, to me, was the only mistress I could have, and all other attempts at pleasure would only leech from me my powers and abilities, my sacred time and effort. With resolve that was, I admit, at times tested, I vowed never to take to bed another conquest. Eventually, of course, I was forced to take an even more drastic measure, which has proved most efficacious.

At Krakow, the feast began and the Elbow-High entered from a side door as the meal was already underway. His name was, if anything, a compliment. Whose elbow was used to measure him for his moniker must have been himself enfeebled, for the man himself was the like of a child. I had a sudden and grave misgiving that a man of his stature could ever become overlord of a troupe of jongleurs, much less of Poland itself. I very nearly left the conclave without pledging my father's fealty, but I had to recollect myself that this little fellow had bested several armies and was now the undisputed lord of Lesser Poland, no small feat, allowing the forgiveness of the term.

Roast duck and pheasant, boiled potatoes, bread and wine and cheese. He certainly feasted like a great lord. The wenches were not as comely as in my father's court, but I suspected that perhaps because his wife's mother was a Catholic saint, the Elbow-High elected to not face his temptations dead-on. And as it was late in the summer, the Elbow-High led us to the courtyard for more wine and mutton. He spoke, once we had all gathered and were pleasantly socializing, arresting our attention with the force and eloquence of his words. He talked of the recent death of the Bohemian pretender, only weeks before, and how it was his intent to, in the years ahead, amass and grow from the soil, as he said, a nation of one people, not the disparate warring lords of that time. He elaborated his vision of a united Poland, a great and vast nation that ran from the Baltic to the Carpathians. His strength of vision was compelling enough, but when he began on his long litany of the advantages he already had over the lords we represented, I could feel any remaining opposition slipping away on the wind.

It was then mostly a formality, when the next morning, still flushed from his speech of the evening before, that we assembled lords pledged ourselves to his cause and his lordship. The ceremony was over and done quickly, and with my the greater part of my business concluded, I approached the steward of the Elbow-High, to arrange for the ladies of my entourage to be found places in his court.

My purposes were complete. My father was now free to live out his life as Duke of Masovia, none of his greater ambition threatening my own life. I had, in the bargain, gained six servants through the generosity of my fellow nobles, who assumed I was taking them for their wombs or backsides. In the end, I sent them all to Wiskitki, where eventually I was able to study them each independently and in pairings. The embassy could not have been a greater success for me personally in my scientific work, for as it happened, one of the new servants was a boy called Adam, a herald for one of the other lords. He had been captured by Cossacks when still very young as his family was fleeing into Poland from Russia. They had gelded him and made him a slave until he was rescued by his master only three years before.

When I found this, I devoted much study to him, examining him closely. I recorded in detail the pattern and location of his scars, his description of what he could recall of the procedure, the instruments and how they were used and cleaned and readied, the effects on his health and growth, on his thought and desires, his life in general. He was hale and healthy, if somewhat feminine in appearance and affect. I began to wonder if science was capable of altering the natural desires and states of the human mind and person, if properly manipulated. There seemed, as still to me seem, no limits to the power of science to change and to better the human condition.

I returned to Płock, my laboratory, the Diacodus, science. In earnest, in the next few weeks following my return, I made extensive scientific inquiries into the internal mysteries of the human, as well as the animal, creature. A serving girl was with child, and I persuaded her to allow me to birth her babe. It was an arduous effort, and her exertions proved unworthy. I gave her a tea brewed with raspberry leaf to ease her struggle, and after some small time, the babe began to crown. Eventually, with great labor, the babe emerged. I wrapped him in swaddling and handed him into his mother's arms. Shortly thereafter, I caught her afterbirth in a silver dish and secreted it away for later use. Additionally, she had bled rather profusely and I was able to collect some of this as well, for the blood of a mother harvested during birthing was a potent base for many potions. The babe, I can report, grew hale and strong and lived a long and happy life at Płock Castle until his manhood.

Other girls were examined, village or farm girls. I studied the cycle of the moon that afflicted them, the difference in skeletal structure, internal structure and the like. I endeavored in one case to affix to one boy an additional rib, taken from the body of a girl of like age, to see whether his Adamic advantages would disappear over the course of time, should he be so gifted as Eve. Unfortunately, neither subject survived the transplanting, although perhaps tellingly, it was the girl who lingered longer.

I was filling my volumes rapidly. My experimental journals overtook the cabinet in which they were stored, and I arranged to have another, more capacious, built for me by a woodworker in Płock. I initiated my long and mutually beneficial correspondence with several of the renowned scholars of the day, most importantly, Vermundr Karl, whom I had already written on a few occasions. I shared with him some of the less provocative experiments I had conducted, and he was gracious enough to reply in kind, allowing me to expand my own stores of knowledge, especially in areas to which I had serious, self-acknowledged deficits, most especially in the realm of those afflicted by diseases that render them animalistic.

I had little experience of such things, having not encountered any sort of creature so afflicted, merely having read accounts of them in scholarly works; Vermundr also intimated he was working on a treatise on the subject of lycanthropy, and though I beseeched him over the years to allow me to read a page here or there, he was close with his work, and I had to wait many decades to read the finished work, which, in any event, caused somewhat of a stir in certain circles.

In a similar vein, I conducted an experiment in the autumn of Our Lord's Year 1306. Like any true scientist, I myself was not successful at all efforts, and some of my human projects expired. I was able, with the use of a meat cleaver, to parcel out three youths into pieces. Using a scraping knife, I took their flesh from their bones and seasoned it with salt and savory spices from the kitchens. Then, I took the bones and ground them into meal, baking them into cakes. Taking the meat over an open fire, I cooked it in a sauce of wine and oil and then served the roasted meat and cakes to some of the farm workers on one of my father's estates. I had watched them for several days prior to feeding them this meal, and then contrived to watch them for several days after. I was able to ascertain a slight increase in their agitation and in their effort at exertion in the fields over the course of the next day and half after eating the meal. One or two were struck with profound internal distress, but the other three worked like six for a short time.

Over the course of the next fortnight, I made a point to have some small contact with each of them, searching for any sign that they had taken on any particular aspect of the youths whom they had consumed. One of the farmers, hitherto a hale and manly sort, grew decidedly morose and indecisive, aspects I had noted in one of the youths who made up a portion of the meal. A theory began to develop in my mind, that the very aspects of our humanity are stored up in our animalcules and structures, and that even the weakest of us can effect upon the strongest a profound alteration when these minuscule structures are thrown together suddenly and without warning.

The winter came and I retreated to Wiskitki, where the lodge was comfortable and secluded and allowed me more time for my studies than did the hectic court of my father in Płock. Over the course of the summer and autumn, as somewhat referred to earlier, I had taken into the lodge fifteen new servants, whom I intended to use as a starting stock for a series of human experimentation that would extend the frontiers of what science had to that time accomplished.

One night, very late, my eyes were growing heavier and heavier as they pored over a near-faded text in Slavonic, itself taken from the Preslav Literary School, a translation of a Byzantine manual of Circumstances.[34] I was in the midst of study when my eyes closed. I blinked them open some few seconds later, but anger and rage suddenly overwhelmed me that I was not the master of myself, that I was still a slave to something so simple and delicate as sleep. I stood and stormed about the room, obliterating from my head any further desire for sleep as I did, but racking my brain for a permanent solution to this problem. Surely, I had wasted countless hours of my valuable time asleep, time when I could have been unlocking mysteries that would benefit the whole of mankind. I needed to find a way to live without sleeping. Every hour of every day I could then devote to the exploration of the Great Art. As Isaiah said, There is no rest for the wicked, and although some may see my life and work as such, my wickedness has only ever served the greater glory and goodness of all men.

I had studied before, over the years, the mechanics of sleep. As a youth, I had kept a series of animals from periods of rest to the point where they were incapable of normal living. Rabbits fared the worst, lasting only some few days, with dogs and cats faring slightly better. I never proceeded to the point of mortality, although it was my suspicion that if deprived of sleep long enough, they surely would have died. Being a human and thus superior to the animal, I set about creating a formula that would allow me to exist and function at my normal capacity without need of sleep. I pored over mathematical tables related to the length of

---

34   The Preslav Literary School was founded in the late 800's in the Bulgarian Empire; it served mostly as a center for translating Byzantine works of science and poetry. The Circumstances referred to are a complex and time-consuming series of calculations that certain magicians are required to make while casting spells, and are influenced by a vast array of circumstances, from the weather, etc. in the place the spell is cast, to the hour and day and minute and angle of the sun or moon or declination of Antares, etc. in the place the spell is to take effect. The Chart of Circumstances for some spells can go on for hundreds of pages. It is a joyless task for most magicians to memorize the Circumstances for their spells.

sleep, the number of breaths a man takes while asleep, the number of heartbeats. I worked for several days, developing a scale to measure the depth of sleep and the levels to which consciousness descends. It was this declining scale that I worked to obliterate.

Consulting my notes from the animal experiments, I elected to use my own person for a human subject. I read what I could of Galen and Hippocrates on the brain and the centers of sleep. I knew by heart the potions and elixirs that could, for some short time, keep a man in the world of the waking. Eventually, through trial and error, I refined what I had already determined, and, satisfied, made ready to take my first steps into a world unbounded by the need for respite.

My laboratory in Wiskitki was larger and more elaborate than the one which I had created in my quarters of Płock Castle, and it was around this time that I began to dismantle the laboratory at Płock and spend more and more time at Wiskitki. The Athanor I had built in Wiskitki was massive; it dwarfed the one I had used as a furnace in Płock, and there was more space for the storage of samples and more working space than at the castle. Once I had moved my scientific work to Wiskitki, there would be nothing, I felt, that I would be unable to accomplish.

The conquest of sleep, for example. In my laboratory in Wiskitki, improved and expanded with the tools and apparatus I had brought from Płock, I set to work, setting aside all my other projects. For, as I saw it, there would be nothing but time for my other works once I had banished from myself forever the need to waste precious hours and whole vast pieces of time insensate and idle.

I set about collecting the herbs and ingredients I would need to kindle the Athanor: aniseed, sage, birch twigs, salt and sand. From the swift-moving creek that ran through the grounds of the lodge, I filled a silver dish with clear, cold water and, in the laboratory, set it atop a tripod, whose legs were of iron etched with ancient runes. I laid out the tools I would need on the stone counter and from one of the hidden vaults, I took a cedar cask filled with ashes, the remains of a wooden Madonna that had been gifted me by a village priest some years ago, along with the charred remnants of several pages of the Bible.

When this was done, I prepared my body. I washed my skin with holy water and then stood with my right foot in a golden dish filled with soil, to keep myself grounded in the earth and to not lose myself in the world of dreams. From my forehead, I cut a lock of hair with the Knife of Solomon, and threw it as well into the Athanor, to add a portion of my thought into the preparatory smoke that was slowly guttering upward. I plucked one eyelash and pared one fingernail and also these I threw into the orange fire, for I wanted never-ceasing sight and the work of my hands to be consecrated. Finally, dipping one fingertip in a silver thimble containing the blood of a virgin's deflowering, I wrote upon my chest and arms the sigils and signs that I would later have to make permanent upon my skin.

Preparations done, I chanted the incantation that would begin what I hoped would become my longest day, one that would never cease. The flames of the Athanor were still orange; they had not burned hot enough yet to consume their own basest nature. I still had to wait. With tongs of iron, I took an ingot of gold and held it over the Athanor, throwing dried rosemary upon the fire. The heat of the fire made sweat course down my body and I knew the fire was growing stronger, eager to pass through its lower form and into its more refined nature.

Chanting louder, I watched as a droplet of molten gold rained into the Athanor. Quickly, not wishing to waste any of my precious gold, and knowing that even two droplets would alter the process and drastically change the recipe of the work, I withdrew the ingot and set it sizzling in a silver bowl of holy water. The steam that exploded upward I bent to inhale, tasting the savor on my tongue of lemon and cold water. Straightening, I threw the rest of the ingredients into the Athanor and stood back as a great blue tongue of cold fire leapt upward. I had created the Cold and Negating Fire, the first real step on the path to ever-wakefulness.

The Cold and Negating Fire quickly sucked the heat from the room, and the sweat that had been pouring from my body turned almost at once clammy and chill, and my teeth began to rattle in my head and my joints to stiffen. I watched as a rime of frost began to form on the rim of the Athanor, which only seconds ago had been fiery and pulsing with heat. All was ready for the next part of the process. I lifted from the stone counter a small cauldron and into it I poured the solutions I had made, the potions and elixirs that would bring sleep to them that wished it. The morphean brew contained nightshade and chamomile and valerian and poppy. It contained the blood of a hibernating bear, dearly collected.

Into the Athanor I laid the cauldron and waited. Shivering, I stood back from the icy flames and listened as the Cold Fire devoured the solution, eating away at its potent elements, feasting on the vital and then converting them in its Negating flame into the very opposite of the that which had gone in. I watched as the Cold and Negating Fire within the Athanor blazed a cobalt blue, then nearly white, the conversion process nearly complete. Finally, in a shower of sparks that fell about me like snowflakes, it was done, and I withdrew the cauldron from the Athanor with heavy woolen mitts, although still had I not placed it down almost at once, frostbite would have claimed my hands.

I peered in at the solution. It was a thick black syrup, ready for the final stage. I took up the Needle of Canopus and dipped its tip into the solution. Over and over again, I pricked the Needle into my flesh, going over and over the sigils and signs and runes I had drawn earlier on myself in ash. Like ink, it set into my flesh, as though I were writing a book upon my very skin, which in a way I suppose I was. Muttering the incants as I went, I pricked up and down my arms, over my chest, leaving the final sigil, at the base of my throat, for last.

It was this sigil, the Vorthyn, that would seal all I had done before.[35] My hand did not falter as I held it to my throat, but for a brief second, a thought came to me that perhaps a second line of defense against sleep was warranted. Thus, into the dish of creek water, I lay the Diacodus, newly garnered and as yet untested. The water remained calm for a brief second as the stone nestled at the bottom, the water just barely covering its crown.

Then suddenly, a brilliant tyrian light began to emanate from the dish, as though the water had been colored with dye. The air above the water began to shimmer with faint, dark forms, twisting and writhing, each so small that even a hundred of them could perhaps dance on the head of a pin. But as I looked, I could see to great degree each detail of them. Their skins were black, although some had inlay of silver worked through them, like carving, and some had bands of red about their arms and necks. Their eyes burned in their small faces, some bright blue, others fire red, still others milk white. Their bodies and arms and legs were thin, their fingers elongated, some with claws at their tips. Some had wings of leather, others had scales covering them. They were demons, of course, and knowing which I desired, I

---

35 The Vorthyn, an ancient pagan rune, likely of Viking derivation, resembles an unclosed circle with an angled slash along its lower half, somewhat like a crude capital-G. A Danish survey conducted in the 1890's by the University of Copenhagen, speculated that the Vorthyn was pronounced somewhat with an "amn" sound, leading them to conclude it was the Viking equivalent of "amen". The Needle of Canopus is an alchemical tool used for binding tattoos and ink-marking on skin or vellum. It is often little more than an ornately decorated knitting needle.

called it forth.

Speaking its name surprised it, for it is well known amongst them that the race of Man do not know their names, but I was no longer of the race of Men, I was a New Man. It came forth, and the others faded into nothingness, the glow of the water receding to barely a faint shimmer. It stood, peering up at me from the dish, seeming lost and confused, and I spoke to it and claimed it as my own, speaking over it a binding word before it was able to fully comprehend me.

True, had this been a stronger, more powerful demon, I would like as not have been able to so much as draw it forward, much less bind it to me. But, I had purposely chosen this demon from the lowest caste because I had suspected my strength would overmatch it. Belphoram, it was called, a lesser demon of sleep, one of the thousand and one sons of the Lord of Evening and the Queen of the Dawn, two greater demons who, though despite their lofty titles, were really no more than vassals of vastly more powerful devils.

Within the Vorthyn, I now carved the binding rune that would keep Belphoram trapped within me forever. Though for a demon he was a weakling, his powers over sleep far surpassed my own. I ventured that a day would come when I would no longer need him bound to me, but I was risking nothing at that early stage. I inked the rune, and completed the Vorthyn. A rush of cold wind passed through the room, whipping my hair and robes about me like a tempest. The candles went out and even the Athanor's flames, now back to a glowing orange, dipped slightly and went low.

The cobwebs at the corners of my mind were instantly gone in that rush of wind. The invigoration I felt was instant, and the weariness that had afflicted my limbs and joints over the past weeks of study were gone, leeching from me into the night air like grains of sand pulled from a beach into the sea. Faintly, in my ears, I heard Belphoram's voice, a raspy whisper, a new tenant inspecting his lodgings, cursing himself for his slowness and abasing himself before his new master. In years to come, I would grow to find Belphoram a coward and a craven and although occasionally a helpful guide in certain nefarious efforts, overall quite like an insolent child, but in those first moments, as the reality of what I had done overtook me, the realization that I now had a demon, however small and minor and weak, bound within me forever, I felt a flowering sense of greatness blossoming in my heart, and from that day to this, I have never ceased feeling it, although at times I admit it is tinged with a small fear, a nagging at its edges that is simple enough to ignore.

With solvent of alkahest, I cleaned my tools and the Athanor, collecting up the ash from my furnace and storing it in a different cedar chest. The ingot I locked away, the herbs and else I repacked in their phials or sleeves. Much of the night and the morning had passed during the process, and I looked out the window to see a bright, full sun glowing over the fields and farms of Wiskitki. I went to the window and peered down at the rocky escarpment on which the lodge had been built. A she-goat and her kids picked their way carefully over the ridges and stones, going who knew where but eventually to my plate. Farther out, I saw the men of the fields with their scythes flashing in the sunlight, rapid glints of gold that put me in mind of the molten droplet that fell from my ingot. The sounds of the working world drifted up to my ears, and all went on as it had the day before, the heaven overhead watching down benign and clear, the river laid down like a silver ribbon on the land, and the men and the women and the children of the town lived and went on and soon they would sleep and rise and tomorrow begin anew. I smiled, incomparably happy.

The evening came, giving way to night. My eye did not grow heavy, nor did my mind falter. I was awake, my mind alert and unhindered. I could not help myself; I began to laugh. I did not sleep that night, nor the night after. Although there are times when I must close my eyes and collect my thoughts, reorganize in my mind the work I am always pondering, I have not slept as a man does in more than forty years.

7

[pages omitted][36]

...[with]out delay. Forthwith, I called my horse and went out of the castle grounds to the small farm where the girl toiled in childbirth. The goodwife of the house had given over a small corner of her root cellar and piled a small quantity of hay for the girl to lay upon and labor. She was alone with her husband, a youth who also worked the farm. He was kneeling beside her, mopping her brow and muttering to her softly. He looked up at my arrival, but made no sign to me, returning his attention to the girl on the straw.

A candle guttered on a rickety wooden table, and the light it cast was barely enough to illuminate the scene. The girl was sobbing, sheened in sweat, her hair ragged and unkempt. She lay with her back against the wall, knees drawn up, her enormous belly swelling against the soiled linen dress she wore. At intervals, she would cry and scream in distress, as the babe inside her attempted its course.

For several moments, I stood outside the circle of dim candlelight, watching her. She was too far into her pains to have noted my coming into the room, and so when I finally stepped into the light, and she lifted her face at the movement, her eyes went wide and she began anew with

---

36   At this point, the manuscript is heavily edited by hand, several pages rendered utterly illegible either through intent or circumstance. A thick, tar-like substance has even been affixed to many of the pages, obliterating whatever was written beneath. Some of the vellum sheets even show evidence of sections being removed with a knife or blade, some scratched out completely while others have actually been excised. The best estimate that can be made is that some forty-one pages of the manuscript have been rendered unintelligible, although of note, one page of this section survived intact and was found in the bombed-out ruins of Schloss Hexenagger, in rural Bavaria, after the Second World War. The castle had been an SS headquarters and archives. The single page is reproduced here, although there are very few indications as to when in the life of Siemowit the events occur.

whimpering and fierce sobbing.

I went to the girl's side, lightly pushing aside the farm boy. I lifted her dress and examined her; the babe was near to crowning. The time was very close. I called up to a servant girl and demanded of her a quantity of hot water and a sharp knife. The girl's hands kneaded handfuls of straw as she withstood the pains of labor, coming and going like the waves of the sea. She would arch her back, throw her head back and wail, then all her bones seemed to turn to water and she would collapse upon herself, exhausted with the effort of enduring another spasm of the birthing.

The servant girl came after a time with a tub of hot water and a carving knife, which I took from her and held over the candle flame, several moments on each side and on the blade. The youth had gone back to the girl's side, and I overheard him speaking endearments to her in the low speech of whatever place they hailed from. The sound of his voice, overwhelmed by her screaming and pain, washed over me like rain; it was as though they were characters in a mummer's show, going through their paces, and more than that, a show I had seen innumerable times, so that the performances were known to me intimately and thus had lost all semblance of interest.

I came to myself again, and went to the girl's side, again moving the youth from her. I lifted her dress again; the babe was distending her nether area fearsomely. I drew from my cloak a square of clean linen and lay the knife upon it, then set it beside us on the floor. Then, I took my place between her knees, pulling them apart. I instructed her to push at the next wave of pain, and to continue through it. She did so, and for the next several hours, she proved her strength as a formidable girl and as a vessel of science, pushing with might and endurance.

At length, the babe came forth. I grasped the head of the babe as it left her, pulling it by the crown and shoulders.

I quickly cleaned its face and body, turning it over and peering closely at it. I ordered the youth to bring the candle over so I could see the babe all the better. Under the flickering, dancing, pale orange light of the smoking candle, I saw my efforts brought to fruition.

The babe's skin, on its back, was akin to scales, as on a fish, although larger. The scales were hard to the touch, not the soft silkiness which a newborn babe's should be. I rapped on them, and my knuckles felt as though they were knocking upon a stone; the babe let out a mewl. I turned it over, lifting its arms, peering into its ears, nose, mouth. To all other appearances, the babe seemed a normal newling. It was merely upon its back that the marks of science were to be found. I took the candle roughly from the youth's hand and held it close to the scaly back of the babe, waiting. The youth and the girl were by now in tears, huddling together and whispering to one another, fearsome tones in their words, but I paid them no mind. The babe, though, seemed to take no heed of the candle's flame.

Delighted, I took up the knife and cut the babe's navel string, and tied off the excess. At this point, I noted the babe was a boy. I lay the babe upon the hay, away from the bloody effluent of his mother, and examined the soles of its feet. Again, my heart leapt in my chest: the scales were there, too. Excitedly, I turned the babe onto its stomach. The babe's back showed, of course, the most pronounced scales, but the shade and coloring of the backs of the legs and buttocks showed a similar graying, indicating to me that in time, the entirety of the babe's back half would be so endowed.

Smiling broadly, I withdrew from my cloak a large leathern sack of gold florins, the price heretofore agreed upon by the husband and myself. Again, I cleaned the babe with water and wrapped it tightly in the linen. I allowed the girl to give the babe suck for some time, while the youth huddled himself to the girl, holding her to himself and

85

cooing over the babe, kissing and stroking its head, and the girl's.

I am not a cruel man, and so I left them to themselves for some time, moving off outside the circle of light afforded by the candle. I even attempted to shut my ears to their whimpers and cries, but the maudlin scene was never far from my ears. The babe's squalling had lessened, especially upon the tit. Soon, though, I stood up and moved to them again, my hands outstretched. I told the youth that the time had come to give up the babe, and reminded him of the bargain he had struck.

With tears and kisses, the youth and the girl parted their babe from themselves and into my arms. The babe was asleep shortly, and I went toward the stairs that would lead out of the cellar. I asked the youth how they had planned to call the babe, and he told me, through sobs, that they had intended to christen the babe and call it after the girl's father, and so I promised him that I would abide by his wishes and the babe would be called Lukasz.

I went from the farmhouse and back to the castle, summoning Gudmunda shortly after my arrival. I informed her of the strange nature of the child, fabricating a tale to her that I had rescued the babe from a foundling's house, where his parents had left him because of the oddness of his pallor and hardness of skin, and that given time I could cure the babe of his affliction. I told Gudmunda to give the babe suck as needed, but that the babe should be given a place in the nursery of its own, and I would attend to its growth and health.

I could hardly be more pleased with this scientific victory. The womb had been conquered, it seemed to me. My effort at manipulating the very mechanisms that formed life within a mother's confines had proved astonishingly successful; the babe had been born exactly as I had hoped, scaled and impervious to fire. In time, I hoped the scales would envelop his whole skin, but I was satisfied with the partiality of the coverage. Who knew what maturity would bring to the child Lukasz?

Someday, perhaps, there would come a time when....[37]

---

37   The page ends here, and the method by which Siemowit "created" the boy Lukasz is never explained, though further references to his development and growth, even his existence in utero, can be gleaned from later entries in the Duke's memoir. The boy Lukasz is, in fact, raised at Płock Castle, ostensibly by Siemowit, but most likely by an understanding Gudmunda. The Duke steadfastly looks upon the boy as an experiment, indeed using the boy later in life as a basis for several scientific explorations. What the boy thought of the Duke, however, remains a mystery for the ages.

8

[pages omitted][38]

...[An]ima. The work engrossed me, and I filled the first dozen pages of the vellum that first night.[39] By candlelight, my quill scratched ceaselessly and I only stopped when the stiffness of my fingers prevented me from holding the pen any longer.

The morning found me still at my desk, attempting to perfect one of the recipes I had developed for a tonic which I hoped would dissolve stones of the gall. I broke my fast with a flagon of dark wine with bread and cheese, and then went straightaway to the village where I had arranged to meet with a lay brother of the Teutonic Knights, who was called Nicolas, and was a Fleming.

The inn where I was to meet him was the Flayed Goat, and it was the finest establishment of its kind at the time. I entered, leaving my steward to see to the horses at the inn's stable, and was immediately presented by a large open hall, with several long tables and a vast fireplace. The floor was dusted with wood shavings, and the whole place smelled

---

38   At the next point where the manuscript becomes legible, it is much further along in the Duke's life. His father has died, and thus has he become Duke of Masovia, Warsaw, Liw and Rawa. As part of his father's will, however, Siemowit's brother Wenceslaus became Duke of Płock, and Siemowit was forced to remove from the castle where he had spent much of his life. He relocated to the capital of Masovia, Rawa Mazowiecka, but spent much of his time at Wiskitki. His experiments continued almost ceaselessly, several being conducted at one time; it appears he had at this time mastered the arts of herbalism and healing, and had made immense progress in the arts of metallurgy and alchemy. His darker work, including the binding of demons and the investigation into shape-changers, expanded in this time period dramatically; it is estimated the memoir resumes in the spring of 1319.

39   The first reference to Siemowit's magnum opus, Lex Humana, or The Human Law, in which he expounds all his theories, first and foremost amongst them the Quinque Gradus Anima, or Five Planes of Anima.

of spilt ale, sweat, musty clothing and urine. I took a place near the fire after telling the wench I wanted ale and meats brought.

I settled in and waited for the Fleming. I had met him some days before, as his company of Knights trooped through the countryside on their way to a garrison in Radzyń, near to the northwest. Several of the nights and lay brothers had lodged at my estate, and I had opportunity to make the acquaintance of this Fleming and some of his cohort.

We conversed easily in Latin, while his Knight brethren were usually lost, speaking in their own native tongues amongst each other: mostly they were Germans, but three were Poles, and eventually, they and I also engaged easily. They had marched off the day previous, but the Fleming had stayed behind, ostensibly to learn from me of healing herbs and concoctions, but I intended another bargain with him.

The Knights were the warriors of Christ, the army of the Catholic world, and that they endeavored to liberate the Holy Land from the infidel and to defend the faith from all its foes. I ventured that the lay brother would be interested in some of the relics I had acquired over the years, and to that end, I had arranged to meet him at the inn, where we could discuss such things. In fact, I had brought with me a gilded finger bone of Saint Jerome, to gift the lay brother with. I had laid several enchantments upon the relic, which I had bought from a Roman Gypsy some years before, who had it from a priest at the Maria Maggiore where the saint's relics were cloistered.

The Fleming arrived and we ate and drank convivially, and then retired to an upstairs room for our private discussion. The room was spare, with a rickety bed and a small table beneath the window, a bowl of fruit incongruous on its surface. I settled myself on the edge of the table and the brother took a seat upon the bed; it creaked loudly as he eased himself down.

The pleasantries had been accomplished downstairs, and so now we were here to conduct business. I took from my cloak the finger bone, wrapped in delicate, damasked silk, and held it out to him, giving him no indication as to what it contained. I watched his face as he delicately unwrapped the silk, laying the square of fabric on his narrow lap. The features of his face were a study in concentration, as he peered closely at the relic. Using the silk to cover his fingers, he lifted the bone up to his eyes, to the light.

He guessed rightly as to its nature, although when I informed him it was of Jerome, he was taken aback and expressed his amazement repeatedly, after I had assured him many times of the relic's veracity and provenance. It was nothing to me, of course, a pretty bauble, a gruesome trinket, but I knew to him, it would be a treasure. The power of things can only be measured by the belief that is granted them; if a thing is suspect, it has no power. In the hands of this lay brother, at least to his mind, the gilded bone had great power, and it was this that I intended to trade upon.

This Fleming had made a throwaway comment while we had been talking several evenings before, about the rumors that had come to his ears while the Knights were marching through the Black Forest in Germany, about shape-changing men, specifically of men who transform into wolves. He told the tale in a light-hearted manner, but I detected in his voice the faintest whispers of fear and trepidation. I wanted to know more, and I was willing to part with a useless piece of bone to do so.

He knew I was a scientist, and I also had brought several vellums I had made for him on the subject of healing herbs and tinctures, our stated reason for meeting. But, I steered the conversation back to the story he had told of the shape-changers. He laughed, but it was tinged with a nervousness that belied him. I urged him to tell me the story again, recounting every detail he could recall.

According to the brother, his troop had, several months before, been crossing the Black Forest, on their way here to Poland. They had made encampment at a place that barely qualified as a village, merely a cluster of huts that had been built in a hacked-out clearing of the thick forest. The brother had gone to the little church that served the village and had celebrated the Mass for the Knights and the townspeople. After, he was hearing their confessions, and one of the villagers, an old woman, took him aside and asked him to pray for her son, who was afflicted with some strangeness that caused him to devolve to a wolf. The brother, of course, scoffed at the woman, who went away angry and cursing, but the next morning, as the Knights were preparing to march on, several of the townsfolk approached the brother and the Captain, stating that in the night, a wolf had attacked a man on the road and he was dead. The Captain and the brother and several Knights followed some of the men to the place of the attack, and indeed found a man who had been savaged by some wild animal, possibly a wolf. The Knights brought the man back to the village and there he was identified and cleaned and readied for burial. The brother performed a funeral service for the man, and when it ended, the Knights made ready to march off. The Captain advised the townsfolk to post guards at night and kill any wolves or wild beasts who ventured near the village. As the troop was marching out, however, two men approached the brother, a youth and an older fellow. They took him aside, and told him that indeed, the man who had been killed on the road had been attacked by the old woman's son, who was called Hans. This Hans was missing all night, according to his mother, and had stumbled home during the funeral, covered in blood and having no memory of the night before. The brother agreed to meet with Hans, telling the Captain he would catch up to the troop later. Upon seeing the young Hans, the brother was aghast: his clothing was shredded and his face and hands were caked in dried blood. He could make no coherent speech, and when the old woman was questioned, she merely broke into tears and was unable to answer, save that her son was a shape-changer, but he had never killed a man before, only other animals. The brother was taken aback, and knew not how to proceed. He made the Sign of the Cross over the young Hans, and debated whether to perform an exorcism, but he did not know the rites well enough. He advised the young man and the older fellow to tie Hans to the bed and restrict him from leaving the house for several days. Then, he left and overtook the Knights several hours later. It was not until they reached the larger town of Altensteig the next night, that the rumors caught them of a wolf attack that had killed several people in the village they had just left, including the young man, and several other townsfolk.

The brother concluded his story and a chill ran down him; I saw him shudder. For my part, I gave his tale some small credence, owing mostly to my correspondence with Vermundr Karl, who I considered an expert in the field. I had grown more and more interested in these tales of shape-changing men, and I had gathered several from across Europe over the previous few years. Far and away, the majority of these described men devolving to a wolf, but from a Finn I had heard tale of a man devolving to a bear, and from a Russian visitor, of a man devolving to a bat. Nothing, I knew, was impossible for the human machine to achieve; it was only a matter of understanding the mechanism and its ability.

I knew, from our earlier discussion, that the Fleming was to return to Aachen with another troop of Knights once the group he was traveling with reached their destination; it was his role, he told me, mostly to serve as a wandering confessor to the armies of Christ that marched across the continent. I urged him to return to my estate on his journey back west, promising him lodging and fine food for himself and as many of his Knights as I was able to accommodate.

In addition, I left hanging the suggestion of a gift of another relic. I could see himself in his own eyes, enlarged in the view of his Knights by the mere possession of a gilded finger bone; the possibilities for his own greatness, I could see dancing in his mind.

We parted, and I took several ales with the Knights collected in the main room of the inn, acting the gregarious lord but in actuality sizing up each as a potential specimen. There was one who particularly caught my interest. He was a large brute of a man, but youthful and, in his own words, new to the Order and on his first march. He was a Dane, called Jorgen. His land, he told me, was inhospitable to the Church, still hard in the grip of the heathen gods, and so it had served as a crucible, to melt away the doubt and inconstancy that afflicted the weak-hearted, and to make him an earnest servant and warrior of God.

All well and good for him, but for me the only church was science. In fact, I could only bear to listen to so much of his proselytizing autobiography before I slipped into a reverie of opening his chest to affix therein the mechanical heart I had built and closing him up again to see how a man of his size and strength could function given the power of two hearts, one natural and other gifted by science.[40] I confess that he had stopped speaking, apparently for some moments, awaiting my response, while I was still deep in my vision, and it was with a feigned headache that I dismissed

---

40 The mechanical heart to which the Duke refers was a very crude, ungainly pump: a hollow canister of metal halved by a bellows, tubes and coils protruding from numerous points, springs and bladders affixed. The entire apparatus was the approximately the size of a loaf of bread, and would theoretically be powered by the movement of the body itself, which would start the flow of blood into the canister, which would in turn churn the bellows and direct the blood through the tubes, attached as they were to arteries and veins. Visionary, undoubtedly, but impractical in the extreme, the Duke spent the rest of his life tinkering with the design and, almost unbelievably, made a successful implantation at Wiskitki around 1337.

my inattention and invited the fellow back to my estate, with the offer of provisioning him and his fellows with some smoked venison I had laid by. The Dane demurred, saying such things were the purview of another functionary, and he could not impose upon me further. I elected not to press the invitation, and bid the warriors farewell and godspeed.

The interval passed unremarkably but for the continuation of my experiments. By this time, I had a veritable stable of subjects at Wiskitki, most of them bought as servants, others brought into my household by other means. One or two of them were the results of the breeding program I had instituted in the first year of my overlordship of Wiskitki. In sum, according to the census I took at the beginning of the year, there were twenty-six men, women and children at the lodge, ranging in age from three months to four-and-fifty.

The fertility of women was a project in which I had made great advances. Several of the females had arrived at my household as mere girls, and as soon as they had arrived, I had started them on a diet I had crafted to influence and increase their female abilities. To break their fast, they were to drink nothing but nettle broth. They were then to spend the morning working in the henyard, attending to the eggs and chicks, or to spend as much time as possible in the presence of women already carrying with child, to saturate their very animalcules with the airs and humors of burgeoning fertility. Weekly, I would examine each girl intimately, marking their progress of lack of same. At midday, they would be given a soup which was based off the moon blood of older mothers in the household, a bread of alfalfa and clover, after which I would knead into their lower abdomens and nether areas oil of primrose. In the evenings, I allowed them a treat of a sherbet of yarrow and aniseed, and they were instructed to stay awake all night upon the full moon, but the sleep on all other nights a minimum of four hours.

I began to see positive results within the first year of the experiment, the younger girls flowering earlier than normal, and I subsequently, if they proved strong and healthy enough, added them to the breeding program. Even today, decades later, the progeny of my breeding program scamper about the lodge here at Wiskitki, and although I never sired children of my own, I cannot help but feel the pride I imagine a true parent would feel whenever I see these creations of mine dash past me.

Some two months later, the Fleming returned to my estate, on his way west to Aachen with another marching troop of Christ's army. He called near sundown, and I welcomed him as a long-absent friend. I had not been idle in the meantime; I had been preparing for his return by compiling all my related correspondence with Vermundr Karl on the subject into one volume, and studied it to the point of memorization. Additionally, I had outfitted myself for a long journey, equipping a wagon and packing several trunks with warm clothing, dried food, and various weapons and scientific instruments. I intended to make the journey with the Knights as far as the Black Forest, indeed to the very village where this shape-changer Hans was alleged to live, if he had indeed been suffered to live by the townsfolk or nature.

As we sat to table, I inquired to the Fleming after the Dane called Jorgen, the hulking man whom I had envisioned twin-hearted, and was told he had felled five men at a stroke in a battle with a Bohemian advance party. I credited the tale with amazement, though I cannot say the claim surprised me much; in fact I wondered that it was only five. Again, my mind began to wander to thoughts of all I could accomplish were I ever so blessed as to avail myself of such a specimen.

We talked over the meal and eventually, the conversation came to the subject of the ugliness of war itself and the suffering of the men injured and wounded therein. He recounted to me several of the most horrific wounds he had seen in the battle against the Bohemians: a man whose arm had been lopped off and been left screaming in sheer agony as he bled to death in the mud, another whose face was split down the middle by a blow from an axe and yet still did not die, but wandered about the battlefield, dazed, face awash in blood, a deep cleft halving his head. Yet another had been impaled at the groin by a bolt shot at close range, in lingering, ever-worsening pain, waiting to die of some sickness or loss of blood.

I had fought in several battles, mostly small skirmishes, in my time, none so notably as that first which I have already related, but the Fleming's words rang true: there seemed no peace nor hope for those men who were not instantly dispatched in the course of war. The wounds of war were, it seemed, as sure a killer as the true blow from the sword, yet slower and more painful.

Imagine... I suddenly thought, and in thinking, I was so aroused by the brilliance of the idea that I voiced it aloud... imagine if a man could feel no pain? A man who felt no pain could not be crippled by pain, his inaction nullified. He could fight on, and perhaps even fell the man who wounded him in turn. An army of the painless could be near invincible, until at least such time as the blood emptied from them, could they not? Pain was merely the physical manifestation of fear, and without pain, there is no fear. If pain is removed, a man will be fearless, and a fearless warrior is deadlier than a scythe.

The meal and evening went on, but I confess to remembering little, as I was consumed by this new revelation. A man who could live without pain. A soldier who could fight and rally even after receiving dread wounds. The more I thought about it, the more I found applications outside the military realm. A farmer who sliced off a toe while hoeing his field would only need to bind up the stump and continue on at work, and the day would not be lost, the field would be readied for sowing. A woodsman who gored himself while cutting wood would again merely need to staunch himself and return to his task, and again the work would be saved, the wood piled up and the woodsman's family assured of another night of warmth against the winter. Even a barber-surgeon who pricked himself in a bloodletting would be able to continue on and heal his man, instead of risking the patient's life while attending to his own worry. The very world itself could be made immeasurably better, more productive, more healthy I even wagered, if only pain could be overcome. If sleep could be overcome, surely a thing like pain could as well.

As the Knights and the Fleming retired to sleep, I flew to my laboratory, pulling down every scroll and vellum I could find that applied to the brain and the body and its responses to pain. Even my own notes on pain I consulted, having done numerous experiments on pain threshold in the past. I had developed a scale, and found that the average man could not endure much over three-of-seven. If I could find a way to raise that tolerance, even to a five-of-seven, the benefits could be profound. My thoughts drifted to the boy Lukasz, whose skin was impervious to fire. I realized the boy could be used as a base from which to launch further investigations into the nature and defeat of pain.

All that night I pored over the notes of my own and the works of minds more learned than my own. The seed had been planted in my brain and I could not uproot it, though I had no desire to. In the morning, I went down and broke my fast with the Fleming. His knights were bathing in the river; I could hear them through the open windows of the kitchen, laughing, splashing, cavorting. I wondered how many of them would be felled by an enemy sword, burned by hot oil, speared by an arrow's flight, crushed beneath a catapult's stone. Later life would be bring me no cause to love the Teutonic Knights, but upon that morning, I grew weary with trepidation for those young, strong men in the river, numbered in their days as are we all, yet theirs under so much greater threat.

In the afternoon, I took the Fleming for a ride through the countryside around Wiskitki, taking especial care to point out each church we passed in the small villages. He seemed well pleased, and eventually we came to a watermill beside a swift-rushing stream. The man who operated the mill was known to me, as I often sent some of my estate grain to him for milling, allowing him to keep a portion as his payment; I sold the rest to bakers in my father's growing Warsaw. The miller was an old man, crippled, missing an arm at the elbow from a childhood accident that should have killed him. Years before I had built him a false arm of oak and leather straps, a crudely carved hand affixed at the end, and while it aided him little in his work of milling, he was always quick to enumerate for me the things he could do with it, that he had been unable to do before without difficulty: rake a flower bed, carry two buckets, churn butter. As such, he was invariably glad to see me, in addition to my being his lord.

I imposed ourselves upon the miller's hospitality, and he soon brought forth a fine bread for us. For a peasant, the miller was a fine man and true, and I had once given him a gift of a damasked sword, rusted and like to shatter if ever used. But it was a Crusader sword, brought back from the Palestine by a Polish knight some century before and given me as a fealty by some village hetman upon my accession as Duke. I found it unseemly and crude, and was thus not averse to giving it to this miller as a token of appreciation for the fine work he made of milling my flour.

I had the miller fetch the sword while the Fleming and I ate the bread. He went and brought it, laying it upon the board before us. If anything, it had worsened in quality over the years. The rust had eaten through the blade in many places, like moths through linen. The jewels in the hilt had been pried loose even before it had been given me, but now the thing looked forlorn and ugly. But through the rust could still be made out the Arabian inscription on the blade, and the fine crafting of the sword could not be doubted.

Gesturing to it, I told the Fleming the tale that had been told me when it had been given unto me, that it was the sword of the guardsman of the great heathen lord Saladin, who had been victorious in the Holy Land and reigned over his Arab empire from a throne of Crusader skulls. The guardsman whose sword it had been had fallen, it was told me, felling a brave Frankish knight who had come unto the person of Saladin feigning peace, with the intent of assassinating him. Upon seeing the Frank withdraw a secret blade for the purpose, the guardsman had struck him down, and thus the sword was sanctified with the blood of a true Christian warrior that had died in the ultimate act of preserving the Faith.

Whether or not I believed the tale, it could not do less than invigorate the mind of the Fleming, who gazed upon the sword as though seeing the blade itself tear the flesh of the brave Frankish knight, seeing the crimson glisten of his martyr's blood still wet upon the steel. I took up the sword and held the hilt toward the Fleming, proffering another gift. He hefted it lightly, as though afraid it would be heavier than it was, or perhaps more delicate. He marveled at it in his hand, staring wide-eyed, ensnared.

With a leather pouch of five gold florins to compensate the miller, I sent him away and told the Fleming of my intent to accompany him and his troop to the Black Forest. I cannot even now tell if he heard me or not, whether he was enthralled in visions of a blood-stained throne room or not. He wrapped the sword carefully in his riding cloak, and shortly thereafter we left the miller, returning to the lodge at Wiskitki in time for the evening meal.

Within a fortnight, I had left with the Knights westward. I had no other goal in mind but to see for myself one of these shape-changers, and I hoped this Hans was still alive, that he had not been claimed by the malice of ignorant minds. The weather was fine and the roads were in good condition; the normal fears of the solitary traveler of highwaymen and bandits were unfounded when in the company of a troop of Teutonic Knights. We made excellent time, the soldiers well used to covering long distances in the span of a day. Still and all, it took nearly three weeks for us to breach the border of the Black Forest, and I was sorely ready to be for a time stationary.

The Fleming and a small cohort of Knights led me to the village where they had encamped before, where the infamous Hans had lived. Several of the elders in the village remembered the Fleming, and seemed very happy to see him, and the presence of more Knights visibly put them at ease. This had been a place living in fear, it was palpable in the air, in the stares of the young and old, especially the womenfolk. My heart fairly rushed up my throat at the possibility that Hans was still alive, still here, kept as some kind of captive. I had half a mind to force the Fleming to take me to him at once.

Instead, I allowed myself to be led along with the Fleming and the Knights to a small inn, where we were treated with rustic hospitality. I knew very little of the German tongue, and thus was unable to follow much of the conversation, which had all the feel of catching-up and small talk. At length, I asked the Fleming to inquire after the creature Hans, and perhaps where he could be found.

It was arranged that the Fleming and I would be taken to the house of the old woman, who had claimed to be Hans' mother later in the evening, after dark. It was said she did not leave the house anymore, sending a boy out to buy bread and meat for her every few days. Though it had only been a matter of some two months, it was said she was turning toward hermitage in the little hovel.

I wondered how she would receive two unexpected visitors, but I hoped the presence of the Fleming, whom had done her a service in her eyes, would stand us in her good graces. Anxiously, in boredom, I awaited the setting of the sun. There was nothing of interest to me in the village, which was sparsely populated; some of the children showed tell-tale signs of being inbred. I passed the time in an empty corner of the inn, crafting in my mind the plan I hoped to enact upon meeting the creature Hans.

I drank ale, so as not to appear ostentatious in abstaining, for it was the odd man, I have found, who does not imbibe with his fellows. At length, the Fleming came to my table, bringing me a plate of food: a mutton leg, roasted potatoes, a pheasant steak, mashed turnips and bread. I looked about and noted most of the others were making do with a thick stew. Quickly, I devoured the meal, and the Fleming and I fell into conversation about Hans and his nature.

As we talked, I realized I had judged this Fleming perhaps too lightly; I had seen him merely as an end to my means, a willing servant to be bought and led with saint's bones and Crusader swords, a perhaps-awestruck young man who could be bent to my will and interest. As it happened, in that German village, I realized I had found another kindred spirit, one who reminded me so fully and completely of my first true helper, the boy Kazimir who I missed deeply. The Fleming spoke eloquently on the subject of shape-changers, far more in-depth than he had ever let on before. He elucidated his own theories on the nature of these beings, which differed from those of Vermundr Karl. Namely, the Fleming was of the opinion that these creatures were cursed by God and therefore bore the mark of His displeasure by devolving into a baser beast, yet all the while retaining their human mind and sensibility, so as to reiterate their true inhumanity.

Needless to say I found his theory as ridiculous as I found Vermundr's. My own mind went to the idea that these beings were an entirely different species of man, a branching off in a similar vein as the house-cat from the mountain lion. I did not wish to engage the Fleming in a debate, however, and merely praised the logic and originality of his argument. But the greater questions to me at the moment was, how and why had the Fleming developed such an interest in such creatures? I dared to hope, correctly as it happened, that the lay brother was a man whose heart had also been kindled by the light of knowledge and striving.

He was a religious man, very much so, he told me. His own father had been a mason, and had helped to build the great cathedral of St. Rumbold in Mechelen. The Fleming had grown up amidst the rising stone towers and soaring spires of the massive fortress of God, running about the flagstones of the floor, dodging around huge blocks of granite and marble stacked and stored in what would become the nave of the great church, while high above on rickety wooden scaffolds, strong men with hunched backs piled with stone or wood seemingly cavorted in the ever-expanding rafters and ceilings. His father was one of those men, and usually he worked outside, piling shaped stone ever higher, building the tower that much higher to heaven.

The Fleming had been playing in the field beside the cathedral's husk with another boy, and so he was spared the sight of his father falling, falling down to earth like a cast-off angel. His mother could not afford to keep him at home and so he was sent to the monks at a nearby monastery. He was seven years old when he arrived, and was taken under the tutelage of a harsh Dutch brother called Walder. This Walder was cruel and prone to drink. One evening, perhaps a year after his arrival, the abbot sent him to fetch Walder from the monastery's apiary. When the boy arrived, he did not see Walder anyplace and looked about for him, finally following the sounds of whimpering coming from tall grass nearby. He came upon the old monk fornicating roughly with a milkmaid, and several empty bottles of wine scattered about them.

Walder, seeing the boy, threw himself upon him, heedless of his own shame and sin, and throttled the Fleming violently, in the meanwhile the milkmaid gathering herself off. Walder dragged the boy by his hair the long distance back to the monastery, threatening to kill him many times over if he revealed to anyone what he had seen. The boy spent many days in the infirmary, and when he finally emerged, Walder was nowhere to be found.

The shame the boy felt at his treatment, the anger in his heart at being victimized and humiliated by a man of God who himself was a base sinner, roiled in his heart and his mind, and the monks would find the young boy in prayer many times a day, sunk so deep in the mysteries of the faith that sometimes they were not even able to rouse him for meals or chores. His zeal was noted, however, by the abbot, and in time, the young Fleming was sent to a school run by the order in Cologne.

He became, through diligence and study and prayer, the valet to Heinrich Virneburg, the provost of Cologne Cathedral.[41] His life, though still one of study and chores and silence, was simple, and there were many hours in the day in which his mind turned not to God, but instead to Walder. Over and over, he rehearsed in his fantasy the gruesome deaths that would come to the old sinner at his own hands, and more and more he became consumed by these dreams, until finally, one morning some two years after his arrival in Cologne, he walked out the gates and never returned,

---

41   In 1314, Heinrich Virneburg, as Archbishop of Cologne, would crown Frederick the Fair as Emperor.

making his way back to Flanders under another name.

For the better part of five years, he searched out the old monk, himself posing as a lay brother with the Franciscans. Finally, back in Mechelen with yet another name and the face of a youth rather than a boy, he found the man he was looking for, working as a hostler. He stumbled upon the man after a day of riding, trotting his weary horse to the candle-lit lean-to outside of the city that catered to travelers of modest means. The old fellow who hobbled out to take the horse's rein from him could have been no other, and the Fleming's heart leapt in his chest at the unexpected sight of the man.

Time had ravaged him, true, but it was more than that, for it had not been so much time. His face and arms were scarred deeply, lines running like empty riverbeds down his cheeks and neck and forearms. The limp he walked with was severe, and although most would assume it had come in the line of being a hostler and making one's living with stranger's horses who were likely to kick and stamp, something about the man's gait told the Fleming it had been something else that had done it to him; for a horse would have shattered his leg and likely he would have lost it, but the old man moved as though the tendons and muscle of his leg had been torn and healed in a contracted way.

The Fleming, satisfied the old man had no recollection of him, inquired after the man's injuries, guessing perhaps he had been in a war. But the old fellow merely grunted and stated he had been hurt in the Alps while crossing to Italy on his way to Venice. An avalanche? No, had been the answer. The Fleming did not wish to arouse the old man's suspicion and so let the subject fall. But later that night, he called on the old fellow at his place beside the stable with a large flagon of wine.

They drank until the very dark of the night came upon them, and old Walder's tongue loosened as they did. He told the story warily, but well, and the Fleming had the distinct impression he told it often when in his cups. Walder had crossed the Alps with a youth; they were both hoping to make their fortunes in Venice. Late in the night as they camped high in the passes, Walder still hungry for their food had grown meager, the youth eyed Walder strangely then went off to the trees to make his water. Only when he returned, he had assumed the aspect of a wolf and savagely attacked Walder, taking great pieces of his leg and backside before the old fellow was able to fight him off with a burning stick from the fire. The wolf ran off and Walder waited to bleed to death.

Instead, he was found in the morning; the cold of the night had frozen his wound shut. He was taken to a small village and sewn up by a woman. Eventually, his health rallied and he turned back home, forswearing Venice and his fortunes, leaving the sinking city to its cursed invader.

He showed the Fleming the marks of his attack, and then drank off the rest of the wine. The Fleming waited until the old man had fallen into his stupor, then stood over him, wonderingly. The tale had been so matter-of-fact, told so earnestly and without fear of disbelief. Try as he could, he was not able to put out from his head these fancies of shape-changing men, who could devolve to a wolf and back again. He later joined the Knights, crisscrossing Europe, hearing stories and legends in disparate places of such things as his old tormentor had told him.

The Fleming finished his tale, and I could still see the wide-eyed wonder on his face as the memory of Walder's story played again in his mind. I let a moment pass before I asked him whether he had ever seen or met one such, and the smile that came to his face when he answered that he was only waiting for the sun to set was akin to that of a child's upon receiving a treasured gift.[42]

We parted, each retiring in high spirits, agreeing to meet again at the inn shortly after sunset. I took a walk in the village, but this took only a matter of moments until I was swallowed up by the thick evergreens of the Black Forest. I heard sheep bleating, and came across a young shepherd boy tending his tiny flock amongst the clover that grew on the forest floor. I hailed him in broken German and he waved cheerfully as I passed by. I wondered if Hans would prefer his meat or that of the lambs.

After an interminable wait, the sun itself seeming to conspire to slow its arc across the sky, I made my way back to the little inn to await the Fleming. Shortly after, he arrived and we departed for the house of the old woman. It was away from the village somewhat, tucked away in the trees, which I'm sure suited the folk very well—and the old woman nicely for that matter, burgeoning hermit that she was. Smoke curled from the stone chimney as we neared, and an unmistakable scent of offal grew stronger and stronger the closer we came.

The mother came out before we were even before her place. She was not as old as I had pictured, merely a woman worn down by hard living. Perhaps, she was in her middle-womanhood. She greeted the Fleming with a warm embrace and called him Father, as though he were a real priest and not a lay brother; the Fleming, I noted, made no move to correct her. He then turned to me and I bowed, and he introduced me as a barber-surgeon from Bohemia, which accounted for my lack of her speech. This seemed to please her to a great degree, and she ushered us into the small house.

---

42 Walder Breggeneden, a former monk and hostler, was found murdered in his shed in the fall of 1313. A "violent and viscous man with many enemies", according to the city archives of Mechelen. His murder was unsolved and given only token investigation.

Inside, it was warm and rustic, pleasant in its way. There was a fire in the hearth, and a large iron kettle hung over it; I could hear something bubbling inside. The floor was of hard-packed dirt and sawdust. From a wall hung a large carved wooden crucifix, and beneath it a candle flickered. Between it and the fire, there was no other light in the room.

She led us through the room to where a carpet was hung to cover a doorframe. Pulling it back, she ushered us into a tiny room with stone walls and a barred window. In the room was a wooden pallet, and two iron rings were set into the stone wall at the head of the bed. On the bed was a youth, asleep, his arms above his head, chained to the wall by braces about his wrist.

He looked emaciated and wan. Through the bars, the starlight shone through, and it made his skin appear milky and phantasmic, as though he were some sort of ghost. His hair was long and thick, black as jet, and he was bearded, but underneath it could still be glimpsed a hollow, haggard face. He had been dressed in a linen tunic, filthy and covered with grime. At a glance, I noticed his hands: the fingers were crusted with dried blood. Lifting the thin blanket covering him, I saw the same was true of his toes, and that his legs were lean and muscled, and hairy.

Under my guise as a barber-surgeon, I ushered the woman from the room and with the Fleming, began my examination of the creature called Hans. He slept, deeply, and I pulled his lids up to check his eyes, and he did not awaken nor ever stir. Carefully, I pried open his mouth, expecting it to snap shut over my fingers at any second, and peered in at the teeth as the Fleming held a candle over me. Hans' teeth were ragged and some were worn down to mere stumps; his tongue lolled an ugly shade of brown-black, and his breath stank of rotting meat.

His limbs and trunk were healthy in appearance; he was lithe and looked as though, were he to suddenly spring awake and find us examining him, he could jump and run like a rabbit and we would lose him forever into the night and the forest. But he was woefully thin, as though he had not eaten properly for weeks. Using the Fleming as interpreter, I called the woman back into the room and asked her what he ate and how much.

At this, she began to sob, and explained that he slept for most of the day and night, being awake perhaps only two hours in a day, and it was in those brief periods of wakefulness that she tried to make him eat but the only thing he could tolerate was raw meat: chicken and other poultry and the occasional lamb, if she could get it. The things she had had to do to get her son his meat, I can only imagine; there were no cattle in the forest, and the lambs I had seen were few and far between. Chickens ran amok, and I imagined she had used up her own flock long before.

He had been kept, she told us, chained to the wall in the small room since the Fleming and the Knights had left them, and that he did not speak and never had. She tried to get him up to exercise his limbs when he waked, but often he was listless and wanted no part of it. She said he would not let her shave or bathe him. I told her, frankly, that the youth was like to starve to death.

Then, I could no longer avoid the subject, and demanded to know why the old woman felt her son was a shape-changer. At this, the sobbing that had started when I had mentioned starving abruptly stopped and she looked at me squarely in the face, and although it was the Fleming who spoke her words to me, I knew them in my heart before I even needed his translation: I have seen it, she said.

It was rare, she said, he did not do it often. The last time had indeed been when the Knights had been in the village before, but prior to that, it had been some eight months. When it happened, she described, he shook all over, as though in a fit, and then his body and limbs began to elongate, along with his jaw, and his very aspect altered, his frame and bones grew and shrank and folded in on themselves until he had abandoned the form of a man and devolved to that of a wolf. Hair covered his body, and he was far taller than he had been, and his legs more powerful, his hands larger and fingers more like claws. The teeth in his mouth grew to fangs and his nose and jaw seemed to fuse and create a snout.

When his transformation was complete, she said, he would spring away like a scared animal and dash off into the forest, and he would be gone for hours or days and return to the house in a daze, covered in blood, naked, unable to recall a thing since before his change. He would spend the first night back home vomiting and spewing from his backside, curled on the floor with a stabbing pain in his gut, but after usually a day, he would get up and go to his bed and sleep for days on end, without eating, without washing, emptying his bowels all over himself.

Fascinated, I asked her when was the first time she had seen such a thing, and she replied he had been a youth of perhaps twelve; Hans was seventeen at that present time. Had she been afraid? At this question, she shook her head, and said she had not, and I found this odd and told her so. She explained she was a Gypsy, and had heard of such things before, and that even one of her uncles had been so, that she had seen him change as a girl.

I asked her then about how the birthing of him had passed, whether it had been hard or light, long or fast. She lowered her head, and preying upon the peasant's underlying fear of the barber-surgeon, I pressed her until she admitted that Hans was not her son, but a foundling that had been given her. She refused to reveal who this woman had been, nor where it had occurred, but she swore upon the Holy Faith that she loved Hans as her son, and prayed for him as one of her own blood.

The admission seemed to take the will from her and she excused herself and left the room. The Fleming and I exchanged a glance and he went out to her. Alone with Hans, I wasted no time. Withdrawing from my cloak several instruments and glass phials, I went to work, quickly and adeptly, making the least noise I could for fear of arousing the attention of either the woman or the Fleming.

I made a small, deep incision in the youth's forearm and collected three phials of his blood; it flowed slow and thick, and I stopped the flow with a daub of sap I had brought for the purpose. I took several locks of his hair, pried a loose tooth from his jaw, pared a finger- and toe-nail. The blood, though, was the prize. I quickly secreted the tools and phials back into my cloak and made sure the youth did not look as though he had been disturbed.

I went to the other side of his bed to peer out the barred window; it looked out upon the thick forest. Moonlight now fell from the sky, making the grass and clover of the forest floor look snowy and frozen. I turned back to Hans and started; his eyes were open, looking at me. For a moment, I was as a statue, unmoving, staring down at the creature, and all at once I went to my knees and whispered at his ear.

In Latin, in Vulgara, in Russian, I asked and repeated over and over the same questions. What are you? Where are you from? Where are the rest of you? He turned his head, but his face expressed no comprehension. I was almost ready to collapse in frustration, I could feel a well of helplessness and defeat rising in my gut, when something from the Fleming's tale sprang to my mind. On a whim, I asked again in Italian, a language I had only recently started to study.

The youth's face lit, his eyes widened. Gian, he had answered in a whisper, Gian. Gian, which was the Italian version of Hans. Trebizond, he said, Venice. I took it to mean he had been born a Byzantine and later lived in Venice. Everywhere, he answered, we are everywhere. And then he smiled, baring his awful teeth; a trickle of grey slaver ran from the corner of his mouth. With a great effort, he thrashed his arms in their chains, rattling them against the stone loudly. The Fleming and the woman came rushing in; she screamed to see him awake, and made to usher us from the room, fear in her eyes.

The Fleming rushed out without haste. The woman looked to me beseechingly, urging me in German to leave, to go. I replied to her calmly in Italian, as Hans thrashed violently on the bed, lifting his body in spasms and arcs, crashing down again, near to sending the bed frame into splinters. The chains rattled against the wall, and the braces about his wrists chafed his skin to the point that blood flowed.

I am staying, I told her. And from my cloak I drew my long dagger, and pointed it at the creature, saying again, And I will kill him if you do not tell me all you know of him. I will saw his head from his neck. Her eyes went wild and she lunged at me. I knocked her to the ground with a strong blow to the side of her head; she groaned and rolled upon the floor.

The priest, she said when she recovered, told me you could cure him. I told her it was not so, and went to the youth's side, laying the flat of my blade against his neck. His thrashing and trembling slowed at its touch and he stared up at me in terror. He spat at me, cursing me in several tongues I did not recognize. The woman still sat hunched on the floor, knees hugged to her breast, watching me intently.

He is my sister's child, she said finally. She died birthing him. A changer had raped her, and she had tried to destroy the babe in her womb, but it had been too strong, and so she prayed she would die birthing it, and the Lord granted her that. Her family were Gypsies, she said, from the hill country east of Trebizond far to the east. She and the infant had been captured by raiders one spring and sent off as slaves to the market at Venice. She had escaped with the boy, and hidden in the countryside and forests of northern Italy, in the Alpine foothills. She had heard from other Gypsies that the boy's kind was common in middle Europe and so she intended to make her way to Germany. Somehow, the two had fallen into a small pack, the term she used, of other changers, and they lived with them in the thickly wooded forests that carpeted those Alpine hills. There were three of them, not including the boy and herself, she said, who was not a changer. Two of them were twin brothers, she said, and the group of them wandered far and wide for many years, through the Alps and into Hungary, Austria, Switzerland, and back to Italy. Back and forth across the waist of Europe, always hiding in the forests or in caves, doing all they could to avoid men and towns, for they were sure there they would be killed. Or burned.

One winter night, the other one, who was not one of the brothers, attacked and killed a goat on a farm, and the sound of the slaughter had brought the farmer out, and he killed the youth. The rest of them fled, the two brothers she knew not where, she and the boy she now called Hans over the passes again and into the Black Forest, where they had settled in this village, and where the boy had grown up into the youth against whose neck I pressed my blade.

I made her describe the twin brothers to me, and after a time I hid the dagger away again in my cloak. As I withdrew my hand again, I dangled before her a leather sack of gold florins. I told her, as she took it, opening it wide-eyed, that if she and Hans wished to return to Poland with me, they would be safe there. But if they chose not to come, the gold was enough for them to start another life someplace else, someplace perhaps in the Alpine foothills, nearer their kind.

She looked up at me but I did not await her answer. I returned to the inn, where I found the Fleming, cowering in a stein of ale. I invented a tale for him and we parted for the night.

In the morning, the Knights and the Fleming left for Aachen, and I called at the woman's house. There was no answer to my knock, and so I went inside. There was no sign of her there, so I went to Hans' stone room, through the hanging carpet.

She was dead, disemboweled on the dirt floor, large pieces of her flesh gone, bitten off. Flies buzzed about her and a dark spreading stain muddied the ground. The chains hung from the wall, the braces opened, unlocked. There was no sign of Hans, nor of the gold florins.

9

Since the time of my accession as Duke of Masovia, I came to rely on trusted individuals who would assist me in my scientific works. Of course, the Fleming grew to be one of these, and the trust I had placed in him early in our acquaintanceship only grew as the years went on, to the point that, at times when I spoke to him, I had the strange sensation that I was actually merely having a conversation with myself, with some other aspect of my person. I could send him forth with my instructions, and he would return with all I had asked for and more, even anticipating me in some degree, garnering for me certain items or subjects that I would have use of in the future.

The day-to-day administration of Masovia, however, would not allow me to roam afield, searching for likely candidates or useful ingredients as often as I had when merely the heir. The Fleming, in his capacity as a traveling Knight, traversed Europe, and each time his journeys brought him to Poland, he would endeavor to visit me, and each time he brought me news of some incredible thing, or some amazing item or relic, some rare herb or item. As often as six times a year, I opened my estate at Wiskitki to him, and treated him as one of my own household, feasting him and whichever Knights he had brought with him as honored guests, taking them hunting and game-hawking. I can only hope that the Fleming enjoyed his time at my lodge as much as I enjoyed having him there. If anyone, centuries hence, wishes to find in my life what could be termed a turning point, where the fulcrum of things shifted and the balance was changed and all that I had been before altered into something else, it could well be marked by the death of the Fleming, which affected me more greatly than any scientific defeat I had ever suffered.

But, that of course was years hence. I refer now to the springtime of our friendship. It was on one of these early visits to me that the Fleming brought me a creature that I had merely dreamt of, one whose very essence had been a mystery to science since Adam named the animals.

The creature he brought me was sickly; it had not traveled well. He had it, he said, from a bazaar in the Russian frontier, where it was descended, as was told him, from the stronger ancestors that had come across the Caucasus with the Khan of the Huns. He had wrapped it in a silken blanket, itself no small fortune, and laid it before me on the table, when his Knights had gone and it was only he and I.

I unwrapped the thing; it was moving, ever so slightly, under the fabric. The silk fell away and I beheld the tiny thing, little larger that my two hands placed side-by-side. It was indisputably a dragon, thin and feeble, barely breathing. My heart clutched in my chest, I could not believe what I was holding in my very hands. The dragon was parti-colored, pale orange and green and silver and purple, like a brilliant sunset had been spilled over it. The head lolled, the thing panted like a dog in summer. The eyes were black as jet and wet, as though the creature were about to cry. The snout and jaw looked brittle, and as it panted, I could see in its mouth the rows of tiny but very sharp teeth. It had a long tail that it had curled up against its body, and I took it and uncurled it to its length, and the thing made a high-pitched whimper until I released it. The four feet were clawed, but the little dragon seemed not able to draw enough strength to slash at us; if he had, the claws would surely have drawn blood. The scales that covered it were lovely, glimmering in the evening light, even as the creature itself seemed ready to expire.

I was, as I say, amazed, and openly wondered what price the Fleming had had to part with for such a treasure as this, but he would not reveal his cost. I confess that I knew little of these beings, what scant knowledge there was of dragons was cloistered in the East, I feared, and very little had seen the light of science and truth here in the civilized world.

There was, I knew, only one treatise on the nature of these creatures available in Europe, written in a Northern tongue. I had seen it once, in my travels to the great university at Heidelberg.[43] I had made a rough copy of a few pages, now in my library, and it was over this that I pored as the night burned on and the Fleming and his Knights slept.

The dragon slept on my writing table as I read the text over and over. I watched it sleep for several moments, and it was as I was doing so that a familiar, yet long-ignored voice whispered in my head. It was the demon Belphoram, whom I rarely listened to although he was often speaking in my mind. The demon spoke, telling me that in the dawn of time, even before the world had been made, in the long emptiness of nothing that preceded Genesis, the star Thuban had been the brightest of the heavens. It shone like silver fire in the vast empty vault of the universe, and the other stars were born as mere reflections of her violent burning light. Even heaven was made, and her floors were made of the starlight of Thuban. The days were ancient, lasting ten thousand years, and as heaven was built up and the first beings of light were made, their blood and bodies made from the same light, though dimmed. And one of these, Belphoram told me, was the Prince Lucifer, who reigned over a large swath of heaven then. Each day and night, the light of Thuban shone down on him and he grew spiteful and avaricious, for its beauty rivaled even his own. He went up to the star Thuban with a sickle of silver and with a mighty swing, cut from the star an arc of light, which he brought back down to the new heaven with him. Seeing what had been done, the Lord was displeased, and made the Prince Lucifer cast the light of Thuban down from heaven, down through the fathomless reaches of sky and aether that separated it from the earth. Plotting in his heart his future revenge, the Prince Lucifer with all his might threw down the bolt of Thuban, and it struck the new-made earth, striking its upper half into the

43 Presumably, this journey to Heidelberg occurred in the missing pages of the memoir.

sea, and its lower into the stone of the earth. A great fissure was made in the face of the world, the demon told me, and it was from this fissure that the dragons emerged.

A fanciful tale, I admit, and from the lips of a demon, I cannot but doubt its truth. But, there was something otherworldly about the little dragon, some aspect to the thing that seemed indeed not to belong to the sordid world of men, that I could not wholly in my heart doubt what the demon had said. In fact, the more I gazed upon the sleeping serpent, the more sure I was that its forebears were celestial. I even took up a quill and wrote down the tale as the demon had told me, adding it to the lore I had before me.

Sadly, though, all the accumulated knowledge about dragons that I had access to helped me little. I did not know how to care for it, how to keep it or use it. The pages I had managed to copy dealt mainly with such things as distinguishing between breeds of dragon and their characteristics. The dragon before me was not among those listed on my copy, however. At some point in the night, the dragon woke and looked about it, as though in confusion. I dripped water into its mouth from a stopper and tried to make it eat some raw meat I had had brought up for the purpose, cut very small and seasoned with salt. It nibbled lightly at a piece from the end of my finger; its tongue was rough, similar to that of a cat.

I had no idea how to care for a sickly dragon, which this was most apparently was. I left it alone as it drifted back to sleep, resisting all the urges of science that screamed in my heart and head to extract a sample of the creature's blood, to pry a scale from it, a claw, a tooth, to tear its tongue out by the root. If I could nurse the thing back to health, I kept repeating to myself, I could have a near-endless supply of these things. I turned my attention back to the copy of the treatise, trying to fill in the gaps with reasonable guesses, using the power of the mind to stop up the gaping holes in my knowledge.

At breakfast next morning, I interrogated the Fleming about the dragon, where exactly he had gotten it, and how, in what condition, from whom. It came from the bazaar, he told me, in the village of Chertyin, deep in the Russian Baltic.[44] The woman selling it was decrepit, old beyond description, Asiatic in mien and aspect, not a Christian he took pains to tell me. According to this crone, the dragon was of the stock that rode west with the Huns bringing fire and death as they came. The Fleming said she tried to embellish the tale by peppering it with the name of Attila, but he made his skepticism plain, and the crone let it lie.

Most of them had died out, she had said, their line not strong here in the West. They could not thrive far from home, it seemed. The Fleming, knowing as little about dragons as I did, accepted this as somewhat logical, and the crone let him examine the one specimen she had. Her other wares were painted eggs and metal trinkets of fine workmanship. She also had a small store of potions and herbs she grew in her own garden, she said, themselves grown from stock brought from the East. She ushered the Fleming into her tent and took up the dragon from a small wooden cage hidden under blankets.

The Fleming was astounded. Like myself, all his knowledge of these creatures was hearsay, or from the pages of a treatise. But, here he held one in his very hands. Truly, it was small and sickly, but there was no doubt, it was a dragon. The crone claimed not to know what ailed the serpent, but it had been sickly from birth. Its parents were dead, she said, they had lived in a small limestone cavern near the place where she lived. She had found the dead body of the mother when out collecting herbs, and taken the eggs with her from the cavern. The others had been stillborn, and

---

44 The village of Chertyin was demolished in 1952 by the Soviet government to make room for the Lysenko Institute of Paleobiology.

she had used the eggs and eaten them, and the strength they had given her had allowed her to survive the coldest winter of her lifetime. One egg hatched a live dragon, and it was this.

She told the Fleming that the Huns had brought with them three dragons, two males and a female. They were strong and healthy when they left, sowing fear and devastation in their path as the army of the Huns marched toward Europe. According to the legends of her people, who were among the marchers, the beasts had grown weaker and weaker as they approached the Caucasus, one of them, a male, dying on the slopes of Elbrus. The female, though, was carrying, and her inner strength seemed to be fired by this, by her maternal instinct. Eventually, when the Huns gained the Russian frontier, the other male died as well and only the female was left.

As her babes grew in her, this she-dragon grew more fierce and ferocious, terrifying even to the Huns who had been her handlers when she was a little one. One day, she broke from them and soared up into the sky and flew away, far away from them to the north, and the Huns never saw her again. The crone assured the Fleming that there were still villages to this day that have tales of the morning when a great winged demon flew over their heads, blackening the sky and sending out a roar to shatter walls of stone.

That had been some thousand years before, she told the Fleming. The female dragon had secreted herself somewhere in the forests of northern Russia and birthed her babes, who in turn bred and made more generations, each a weaker and less powerful version of their parents. This one, the crone assured the Fleming, was the last of the line, the final link to that fabled march from the golden halls far east of the Caspian Sea.

The Fleming admitted he paid the woman a shortweight

of gold from the coffers of the Knights.[45] A princely sum, of course, to the woman, but the Fleming assured me the amount was likely not even to be noticed gone by the Treasurer-General when they arrived at Aachen later. I offered to recompense him the cost of the endeavor, but he gracefully declined; however, I was able to gift him with some small items which I knew he would find priceless, though which to me had little value: a gem from the crown of the Empress Helena, and a finely-carved wooden box containing a goodly sum of frankincense.[46]

As much as I enjoyed his company, I admit I was eager for the Fleming and his Knights to be gone, so I could spend my days learning about the dragon. As it was, I hosted him and his entourage for another week, each day feasting and sporting and touring the countryside. On one such ride, he and I discussed the shape-changer Hans that we had met earlier that year. I inquired whether he had been seen again in the Black Forest village, but the Fleming told me there had been no sightings in the area, although he brought me fresh rumors of such creatures from Bohemia and Switzerland. I openly wondered how many of these fascinating beings there were in the world, and then reminded myself that Hans himself had told me his kind were everywhere.

At length, the Fleming and the Knights departed. I nearly rushed upstairs to my laboratory the moment they disappeared around the bend of the road. The dragon still slept on my writing desk; it moved rarely during the day and spent most hours asleep. It had, however, started eating more than a few bites of the raw meat; in fact, just the evening prior it had managed to consume an entire cube. Little by little, I hoped fervently, the little creature could be

---

45 An archaic unit of measure, approximately three pounds.

46 The Empress Helena, also a Catholic saint, was the mother of Constantine the Great, the Byzantine Emperor. She made a pilgrimage to the Holy Land, where according to legend, she discovered and brought back with her the True Cross.

brought back from the brink of sickness. I had no way of determining its humors, of gauging its blood. All I could do was give it food and water and keep close watch over it.

Weeks went by, and the dragon improved but slightly. It did not sleep so much during the day, and so I let it wander in a secluded courtyard, where it could feel the sun and fresh air upon it; I had also fettered its leg to a bolt in the floor so it could not take wing and fly away. It was still weak, though, and often on its outdoor exploration, it would curl itself up and rest with open eyes darting all about. I watched it catch several flies and insects with its long tongue, and one morning saw it pawing at the dirt, digging up a large worm. It was hunting, I thought. I took it as a good sign.

One morning, I had the idea to bring the boy Lukasz to see the dragon. He was near three years old by this time, and I set him and the dragon together in the courtyard, then retired inside where I could watch them. Theories and ideas regarding Lukasz and the dragon had been fomenting in my mind for some small time, as I had nursed the creature. The boy had grown strong, the scales of his back thick and tough. The backs of his legs and buttocks, too, now showed a thicker layer of the scale than he had at birth. I entertained notions of somehow improving the boy by means of the dragon's blood; I even wondered at the feasibility of breeding one to the other somehow. I watched as the little boy and the little dragon regarded each other in the courtyard. Neither seemed too interested in coming near the other. Then, after nearly an hour had passed with little more than some hard staring, the boy stood and approached the dragon. He reached his hand out and placed it lightly on the snout of the serpent. The dragon flinched, like a scared child, but did not snarl or attack or let fly with a geyser of fire, as I had wondered.

I let the two interact for some small time more, before fetching the boy and returning him to his studies and his tests. The dragon, I rewarded with a large portion of raw meat. For several days running, I let the boy and the dragon interact thus, and I saw in each of them grow a regard for the other, as though each recognizing in the other a kindred spirit of some kind, a sentimental thought I admit to having at the time, though now I recognize it as pure pablum.

Seeing the two thus enamored, though, merely served to stoke the fires of my mind with regard to the seemingly infinite possibilities presented by the merging of man and dragon. Eventually, after some few months, the dragon was healthy enough, and to be honest, docile enough, to allow me to extract a sample of its blood. The task was simple, and it amazed me at how fortunate I was, how expansively the animating spirits of science had smiled upon me, by allowing me access to such an indescribable treasure.

Into the most secret of my vaults I placed the phial of dragon's blood, to be used only at direst need. I felt, in my heart, a weight unsettle and slide away into the air, an unknown burden lost and yet myself bettered and soul-lightened by its departure.

It was late in the summer that I received word from one of my assistants in Italy in regard to the shape-changers. I had paid a trusted fellow handsomely to relocate himself to Venice and send me periodical reports into the rumors and tales surrounding sightings and encounters with the strange creatures as they came to him. His latest report was dated from a month before, excellent speed at any time of year. An illiterate village boy had delivered it to my hand, and after sending him away with a handful of copper, I rushed up to my quarters and tore open the thick stack of vellum. I pored over the elegant, simple handwriting, the entire report put down in a cipher of our own creation.

What I read was fantastical and hyperbolic, for the most part. I had entrusted him to repeat everything he heard of the subject to me in the reports, and he had not failed to encode even the most ridiculous, credence-less, and base tales, more akin to a children's story than anything approaching scientific research. I was about to cast the entire stack into the fireplace, but I resolved to read it through to the end. And a good blessing I had of it, as well.

The final two pages were scantly covered, the details were scarce and the witnesses mildly unreliable and far-between. But, there was no denying the appeal of what he had to tell. According to his report, in the village of Dobbiaco in the South Tyrol Alps, there had been over the late spring and summer several accounts of sheep and small animals being found eviscerated and torn apart in their farm sheds and fields. The lords of the town elected to post a watch in the night, as the farmers assumed the culprits were stalking wolves. For several nights, there were no sightings of any sort of predation, and the farm animals lived in a renewed spirit of safety. However, a fortnight after the watch had started, one of the watchmen was found by morning light to have been savaged and his throat torn out and his innards strewn about the ground all about him. Seemingly, he had wandered off in the night from his watch, some small distance into the woods that carpeted the steep hills that surrounded the town. The watch was increased, and the following night, another man of the watch was found similarly disemboweled, and several more sheep and goats. The next night, not a man of the town was exempted from the watch, and surely enough, in the smallest hours, a commotion was heard and many men rushed toward the sound. They came upon a small wolf savaging a youth, tearing at him with claw and teeth. The youth was already near torn to ribbons, but the men attacked the small wolf with pikes and halberds. The small wolf soon succumbed to its wounds, and to the shock of all the men collected, upon its death the wolf altered in aspect to that of a young boy, perhaps eight or nine years old.

The report concluded that the wolf-boy's corpse had

been burned by the villagers, which I cursed aloud upon reading of it, and that the youth who had been killed was buried in the churchyard. I reflected on the tale for the rest of the night, and question upon question came to me as the stars burned in the darkened heavens. Was the boy a part of a pack? It was hard to believe that a single small wolf had been responsible for attacking at least two grown men. Or did taking upon oneself the aspect of the wolf give one a commensurate strength? Surely, an eight or nine year old wolf was equal to the task of attacking a youth. And what of his reverting back into a human aspect upon death? I could not begin to formulate a theory on any of these queries. I felt, more and more, that I needed to travel to the Tyrol, and investigate on my own.

The likelihood that I could leave at such short notice, given the needs of governing Masovia, though, made the possibility highly unlikely. I had already been, in the course of the previous year, off to the Black Forest and into the Lithuanian hinterlands, not even mentioning the two- or three-day journeys to visit other local nobles at their lodges or estates. I knew well, from history and from hearsay, how quickly an unhappy people can turn against their lords, and the more time I was away from Masovia, the more likely it was that the steward I had left in charge would prove incapable of the task. I needed some pressing cause that could serve as pretext to allow me to spend more time in the pursuit of science.

To that end, and others, I used many pawns on the chessboard of Europe. I do not flatter myself to think that my endeavors have not influenced recent events to some very small degree. I had made friends in the ranks and command of the Teutonic Knights, I had blood ties to Lithuania and Bohemia, I had spent freely and with careful planning a portion of my gold and treasures with scholars and rogues across the continent. I knew what I wanted and I knew how I wanted to accomplish it.

It would take a war, or some other cataclysmic event, to liberate me for the time I needed. I could leave the details to my generals and captains, lead the armies as needed far afield, and linger as I saw fit in the places where I was drawn, searching ever for the golden light that science shone down on the meager world.

As the will of science would have it, I received news shortly after coming to this conclusion that dimmed to a great degree my efforts to create a war, although I would come back to that very plan later in life with greater forethought and incredible results. A herald arrived in the early autumn from the Elbow-High bearing a message that the King of Sweden, the Magnus Ericsson, Fourth of His Name, was to visit Poland, and specifically Warsaw, on his way to meet with the Prince of Novgorod in Kiev near Christmas.[47]

The main effect of the message was that, due to my father's homage to the Elbow-High, my presence was requested by the short fellow to accompany him and the Swedish King for some days at Warsaw before traveling east with the entourage as far as the border with Russia.

The weeks of preparation went quickly, and soon enough I was on my way to the Elbow-High's court at Warsaw. I traveled with a party of only eight servants and footmen, having left the lodge in the capable hands of Gudmunda and the governance of Masovia in my absence to the steward, who had also served my father in such capacity. It was middle autumn and the rains had already settled firmly over Poland, so the roads were a muddy soup, and although the distance to Warsaw was not significant, it took us the better part of three days to reach it.

---

47 This meeting between the Swedish and Novgorodan monarchs, long hinted at in the historical record but never confirmed, apparently did occur, but the fruits were short-lived. The Swedish King invaded Novgorod in 1348.

My father had founded Warsaw and my last memory of it was of wooden houses and muddy fields astride the great river. Now, only a handful of years later, there were strong stone buildings and the city walls were formidable. The palace of the Elbow-High was a series of sturdy towers, a work in progress but still defensible. He seemed resolved to make up in stone what he lacked in stature.

The rampart rose above as we made our way through the iron gates. The courtyard was flanked with armored soldiers, some holding tall pikes, others with pennons. I recognized the banners of several nobles, many of them my hosts earlier in the year. There were a few from the north I did not know well, and only one I did not recognize at all.

I entered the main keep and was greeted by the same steward I had met before, during the ceremony pledging Masovia's support, the one who had obtained the house servants for me. He nodded as I passed and was received by the Elbow-High and then shown to my quarters.

The evening was a banquet, and in the morning a hunt, and then the next day arrived the King of Sweden. He had arrived in the late evening after most of us had retired, in company of a large traveling entourage: nobles and military leaders, knights and squires, and a small assembly of what were later introduced to me as scholars. In the retinue of the Swedish King, I was exceptionally pleased to discover, was his court philosopher, the renowned scientist Count Axel Cronberg. I knew him somewhat tangentially through a brief correspondence, and even more so from his fame in scientific circles, specifically from his work using butter of antimony as a solvent for organic materials. Although I had as yet been unsuccessful in my own attempts to replicate his good fortune, I could see the sound science behind his theory. I made myself known to him, in a private audience that first evening, and we spent much of the night discussing the wonders of the world that had been brought to light by our work. He even told me he had traveled to the Palestine himself some decades before in search of the Great Stone that would alter the very face of existence, but had failed at the final moment; his face, as he told the tale, was etched in deep sorrow, and I knew he still mourned this loss as freshly as though his own children had been slaughtered before him.

A note on the Magnus Ericsson, perhaps, should be forthcoming. The man himself was tall and strong like a bear, bearded and thick-chested with grey eyes like the sleet of his own skies. He had only a crude grasp of Latin and almost none of Polish, hence the need for such scholars as he had brought with him to interpret and translate for him. I endeavored, over the course of the journey, with the help of the Count Cronberg, to learn the rudiments of Swedish. The King, though, made no such gestures in reciprocation, and often a simple conversation with His Highness would drag on for some time while words were exchanged from one tongue, drawn from a different one, a strange sort of science of speech, a transmuting of one set of sounds into another set that sounded utterly different and yet held near the same meaning. In all, though, the Magnus Ericsson was gregarious and fond of drinking and feasting and battle, a true heir to his Viking forebears, I imagine. Sadly, I would have no cause to see the King in battle, but the reports I heard as to his prowess were such that I have not a doubt that his valor would shame even my milk-blooded cousin of Bohemia.[48]

If truth can be admitted, I would rather have spent the next month in the illustrious company of the Count Cronberg than of his King and lord. We spent some five days at the palace of the Elbow-High before leaving for the eastern frontier, and the Count and I spent each evening

---

48 Yet another insult directed at John of Luxembourg, the thorn in Siemowit's side for most of his middle years. John was notoriously a brave fighter, even leading troops into war when completely blind.

together talking about our science, and when the Count would plead tiredness, he would go off to his quarters, and I would rush off to mine and stay up the remainder of the night, putting down in my journals all I could remember of his experiments and his theories. If there is any justice in this world, the name of Axel Cronberg would be exalted in every court and university in Europe.

10

[pages missing][49]

The winter came down upon us early that year; autumn had barely entered her throes when the first snows began to fall. We in the King's train were still a short distance from the border of Novgorod, but in a matter of some two days, several ells of snow had fallen, and we had been forced to take the hospitality of a local lord, the Zagonowa of Łusuków.[50] The place was not equipped for an entourage of our size or bearing, but the lord acquitted himself well enough under the circumstance, and I availed myself of purchasing for my service a pair of twin boys from a sickly mother who worked in the house and could not foresee herself being a fit mother. I recompensed her out of proportion and hired the services of a town woman, a young and unmarried spinster, to tend them until we returned to Wiskitki, where she as well would be welcome.

Marching onward in the snow, we reached finally the Novgorod border and were met there by a detachment of that Prince's honor guard who were to convey the Swedes to the meeting-place. It was where my role in the procession ended, and I was indeed ready to turn back toward home and the warm fires therein. My mind thus occupied, I was

---

49 At this point, three pages of the manuscript are missing. They had been assumed lost to the vagaries and whims of time; however, in 1856, the several-times-great-grandson of Count Axel Cronberg died without an heir, and in his effects were found these pages, which were inherited by the next of kin, a cousin who happened to be a minister to the King at the time, Oscar I, godson of Napoleon Bonaparte, incidentally. The pages were sealed in a vault at the National Library in Stockholm in 1877 and have not been made public. Numerous requests by the Editor and representatives of the publisher to examine the pages were ignored and/or declined. The manuscript resumes some weeks later.

50 A Zagonowa is a petty noble in the structure of the Polish ruling class of the time. The name derives from zagon, a small unit of land measure, and thus implying the Zagonowa is little more than the owner of a smallish estate- Trans.

unprepared for what came next.

One of the Novgorod soldiers was thrown from his horse, the beast being frightened by a sudden and very near clap of thunder. The young man came down hard on the ground not far from where I myself had reined up, and I heard the tell-tale snap of his neck breaking. A commotion had arisen, and most of the men roundabout were too busy tending to their own frightened mounts to have taken much more notice than that a comrade had fallen. I was the only one near enough to have heard his neck break, and I went to him.

His limbs were heavy and lifeless, limp and with none of the tension of life. His head was crooked at an unsupportable angle, and so I righted it and took off his helm. I beheld a young man, perhaps still a youth, of light blond hair and staring, wide blue eyes. The shock of his fall was permanently upon his face. I felt about his neck and head, down his tunic and onto his shoulders, his upper back, trying to assess the damage that had been done; a jut of bone twisted and poked just beneath the skin at the base of his skull.

At length, a group of soldiers, Swedes and Novgorodan, had gathered about. There was an argument as to what had occurred. The mistrust that boiled between the two sides was on full display, as the Novgorodans accused the Swedes of striking the boy from his horse. There was nearly a brawl until I spoke up and told what had truly happened. Eventually, the two sides agreed that there had been no harm done, and the youth was buried under a cairn a small distance from the encampment where we were to spend the night before returning to Poland in the morning.

In the small of the night, I left the encampment and went the distance on foot to the cairn. It was again snowing heavily, and any tracks I made were quickly covered again. I worked as quickly as I could, partly to stay warm but mostly to accomplish my task the more soon. I dismantled the cairn and took the youth's body, wrapped in his cloak and put it over my shoulder and carried it back to where I had staged my wagon, away from the encampment. I hurriedly placed it in the wagon and piled over it several heavy furs I had brought along to trade.

Before dawn, I made sure we had left, after making proper farewell to the Elbow-High and other lords, who were more concerned with that day's audience with the Prince of Novgorod to take much heed of my departure. The roads were near impassable after the snows and I took it into my head to hire a river boat that would take me quicker toward home.

I came upon a small village just after sunrise and a boy who was carrying a pail of frozen milk from his family's pasture directed me to the river, some short distance away. The river was the Lovat, and it was still navigable, there being no ice floes this early in the year, though the snow had made the land look like deepest Thule. At midmorning, we had gained the river and hired a boatman to take us on his flatboat. The wagon and the few retainers and I piled aboard and the boatman poled us off and let the current of the river take us southward.

The boatman was a grizzled man called Vanya, who said a boat could run this river all the way to Constantinople. He explained the route; the Lovat met the Khunya downstream, which led to the Dneiper, then to the Black Sea and on to Byzantium. He himself had made the route three times, he claimed. The journey took near two months. Impulsively, I paid him a fistful of gold florins to take us as far as his flatboat would safely travel and convey us to the Black Sea. He agreed with a grin as wide as the river.

That first night aboard the flatboat, I went into the back of the wagon alone and uncovered the dead soldier. He had stiffened, in death and in cold. From my cloak and a chest in the wagon I withdrew what tools I needed and set to work. I lay the body out naked on the floor and made the needed incisions, doing what I could to set the wrongness of his neck in order, though I knew even were I successful in what I intended, he would not be freed from an oddness and constant pain there. From a phial, I poured into his chest some grains of saltpeter and into his eyes I dripped an admixture of bile and ash. I cut out his tongue to burn later, and took the fingernail from the little finger of his right hand. I drained a quantity of his blood, though thickened in death, into a small flagon and admixed it with mercury, which I then poured into the other incisions.

I sealed him up and waited. I marked his skin with my sigils, in tiny script along his collarbone and beneath his left armpit, his inner thigh and the back of the neck just under the hairline. I waited again. I spoke into his dead ear his new name, and my own, that of his new master, and chained him with links of iron to the floor of the wagon. I left him and went to the little cabin where the boatman kept his quarters.

His wife and child traveled with him; they made their lives from the river. The woman was far more comely than a boatman's wife had any right to be, and I gave my retainers the strictest orders that she was to be treated with the utmost respect. I intended to free whichever of my men were so inclined to their liberty when we reached the Black Sea, as I had no especial desire to travel with as large an accompaniment as I hitherto had done. I took bread and meat with them, informing them I would restore their provisions at my expense upon reaching the city of Kholm, where the Lovat met the Khunya, and where there was a good market, he told me, for river traffic.

It had been some long time since I had been on a river, traveling at the leisure of the current on a boat—not since my first helper and I had cruised the Vistula that first warm spring together and dragged our little skiff up onto the rocky beach that lay below the hill atop which stood the old cemetery we had intended as our destination. I found the experience utterly rejuvenating. It was relaxing beyond all measure; there was something about our slow but steady progress, at the mercy of the river itself, that calmed the taxing of the mind that constant thought and planning and worry brought upon me. That first night in the boatman's cabin, even though I was fraught with anticipation regarding the dead soldier in the wagon, some part of my mind was becalmed by the journey, and even today, I still think of that boat with the greatest fondness.

After the meal and some small conversation, I left the boatman's cabin and went back to my wagon. I stood before the door, my hand on the bar, waiting, breath caught in my throat. I do not know why I was so nervous; I had done this very thing on two separate occasions, although never so soon after the actual death. I went over in my memory the process I had undertaken, searching out any possible error or oversight, but as is the nature of such things, one could wear themselves out over perceived or invented failures.

I pulled open the door and rushed in, bolting it closed behind me. I turned and held my back against the shut door. The dead soldier was sitting up, still chained to the floor, looking at me with eyes that were now solidly white. His hair, before a pale gold, was now near-white. I estimated I had been in the boatman's cabin for maybe two hours, and so the rapidity of the soldier's awakening and the changing of his aspect seemed to me a hopeful sign.

I stood and watched as he silently filled his lungs, his strong chest filling with air, then falling again. His eyes had the milky look of a blind man, and although he looked directly at me, I was unsure if he actually saw me or anything about him. The wagon was cold, colder than when I had left it; the soldier had made no effort, though, to cover his nakedness with the furs that lay all about him.

Our eyes held each other's for a few seconds and then I spoke the name I had given him, and it was like a trance had been broken. He blinked several times and looked about the wagon, as though searching for the source of the sound that had woken him from waking sleep.

I went through a series of rudimentary commands: lift your arm, shake your head, hold up two fingers. And each time the soldier complied, moving slowly but surely. I went to him and he merely looked up at me as I stood over him. I felt the back of his neck; there was a knot there, like a stone planted beneath the skin, where his spine had snapped and then had been reset. He showed no signs of pain as I poked and prodded him, merely sitting serenely as though it were something he simply had to endure to its finish.

I spent several hours of the night examining the soldier, testing his faculties and responses, his reflexes and the extent to which he could understand me and make himself understood in return. At the end of my examination, I commanded him to sleep, and it was as though he was a marionette whose string had just been cut, for he fell instantly, at the command, into a deep sleep. I covered him with the furs and made sure his chains were secure before leaving the wagon. I barred the door and locked it behind me and went to the brazier that stood at the prow of the flatboat.

The boatman's son was on watch; it was the depths of Matins, perhaps even the first hour of Lauds. The boy sat on a wooden stool, leaning toward the warmth of the glowing fire, looking up every now and again to scan the river for hazards or other traffic, though there was none. I stood in the shadow for a few moments, watching him, watching the night around us, the river and the shores on either side, the sky above us. We seemed to be the only boat moving on the Lovat; any other boats we passed were tied up at the shore. Slowly, silently, we passed the odd village or lone hovel, close enough to the bank to hear the sleepy bleat of a sheep in a yard as we went by. Once, the river curved, and around the bend of it a modest stone nunnery rose up, a darker mass of stone against the darkness of the night, though in a few windows a candle burned. It was a quiet and peaceful night, and but for the soldier in my wagon, it could have been called unremarkable in its banality, or to some, remarkable for the same reason.

At length, I stepped into the swimming firelight and made a small racket so as not to completely frighten the boy. He looked up as I came into his view and he nodded to me and wished me a good night. I returned his greeting and stood before the brazier, warming my hands. We talked briefly, about the river and its course, the weather of the coming months. He had been to Constantinople once with his father, when he had been six or so, he told me. He took me for, and treated me as, a lord, for there were few others so inclined or disposed to make such a journey on a whim. After a while, he stood to make his water over the wale of the boat, and when he was gone I took from my cloak the soldier's tongue, wrapped in linen, and threw it onto the fire.

There was a brief flash of brilliant white flame, and then it burned out and there only remained the orange dancing tongues that had been there before. The night surrounded me, the stars overhead looked down, the quiet wormed into my ears and I smiled to myself, content and alive with purpose. We would reach Constantinople by Epiphany, according to the boatman; we would likely miss the worst of the winter weather, and as we were traveling south, the possibility was even more likely.

After a few days, we reached Kholm, the city at the confluence of the two rivers. It was a bustling place, larger than I had expected, though not even as large as modest Warsaw. The city was mostly formed of tents and wooden long halls along the river, filled with peddlers and hawkers and farmers and tradesmen all crying their wares. I arranged with the boatman the supplies he needed and the payment of them, and then I went off into the city, as we agreed to meet back at the longboat after the middle of day.

It was early enough in the morning that the dirt streets were not crowded, but here and there throngs of wet-nosed boys ran about, ducking around corners as I came near and darting back as I passed. Dogs were everywhere; chickens clucked up and all about the place. I spent the first hours in the marketplace, stocking myself with what herbs and salts I could make use of. There were varieties here that I had never encountered before, and one tent held a crock of paste made from the seed of an Eastern flower called the poppet, which could put a man into indefinite slumber.

The bells of the church rang out the Terce, and there was a sudden yet brief flurry of feet as the devout or the superstitious ran along to their worship. I rounded a corner and came to a long wooden hall, with shopfronts along it. In the door well of one stood a tall, lean, and bearded Jew, who regarded me with squinted, bright blue eyes behind small spectacles.

He wore the black of his kind, a dirty long coat that reached his ankles. Our eyes met, and we held each other's stare. I was accustomed to most folk averting their eyes to me, usually out of deference to their lord, but occasionally, I do not deign to admit, from fear. This Jew, though, knew me not as a lord; I had seen men attired in this village at least as finely as myself, though they were just merchants. I stopped and stood before him, curious.

I spoke a smattering of Hebrew, and tried it on him, offering him the blessing of the day. He grunted and replied in kind. I looked now more closely at this man; I saw the depth in his eyes, and the strange milk-like radiance of his pale skin. The nails of his fingers were crusted with black, as though he had spent years digging in ash and was not able to wash it clean. I saw the hem of his coat was filthy with mud, but the cuffs and sleeve was stained with something more like clay, grey and thick. I saw the back of his hand scarred, like a spatter of hot oil had splashed onto it.

But I knew, suddenly, the wound had not come from oil. I had similar scars of the backs of my hands and upper arms. Many times in the early days of my study had I splashed myself with the Oil of Vitriol[51], and each time I had screamed and wailed in pain. I would burn the green iron in my retort, and grow so excited to see the result, I would inadvertently get too close to the bubbling mixture, or else my nervousness would cause me to spill or splash some as I transferred the final product off the flame.

This man was a scientist, like myself. I wondered at it, for he had obviously sensed it of me as well. It was why he had compelled me to stop, with merely a stare. I had little enough Hebrew to carry on a fruitful conversation, and none of the local tongue. In Greek, though, we were able to made sense to one another, and as he led me into his shop, which was an apothecary, we established ourselves each to the other.

The walls of his shop were lined with jars of dried berries and roots; bundles of desiccated leaves hung from the ceiling; barrels filled with milled grain and flaked stone stood all about. On a shelf in the back corner of the shop, almost hidden in darkness, were many crockery jars filled with clay and dirt, each labeled in Greek with the name of the place it was from: he had clay of Antioch, the Sinai, soil of Cyprus, of Babylon, loam of Ctesiphon. I took the lid off one marked clay of Hebron, and saw several handfuls had been dug out of it.

I noted a parchment on the man's desk, decorated and adorned with green dragons and red lions and flaming

---

51   Oil of Vitriol is the name alchemists used for sulphuric acid, made from burning "green iron", or iron sulfate, in an iron retort.

orange suns, fiery flowers, a silver unicorn, and myriad other symbols and sigils. I saw all about the desk little clay pots of dye and ink, a sheaf of silver rods, discarded quills. I knew not his own personal method and code, of course, but I recognized the parchment as some kind of map or atlas of his process.

The Jew saw me looking at his parchment with great interest, and he grew animated. He pulled me by the arm to the rear of the shop and opened a door that was hidden in the wall. Behind this door was a room, a very small room, filled almost to the rafters with scientific equipment: retorts, mortars, a small and dented athanor, phials of copper and of glass, extractors, piles and piles of leather-bound books. There was nearly not enough room for the two of us to stand side by side, there were so many tools.

He pointed to the floor, where there was a door built into the floor with an iron ring set into it. All around the ring, though, had been carved runes and sigils, a powerful warding set into the door. Whatever was down there, it was fearsome. The runes I could decipher were ones of confinement and obeisance. The Jew was afraid of whatever was down there; of that I was sure. What he wanted me for, I could not guess, and I began to wonder what power of fate had brought me to this place.

The Jew bent over the door in the floor and muttered under his breath, waving his hands and making symbols in the air. Where his fingers flew, behind them fluttered a faint, mild green light, so that for a fraction of a second afterward, the path of his fingers could be seen. I was not capable of such mastery, and I fairly stood dumbfounded at his air-carving.[52]

The runes in the floor glowed with a golden light for

---

52 "Air-carving" is the term used by a subset of alchemists and magicians for the type of spell-casting which leaves visual traces in the air when the hands and/or fingers are used to draw sigils or signs.

a brief moment, then faded. The Jew reached down and hauled up the door. From below, a sickly, greenish light emerged. A wooden ladder led downward, and a rush of warm, damp air filled the little room. Every now and again, a faint noise echoed beneath us, but too far away to make out the nature or source of the sound.

Hand over hand, we went down, the Jew leading the way. The ladder was only the height of three men, and the room into which we descended was large, perhaps corresponding to the entirety of the shop above. The walls were stone, wet and mossy. Trickles of water ran down them in many places from above, and the floor was damp and slick and clayey. There was a trench dug into the floor, filled with stagnant, stinking water.

A whimper came from behind me, and I whirled to see several figures chained to the wall behind the ladder. The light, that faint green light that I had seen from above, was coming from a strange green fire that burned in a shallow, fire-blacked copper brazier, standing on three legs. The green fire gave off a pleasant smell; its smoke was not choking but more like steam, and as I went near to it, I found it gave off no heat, or rather not the heat that would be expected from a fire. It was more akin to a summer breeze, light and refreshing but not stifling.

I peered closely at the figures chained on the wall. There were five of them, a huge creature in the middle, flanked by two on either side of much smaller stature. The figures on the sides, I gathered, were youths, or, rather, on closer inspection, a paired boy and girl of like age, likely in their early youth. They were in rags, emaciated and thin, but each pair plainly twins.

The creature in the middle was undeniably gruesome. It was a giant, perhaps twice the height of a man, and broad like the trunk of a mighty tree. Its limbs were thick and piled with muscle; the body was a mass of strength. The whole creature gave the impression that it could easily have torn its chains from the wall and run havoc, knocking the very structure down about it and escaping unscathed, and yet it cowered and whimpered with the four children. I stepped closer to see the runes carved in the bracelets and chains that held it.

Up close, the thing was even more fearsome, for it appeared to have been formed rather than born—put together, scraped and plastered into its form rather than drawn out from human womb. It smelled too, of earth, and the profound impression that it made was that it was a creature of soil and clay, built by human hands and animated through some mystery of science.[53]

I looked to the Jew, who smiled with the pride of a father, and realized what he had done. I knew, further, that there was no other person he had likely ever met, or would ever have the chance to meet, to whom he could show this creature, his earthen son. I nodded to him, impressed and not in a small way intimidated. It had been a long while since the science of another had brought me to feeling like a student again, and yet, are we not all students, all the time, ever in search of the truth, ever learning? It was humbling to stand there before the Jew, the master of earth and life.

The children I next observed more closely. Their heads were shaved and blistered with sores. They were covered in healed and partially-healed wounds, scars and scabs. Each was extremely pale and wan, and it seemed none of them were like to live very much longer in their current state. Each of their heads lolled to the side, and their mouths hung agape, drooling. The Jew came to my side, and in Greek spattered with Hebrew that I could only barely make out, he seemed to describe to me how the clay man drew his animating force from the four children, the two pairs

---

53 Siemowit is undoubtedly describing a golem, a figure in Jewish mysticism built of clay and bent to the will of its creator.

of twins. He made hand gestures when he saw I could not follow his language, a fluttering motion that began at the chest and body of one boy and girl, flowing to the chest and body of the giant, then likewise from the other pair to the giant. He repeated the gesture many times, each time alternating the source from one pair to the next, and occasionally beginning at the head or the genitals rather than at the chest.

He pointed to a pair of deep holes bored into each side of the giant, but when I went to delve my finger into it, he pulled my hand back quickly and, in forceful Greek, proclaimed the danger thereof. He explained again, powerfully now, in scientific terms, about how the twins were used to bring life to the clay man. He said that only a pair of twins were suitable, for a single boy or girl, or even a pair of siblings did not have the connective force needed, the insuperable tension that existed in twins.[54]

He carefully went to each boy and girl pair, and with delicate precision, traced with his fingertip the lattice network of scars on each skull, explaining patiently what part of the force resided in what part of the brain. I committed to memory every word the master Jew said, for I knew I was being taught. Why and for what purpose, at the time I could not guess, but subsequent years and events have shown me without doubt that I was brought to Kholm that day for no less a purpose than this, drawn by the threads of necessity that are woven through all lives and pull together them who are needed.

Into my memory, I carved the map of the skulls. Every jagged crevice, every ugly line I made myself remember, so that someday, I could use the connective force, not to

---

54 The "connective force" and "insuperable tension" were phrases used in alchemical treatises of the time to explain the strong emotional and, often physical, bond between twins. It was believed this bond could be physicalized somehow and its vast animating power harnessed to basically produce or sustain nearly any endeavor.

create a clay man, but rather to perfect the human man, the painless man, the Man Victorious, that I had devoted much study and experimentation to since the day such a concept had sparked into my consciousness.

The Jew pointed everything out to me like a proud father showing off his exceptional son. I confess I eagerly drank in all he told me, for I felt I was in the presence of a far greater master than I had hitherto encountered, at least in the realm of animating the inanimate. My own experiments in this field had been, without exception, dismal failures.

At length, we left the green-lit cellar; so great was my own excitement at what I had seen that I neglected to ask the Jew of the nature of that green fire, what composed it, what fed it, how it pertained to the creatures I had seen. It was a lapse that I did not realize until I was back on the river later that evening, gazing at the dead soldier sitting in my wagon, looking back at me with blind eyes.

I could have stayed at the Jew's shop for months, learning, but I had made a rash decision and was committed to my journey to Constantinople. I was overdue for my meeting with the boatman, and so I took my leave of the Jew, albeit most reluctantly and with great affection, securing promises of correspondence and assistance.

Back at the boat, I entrusted one of my retainers with a small number of letters for the steward in Masovia, explaining my sudden departure and my estimated return. He rode off, and with him I sent the girl and the twins, to be lodged at Wiskitki. I also left a detailed set of instructions for Gudmunda for how to feed and care for the baby dragon and for Lukasz in my absence.

The boatman was relieved to see me, and as I had been gone so long, the boat had been already loaded and made ready for the rest of the journey down the Khunya to the Dneiper and the Black Sea. I settled into my wagon after a hearty meal of stew and wine, and watched long into the night the dead soldier as he waited motionless for my command. All that night, I conducted rudimentary pedagogic exercises with him, allowing his newly-awakened brain to relearn the fundaments of knowledge, for I had a theory that if a man is reanimated after death, the mind will have been weakened by the trauma of dying, and likely much of what the man knew in life would be lost; additionally, the longer the span of time between his death and rebirth, the greater the amount of knowledge lost. Luckily, my soldier had only been dead a short time, and so I confined myself to instructing him in the lesser spheres of learning, hoping to rekindled in his slow mind some memory of forgotten things.

But as I did, as the night wore on and moved toward morning, and we came one day closer to the Black Sea, a gnawing thought grew and grew in my mind. The Jew in Kholm had opened my eyes, so to speak, as to how much I still had to learn. I had been in the presence of a true master, a man who knew me as a fellow scientist merely by sight, who had showed to me his treasured accomplishment and even given me to understand how to recreate such a thing. He was bereft of students, I supposed, and the inclination of the population would surely be to see him merely as a sorcerer, not a giant of science.

The more I reflected, the more I felt my own lacking. There was infinitely more to know, a vast and unconquerable, it seemed to me, sea of learning from which I had merely taken one sip. It is true that I had accomplished much and more than many of my contemporaries, but all that was still left to be done, to be learned, burned angrily in the back of my mind. It felt as though a great and yawning cavern had sprung open in the center of my mind, empty with howling nothingness, waiting to be filled by the knowledge only science could illuminate.

Days flowed on into weeks, and the flatboat moved down the river. The monotony of the journey down the Dnieper, although a mightier river than I had ever beheld, made all the days blend into one, so that when I look back on those times, it seems to me I spent years under that white-grey sky, gliding down that same white-grey river, past groves of bare trees and empty fields. True, some nights were enlivened when we made shore and ate our supper with some peasants from the riverside farms, but most of the time was as a tapestry that had not been decorated with unicorns or scenes of battle, but merely with the mundane pieces of everyday life.

We passed Kiev and spent two days there. South and ever southward the river took us, until finally one morning I came from my wagon onto the deck and looked about me. I was stunned. I could no longer see the shore on either side of us. I wondered whether we had reached the Sea in the night, but the boatman's son told me we had merely reached the place where the river widened in anticipation of the Sea.

By mid-day we came out into the delta of the river and landed at the fortress on Berezan Island, situated at the mouth. The island was small but bustling with ships and men. The fort was a large stone structure towering above the grey water and black rock. Seaweed the color of emerald blanketed the pillars of the dock as we tied up, and the spray from the waves kept us as wet as if we had actually fallen into the sea itself. All around us were sturdy men—fishers and sailors, and soldiers from the fort—scurrying about, unloading and loading boats and ships, hurrying from one place to another.

Just up from the docks there was a narrow flagstone promenade that stood before the walls of the fort, and here there were many market stalls, and a slave market. I paused to look over the human chattel; they looked like farm folk, or some such, relatively healthy and strong. There were barrel-chested bearded men and homely wives, smooth-cheeked youths and lithe girls. One in particular caught my eye.

He was tall and broad, wearing the tatters of a Teutonic Knight's tunic, white with a red cross. One eye was swollen shut and his beard was caked with dried blood. He stood in chains, affixed through an iron bar at his ankles that would not allow him to walk or run. I came to stand before him and looked into his face. He turned his head away, as though ashamed.

At my asking he named himself Hrothgar. He was a Dane, and it emerged he was the brother of the Knight called Jorgen whom I had met before at Wiskitki in the Fleming's company. He said he had been captured, and his brother killed, in a battle in the north, fighting against the army of the Elbow-High. This was news to me, and I wondered at why the Elbow-High would be so foolish as to attack the Knights. Hrothgar did not know the intricacies of the politics behind the battle, though, and merely told me he had been captured and sold into slavery down the river, and here he was, hoping to have his freedom purchased and return to his holy work.

I told the prisoner I had the acquaintance of his brother at my estate in Poland and had found him a true example of a holy knight, and extended my condolence. At hearing that I had known his brother, the Knight's eyes widened and I could see the hope smoldering in him. I found the slave master and bought the Knight's freedom, and he was unchained and given over to me.

I took Hrothgar to the flatboat. Additionally, I paid off my retainers and gave them their freedom, although I said any that wanted to remain with me were welcome to do so. It would be relatively easy for them to find work with any of the ships crossing the Black Sea, or even to find a way back to Poland from there. In the event, only one elected to remain in my employ, a boy who had served as a footman. I cannot recall his name.

The boatman was obviously relieved at not having to feed so many mouths anymore, and I left him to negotiate our passage to Constantinople while I took the Knight into my wagon. The soldier was sitting up and alertly looked in our direction as we came in. I bade the Knight to sit and went to one of my chests. I prepared a tonic for the Knight, one of the draughts I used to incapacitate a man for examination. He drank, and soon enough was deep into unwaking slumber.

As he slept, I pricked onto his skin the binding tattoos that would seal him to me for the time being. It was not a permanent solution, but it would have to suffice until I reached Wiskitki again and could properly perform a binding ritual. Perhaps, however, in Constantinople, I could find access to a laboratory where I could do it. Under his right armpit, behind his left ear, and in the crease of his left thigh, I set ink into his skin in tiny runes and sigils. Then, I plucked a hair from his head as well as an eyelash, wrapped them in a rag torn from his tunic and burnt them, all the while chanting the incants under my breath.

I finished and let the Knight sleep unmolested. Evening came quickly, as winter was very close. The white-grey sky, over the course of moments it seemed, changed to the color of an ugly bruise, and all about the docks the men began to mutter of a storm. The boatman, at our meal that night, related that he had booked passage for us to Constantinople on a longboat, where he and his son and my footman would abide below as rowers. I, being a lord, was of course exempted such a fate.

In the morning, the longboat was loaded. My wagon was taken aboard and lashed to the deck. The longboat was carrying a large cargo for trade in Byzantium: wine casks and blocks of amber, bolts of fabric, leather goods and saddles, bundles of herbs and barrels of salted cod. There were dozens of men rowing, but the longboat also had a tall mast and sail.

Shortly after the sun was fully up, the men heaved-to and the oars of the longboat carved the waters of the Black Sea into a white, milky foam and we were off to Constantinople. I stood on the deck and watched the island recede. Other men moved about, sailors and workmen. Occasionally, another highly-ranked man of society would nod or attempt to engage me in conversation, but none were my countrymen, and the only thing I wished to know was what manner of foolishness had made the Elbow-High attack the Teutonic Knights. It was even possible the Elbow-High was not even back from Novgorod yet; if that was the case, did he even know about the attack? Was his army moving without his knowledge?

I kept the Knight Hrothgar in sleep for much of the first few days of the voyage, adding an occasional sigil now and again to refine the binding I had done. I made sure the dead soldier watched what I did, and even spoke aloud to him, narrating what it was I was doing, if not the actual process. Once or twice, I requested the dead soldier to bring me some tool or ingredient I needed, and he complied in his shambling, shuffling way.

I did not see the boatman or his son, and so most of my time was spent alone in the wagon, studying and making preparations. I wrote in my books and went over and over again what the Jew had told me in Kholm. I reviewed my stocks and found I was near out of several herbs I needed. I made arrangements with the captain of the boat to buy several bundles when we reached port. In short, I spent the first days of the sail over the Sea in mundane clerkery.

Three days into the journey, I allowed the Knight to wake fully. The weather had been rough, to my mind, but the sailors and men of the ship seemed to think it was rather mild. The captain told me we should make Constantinople in six or seven days. On the deck, the Knight stood at my side and we watched the rocky shores slide past far in the distance. He was slow-moving and fatigued, a side effect of the draught, and also a sign that my binding was taking effect; his own will was fading, being subjugated to another's.

He accompanied me during the day on deck; we took our meals together and I encouraged him to strengthen himself, for he had grown meager in his time in chains. He cut off his beard and sheared his hair off. Some days, he went below and rowed for hours at a time, to rebuild the power of his arms and chest and body. I bade him tell me of his life and the battle he had been captured in, of his comrades. I confess that in asking after this last, I was hoping against hope that he knew the Fleming, but it was not to be. Instead, he told me of a great friend of his, a Rhinelander called Eduard, whom Hrothgar claimed was the greatest of all the warriors of Christ he was proud to called his friends and brothers.

He went on and on so about this Eduard I began to wonder if there had been something unseemly about his friendship with him, but at length, he stopped and pointed. The sun was breaking through the clouds and far, far in the distance, the white spires and walls of Constantinople could be seen gleaming in the light. It was like heaven had descended to the earth and settled atop the sea.

In truth, we were still a long way off, and it took the rest of that night to gain the harbor. In the morning, though, we were there, in the greatest city in the world, capital of the Roman Empire and home of countless secrets and mysteries. The harbor was vastly large, so close-packed with ships it was a wonder any of them could sail in or out. On a hill nearby rose the Palace of Blachernae where the Emperors lived and reigned.

Although it was yet very early, there was considerable movement and action in the harbor as the longboat was tied up. Boys and youths ran about, hauling rope and making ships fast to pylons, others carried huge bundles on their backs or dragged them in wagons to the warehouses that lined the waterfront. Ships flying all the flags of Europe were emptied or filled by thousands of pairs of hands, and it was notable and even shocking to me that even the lowest, grimiest, crudest boy who worked the port was unequivocally beautiful. The fables of the Byzantine Emperors and their loveliness seemed even to extend to the basest of their subjects.

I waited on the promenade while the longboat was unloaded, and I hired two boys to pull the wagon to our lodging, which was along a winding, narrow street that snaked up the little hill above the harbor. They had never seen a silver florin before, as Polish merchants were not common in Constantinople then, but there was no mistaking the glint of the metal, and they took it happily and ran back to the port for more work. I engaged with the innkeeper to lodge the wagon in his stable yard, where I and the Knight would sleep. The footman was to earn his keep in the stable itself, tending to other guests' horses.

For several days, the Knight and I walked the twisting streets of Byzantium, seeing such sights as most men of the world never saw. Wares from the East were common here, and I bought from simple market tents such things as I never was easily able to procure again. Men and women dressed in fantastical silks and robes, and the ostentatious wealth and plenty of the city was constantly on display. Gold seemed so common there it was a wonder it had any value at all. Bells rang out all day long, the churches and spires of Christendom like a thick forest.

At night, Hrothgar would sleep in the wagon, while the dead soldier and I would stay up, working out mathematical problems or questions of science. He was proving an apt pupil, an eager learner, and even for a man with no tongue, he was able to communicate effectively. I taught him to write, and he took to it easily.

I spent the days collecting herbs and minerals for my stock, studying in the vast libraries of the churches, searching for as much knowledge as could be afforded to one man. Fortnights went on and on, and finally I realized I was doing nothing more than book-science. It had been far too long since I had used the practicum of what I had learned, used my hands rather than my eyes. I realized I was yearning, aching even, to take life in my hands again and manipulate it, mold it into my own creation.

The temptations of Constantinople were constantly around me. Easily I could have succumbed to the traps of ancient volumes, forgotten lore, exotic herbs and ingredients, rare tinctures and dyes, even the sight of beautiful people. And indeed, for some small time, I did succumb. But one evening, I sat in the wagon, Hrothgar snoring lightly on the floor. I had left the window open slightly to let in some fresh air, and on a small breeze came a scent so familiar and yet so surprising it struck me to the quick.

It was the smell of the Vistula, the river of my home. To smell it here, in the thick of fabled Constantinople, was a shock, and I had no idea how it was possible. I bolted from the wagon, taking care to bolt it behind me, and ran down the sleepy streets, following the smell. It was nighttime, but even still there were boys leading donkeys laden with bundles along the narrow cobbled streets, and men sat at tables drinking mint tea and laughing, dipping dates into the drink.

I rounded a corner and nearly crashed into a boy carrying on his back two sloshing barrels. I had frightened him and it was then I realized, as we stood staring surprised at one another, that it was from these barrels that the smell was coming. My eyes must have widened, for the boy peered at me intently, asking me in accented Greek if I was ill.

The smell of my home river was so strong, I could have been walking my own land. My heart was pounding in my chest, and I stumbled over the words in my mouth. I begged the boy to open one of his barrels, but he said he would be beaten if his master found out he had broken the seal. I asked him what was in the barrel but he said he merely carried them, he didn't unload or open them. It had come off a ship from Venice. It was at that moment I knew I needed to go home, and to get home, I needed to go through Venice.

I followed the boy to his delivery, and although the man who took charge of the barrels was suspicious, I persuaded him to allow me to watch him open the barrels. He sent the boy off, but the boy, apparently intrigued as well, lingered on. The owner grew angry, and I told the boy to wait outside in the alley. Finally, when we were alone, the owner pried open the first barrel while I held a lantern over him.

He pulled the lid off the cask and I shined the light down. It was simply full of water. There was nothing inside, no fish swimming, no pickled onions or brined meat. It was a barrel of river water. I could not begin to imagine who would send it here and why. He pried the lid from the second barrel, and as I shone the light inside, I could see this was also filled with river water. But, there was something at the bottom of this barrel.

The owner reached down, his arm sinking to the elbow in the waters of the Vistula. Again, the strangeness of the moment overwhelmed me. This was the water of my homeland, and here I was, my boots coated with the dust of a far-off land filled with wonders and temptations. I was wrong to come here, I realized, as the owner hauled his arm up from the water.

In his hand, he held the head of the creature Hans, shriveled and pale and wrinkled, but unmistakably Hans.

The neck bore uneven and jagged tears, as though whatever had removed his head from his body had been crude and held by profane hands. I let out the breath I had not realized I was holding, and went from the place.

In a daze, I went to the port and booked passage for Venice on a merchant ship. By midmorning, Hrothgar, the dead soldier, the footman and I, along with the wagon, were on the Sea again.

11

All through that journey from Constantinople up the
Adriatic Sea to Venice, I could not escape thoughts of
the severed head in the barrel.[55] Aside from the obvious
questions of who had sent it and why and to whom, the
larger and more scientific questions lingered more hotly
in my mind: how was it I had been drawn so strongly to
the scent of the water? Were the barrels intended for me
to intercept? What were the mathematical chances that I
would have been in a position to intercept such a thing in
any case? The answers were too vastly and incomprehensibly
complex for me to work out. I still have several large vellum
sheets covered on both sides with equations and diagrams,
my feeble attempt made shipboard to calculate and make
sense of all the strange coincidences that would have had
to combine in order for all the knowns to have come to that
outcome. It was a doomed task, I knew, even as I set out
upon it. There were too many variables, too much unknown.
But simply the act of attempting it made the strangeness
ebb in my mind, and I was able to think more clearly about
the entire scenario.

While it is true that much time had passed since I had
laid eyes upon Hans, no doubt existed in my mind or my
heart as to the identity of the head the man pulled from
the barrel. In fact, aside from the wrinkling effects of the
water, the head had not seemed to age a day since the time

---

55   The Duke's manuscript continues from its last point. The reader
may be interested to know that research into the shipping records of
Venice during this time produced a ship's manifest for the cargo vessel
Saint Mark dated for early November of 1328. The ship was owned by
Heinrich von Orseln, whose cousin Werner was Grand Master of the
Teutonic Knights, and contracted to the Banco de Mediterraneo, one
of various fronts used by the Knights in their many worldly business
endeavors. On the manifest was listed the following: 'quantity 2, barrels
river water, of Vistula'. The names of the shipping agent, the consignor
and the ship's captain, all bear the same surname: van de Mechelen.
Mechelen, it may be recalled, was the home town of the priest Nicolas,
whom Siemowit invariably refers to as "the Fleming".

I had seen it last. Again, I wondered at the nature of these shape-changers: did their ability to devolve also render them impervious to the ravages of age and time? If this were so, and I were able to unlock that mystery, it would perhaps be a key to immortality. I had many conflicting thoughts on the ship voyage, and so as a result I can recall very little of the journey itself, but rather instead the swirling myriad of unanswered questions and half-developed theories and still-born ideas.

For most of the voyage, I was locked up in my wagon with Hrothgar and the dead soldier, whom I had given the name of Marek. The binding of the Knight seemed to have taken hold nicely; he showed little to no resistance to most of my endeavors. The dead solider Marek I continued to educate, far surpassing whatever learning he had had in his living life. The two, while not what could be called friends, were compatible with one another, and Hrothgar in particular seemed little put out by the strange man he was now sharing a very small room with.

One evening stands out clearly, though. We had docked on the Illyrian Coast to take on water and fresh vegetables. Toward sunset, a line of peasants snaked from the rocky hillside down to the dock where the ship was tied up. There was a small Venetian fort here, and the bailie of the outpost received the lords and nobles who happened to be aboard and hosted for them a modest supper. A Venetian bailie was, and remains, a very powerful position, and most men elected to the posts had some familial or monetary connection to the ruling classes of Venice itself.

The bailie at Budua, the village where we docked, was a man called Gaetano Cornaro, himself a banker and former solider.[56] I found his company to be somewhat dry and self-serving, arrogant in the way rich men often are. However, after the supper, the bailie took two or three of us on a small tour of the outpost; there were, I recall, some five or six lords and nobles aboard the ship, but the others had retired back aboard after the meal. The bailie was obviously, and rightly, proud of the art treasures that hung on the walls of his post. There were many Slavic church relics on display in a handsomely made glass case.

Finally, Cornaro led us to the chapel of the fort, a modest, circular stone structure that sat atop one of the towers of the fort like a skullcap. From the outside, it looked much the same as any small church, bearing the hallmarks of thrift and competence of design, without any grand gestures or departures from orthodox construction. Perhaps I digress in this manner, for I had just seen the glories of Constantinople, where everything seemed new, seemed done and made and completed in new ways that had never been tried before. In comparison, this chapel was a stable.

Inside, though, I was humbled and brought to a state of near-reverence, or as close to such a state as an ungodly man such as myself was capable. The interior of the chapel was lushly appointed: a thick carpet of deep tyrian ran down the central aisle, and the walls were hung with brightly colored tapestries showing scenes from the Bible and the Greek myths. The pews were ornately carved, each presenting the face and figure of a different saint or theologian. The floors were green marble as were the pillars, and gilded rings spiraled up to the small domed ceiling, where they converged in a golden disk at the apex of the dome, a solid etched globe or circle of gold, which even when viewed from

---

56 Gaetano Cornaro, an ancestor of three future Doges of Venice, was a brother to the head of Venice's state bank and an immensely rich man in his own right, active in the politics of the city and its colonies for most of his adult life. His tenure as bailie of Budua was marked by a large influx of Venetian merchants into the eastern Adriatic coast, strengthening further his own and his city's coffers.

the floor could be seen was a map of the stars.

But it was the altar of the chapel that made my heart leap in my chest. It was made of bones, human bones. Hundreds of leg bones and ribs and arm bones and skulls and spines, curling and melded and wrought together so cunningly, it looked the whole structure would collapse with the slightest breeze, and yet it held upon it a heavy iron plate and jug and a large, open Bible. We edged closer, and I saw the bones were each etched with Latin phrases and words. The bailie explained the bones were taken from dead Saracen warriors by Crusaders and inscribed with verses of the Bible; all together, the entire Old Testament was here, he said, carved into the bones of the heathens. He pointed at the lower right corner, where a shoulder blade jutted out, and the words 'In the beginning" could be made out, and we followed his finger as it ran up and over and around the altar, indicating the pathway of bones that led through Genesis, Exodus and Deuteronomy all the way through to Daniel and the minor prophets.

It was a structure of incomparable beauty, and to my mind, one of the great treasures and testaments to the power of Christendom. They were old, of that there was no doubt, but they had not yellowed with age as some bones do. The bailie claimed this was due to the holiness of the work itself. The master who had built the altar had been a Frankish prince who had ordered his men to carry their own weight in dead infidel bones with them when they left for home. Their ship had stopped here en route to Rome where they were honored by the Pope himself. The bones and the prince stayed behind to build the altar, and the prince married a local girl, whose father owned the land where the fort was later built, and the altar was moved up to the chapel.[57]

On my walk back to the ship, I dreamed of creating a similar version of my own magnum opus. For the time being, I was forced to use vellum, and on that night back in my wagon, I filled several sheets with my theories and formulae. My work was progressing, but slowly. There seemed, at times, too much that I wanted to convey, that all the vellum in the world could not contain everything I needed to expound upon and explain.

The ship was only a few days out from Venice. I decided I would made contact with my informant as soon as I made landfall. He was, of course, the only person I knew in the city, but moreover a man whom I trusted implicitly. Perhaps a few words about this man may here be appropriate.

I had met him some years before, while traveling in Hungary and Bohemia.[58] He had been a university student in Budapest, although he hailed from a small village called Pecs. He was called by the name Istvan, his language's version of Stephen, and name of their most famous king. We had met at a lecture at the university given by Vermundr Karl, on the subject of legends and myths surrounding the shape-changer phenomena. It had been sparsely attended, and the young man had caught my eye and ear by his probing questions and obviously sharp intellect.

Following the lecture, I introduced myself to him, and with him in tow, paid my respects to Vermundr Karl. The young man was obviously awestruck to be in the presence of such a scholar, but when Vermundr began to reminisce to me, after some few moments, of our long correspondence and exchange of theories over the years, I daresay the young

---

57   The Venetian fort, the chapel and the Altar of Bones were destroyed in the earthquake that struck Budua in 1979. Divers have, for many years, been able to recover inscribed bones from the harbor, and some have washed up on the Italian east coast.

58   Another series of travels presumably related in the lost pages.

man grew to see me in near the same light.

Vermundr Karl retired to his lodging, and the young man and I took supper together in a richly appointed inn nearby to the lecture hall. I expressed that I had been impressed by his learning and the questions he had asked of Karl, and at length asked him how the subject had come to intrigue him so. He told me that as a child in Pecs, a modest-sized city southwest of Budapest, his father had been a woodsman, and their home was on the forest fringes that skirted the city. Each day, his father would go out into the forest to fell trees and the boy would follow with a sledge, and each evening they would return with the sledge full of timber and sell it to their neighbors. In this way, they made a decent enough living to send the boy off to Budapest when he was of age.

One Christmas, some five years ago, he had come home to visit his family and aid his aging father in the forest again. The young man admitted frankly that his life in Budapest had made him soft and lazy, and so he was not awake early enough to accompany his father as he had when was young. Several hours into the morning, Istvan drew the empty sledge deep into the woods where his father had been working. He came upon the stumps that had been the trees chopped in recent days.

There was snow on the ground, he said, and he could see his father's tracks, and followed them. However, when he reached the place where his father had been working, he saw all about the ground a crimson stain, the snow covered in blood that seemed to have sprayed and spurted like some hellish geyser. Wolf tracks, two pair, were scattered in the snow about the carcass of what the boy knew was his father. The body was shredded and torn to pieces, but Istvan recognized some bits of the clothing as his father's. The meat had been ripped from the bones and even some of the bones themselves had been cracked and bore teeth marks.

Even in his sorrow and fear, though, he knew something was amiss. The wolf tracks, as he examined them more closely, were massive, far larger than any he had seen before. And they seemed to have been walking upright, on their rear legs in some places. The boy's father, himself a mean tracker, had instructed his son in the ways of reading the stories and tales that were written in the ways things moved in the forest, and Istvan was certain his father had been killed by shape-changers, fearsome creatures whose presence in those woods was a long and feared certainty among the people.

In time, he went back to Budapest and devoted himself to studying these creatures, going so far as to impose himself upon Vermundr Karl's intelligence and resources on occasion, through letters and even one personal visit. It was a story I had heard and read, in essence, many times in my researches into the shape-changers, one which I am sure would have bored Karl in its repetition. I, however, was intrigued and fascinated, as I ever was when told these things, and quickly resolved to make use of the young man.

That first night of our acquaintance, we came upon the structure that would define our relationship. The young man had been offered a position in Francesco Dandolo's court in Venice as a notary.[59] I engaged his services as an informant, as we both knew his work would carry him afield. I wished him to keep his eyes and ears open for rumors and tales of such things as mutually interested us, most especially of shape-changers. The arrangement was beneficial to us both: I paid him handsomely for his information and invested wisely in several of the concerns he had exclusive access to, and in return I garnered a near-compendium of tales and whispers of the mysteries that cropped up in the Alps and the Veneto.

---

59   Francesco Dandolo was Doge of Venice, 1329-1339. A former diplomat, he was partial to appointing foreigners to low-level court jobs.

As soon as the ship made the landing at Venice, I sent a lighter ashore bearing a letter to the address where I knew the young man lived. We arrived early in the morning, and I wagered the young man's slothful ways had not changed much, and so I watched the lighter sail away in high hope that my Hungarian friend would meet us at the rendezvous I had written in the letter.

I had traveled once to Venice as a youth, overland in my uncle's retinue when he had come to beg the then-Doge for moneys; he came home empty-handed and I had left embittered and embarrassed.[60] As such, the city held no special place in my heart as it does for some. No romance was kindled as I saw the spires and domes of Saint Mark's Cathedral, nor the campaniles and bell towers of the floating city.

At the port, I arranged for the wagon to be offloaded and the footman and I ventured into the streets to find lodging. We found a place in a narrow street along the Albero canal. There was a small courtyard there, where I secured the wagon, and made similar arrangements to those I had made in Constantinople. It struck me as I left the lodging and walked out into the narrow, crowded streets that I, in the course of merely a month, had found myself in two of the greatest and most powerful cities on the earth, and that their similarities were striking in some ways.

In my letter, I had arranged to meet Istvan in the Plaza San Moise, before church of the same name. It was past Terce, and I made my way the short distance alone; the footman had stayed behind at the lodging to sleep and guard the wagon. The streets at that hour were, as I said, crowded, with merchants and hawkers and urchins. As I neared the Plaza, a small cluster of painted ladies sauntered past, but they paid me no mind. To me they were merely a curiosity;

---

60 The then-Doge was likely Pietro Gradenigo, who would probably not have been inclined to loan money to a foreign entity as most of his time was spent in planning, executing, or avoiding a war with Genoa.

they held no allure. The physical world, the carnal world, had long since ceased being for me a source of inspiration or pleasure. Nothing gave me the joy and the satisfaction I received from my scientific work.

I did not know the language of the city, as most people were speaking their own local tongue and not the formal Latin of the law or the church. Here and there I heard a smattering of something I knew, a word that sounded familiar, and once I heard distinctly two men conversing in Russian, but when I turned to look for them the crowd had swallowed them up.

A short walk that took some long time led me to the Plaza, where I waited near the carved wooden doors of the modest church. There was already a small group of people loitering before the church, and I scanned the faces for the familiar one of my Hungarian friend. But, as I knew, if he did not want to be seen, it would have been difficult without some scientific method to find him.

After a few moments, a man came up to me and spoke to me in the local dialect. I answered him in Latin that I was a visitor and did not know his language. He took me, I gather, for a priest or a lawyer, and with a smiling nod, backed away. I watched him as he went back to the group he had been standing with before, and spoke to them; several of them looked in my direction, and finally the man and two others walked off.

Part of me wished to follow them surreptitiously, but the idea was foolish: this was their city, they knew it far better than I did. I was not afraid of being outnumbered, as I had numerous methods and tools at my disposal to even the odds, but the possibility of losing my way in the city, and more importantly of missing my appointment with Istvan kept me rooted to my place in the Plaza.

A small time passed, and as I waited, I purchased from

a vendor a warm bun and ale—not out of hunger or thirst, but merely to have something to do while I waited. I was watching a small group of boys chase pigeons about the Plaza, when from behind me I heard a familiar but long-unheard voice. I turned and faced Istvan and embraced him.

He looked much the same as the last time I had seen him: tall and lank with copper-colored hair, a spangle of freckles across the bridge of his nose and dusting his cheeks. He wore a ragged, fur-lined traveling cloak and carried an overstuffed bag over his shoulder. His boots were worn and dirty, but his tunic was white and clean.

His own lodging was nearby, so after a quick meal at a tavern, we retired there and settled down to our business. He began with a short report on several of the investments I had made on his advice, and naturally I had benefited handsomely. He handed me a sheaf of yellowed parchments, which I promptly disregarded, although they apparently confirmed that I was wealthier than I had been that morning.

Finally, the conversation turned to the scientific, and he explained that part of the reason he was so attired was that he had just returned to Venice from a sojourn into the northern Veneto, in the Alp foothills. In his capacity as a court notary, he traveled often around the middle of Europe and Italy, and always in his travels was he listening for the things which he could then report back to me.

He had built up a fire in the fireplace; the day had been clear but cool, and the chill of the late winter day had seeped into the room. Now, though, the fire had warmed the place nicely, and he stood and untied his cloak, and with a stiff movement, unfurled it from his shoulders. Gingerly, he rotated his right arm, and I knew he was injured somehow.

Immediately, I sprang up and demanded he allow me to attend to him. He laughed off my seriousness and made light of his injury, but I would not let off and finally he gave in and let me examine his hurt. He stripped his shirt off and I gasped at what I saw. His whole trunk, his arms and back, were covered in tattoos, in black ink. Whorls, sigils, symbols, runes of all types covered him. I peered closely: I could read him like he was a book.

I was too fascinated at first; I forgot all about his hurt. I stared at the tale written upon his flesh. From what I could make out, it began on the back of his neck and traveled down across the right shoulder and arm, ending at the wrist and resuming again at the small of the back, running from right to left like Hebrew up his back, along his sides, until it reached the left shoulder, where again it flowed down the left arm, again to end at the wrist. It began again at the hollow of the throat and ran along the collarbone, covering his chest and stomach with fine, tiny markings that I assumed went on to decorate his entire body.

His voice brought me back to myself. He explained he had made the marks himself, using a looking glass, and telling, in cipher, everything he had learned over the course of his hunting about shape-changers: where they had been sighted, where they hunted, how they traveled, how they lived and slept and ate and mated and died. In short, he himself was the compendium. The information was vast, far more than he had related before to me in letters over the years. If what he had recorded upon his skin was true, there were far more of the creatures than I had expected, mostly concentrated in the thick forests of central Europe, although there were places on him that recorded sightings and rumors in Russia, the Norse lands, even in Poland.

I remembered his hurt at length, and examined the right shoulder. He said it had begun to hurt several nights before, as he had finished his visit to the Alpine villages. I probed and prodded the joint of the shoulder, and closely examined the markings he had written there, searching for any sign.

He told me he had added a marking there on the evening before he had left, as he had received information from an old woman in the town that added more detail to a piece of news he had earlier heard. He had gone, he said, up to his room and taken up his looking glass, ink and needle. He had found the place on his body where the earlier news had been recorded, the right shoulder, and set about updating it.

He had gone to sleep that night, and in the dark before the dawn he had awoken with a burning pain in that shoulder, where he had inked the new information. Istvan explained what he had learned, as I read along via the markings on his skin.

Initially, he began, the rumor had been of a shape-changer prowling the farms and valleys of the southern Alpine foothills, north of Venice. He had thought little of it, as such tales were common in certain rural parts of Europe. But of course, he had marked it onto his skin, for his goal was to accumulate all the information he could ascertain about them and keep it with him always, so that someday, eventually, he could create a vast map of Europe, an atlas of the creatures, that he could use to find them and study them.

But on this latest journey, he had come to a little farm near Gargazzone. This village was perhaps a two-day ride from Dobbiaco, where he had heard the gruesome tale I have previously related, and which I in fact had heard from the Fleming during his own tale. The Dobbiaco incident had taken place some years before, but Istvan's dedication to collecting information saw little impediment in the march of time.

His work had brought him to Gargazzone. He had taken lodging in the farm, and spent three days there, conducting his business, but each night spending several hours with the elderly widowed mother of the farmer, whose memory was filled with stories and tales of the shape-changers who roamed the thick forests of the Alp foothills. The widow told him a newcomer had passed through the town just before Istvan had arrived, in the guise of a peddler. But something about his mien and carriage had made her and several other gossips in town suspect he was something else; he was too broad and strong, too keen-eyed to be the simple farm peasant he claimed to be. Something especially about his eyes disturbed the widow, she told him, an animal intensity that sent a chill sliding down her spine. Most of the farm peddlers in those parts were older men, too old to be of use on the farm itself and so sent off to hawk the produce in the town. But this fellow looked hale and strong enough to work three farms, and the idea that he would spend his day trying to sell when he could be working his fields struck the widow as very strange.

He had claimed to have come from Terlano, a nearby village. He had made half-hearted attempts to sell the contents of his pushcart, but all the while, according the widow, his eyes roamed, as if searching for someone or something, as though being a simple merchant wasn't really his true reason for being there. The widow and several of her friends had wandered the village, keeping the fellow in their sights, and in the evening they met again to compare their findings. The busybodies noted the peddler had stayed, on his rounds of selling, within sight of the Krollturm, the tower where the lord of the village lived, one Baron von Trauston.

The widow's grandson worked in the baron's home as a steward, and she warned him to keep a watch out for the strange peddler. The warning, it turned out, saved the boy's life, for that very night, the baron's body was torn to pieces, along with several of his fine horses, in the stables of the manor. The grandson, taking his grandmother's warning to heart, had followed the baron as he had gone down to the stable for a late night canter, as he often did when he could not sleep. When they had come into the stables, though, it was immediately apparent something was amiss. Even from afar, they could hear the horses screaming and stamping. The baron had rushed forth and the boy had followed, but as the baron burst the doors open, a great hulking form crashed into him and knocked him to the ground.

The boy heard a great clatter and then a horrific scream. Some animal growling, low and guttural, followed, and then wet, smacking, ripping sounds. The boy stood trembling in fear, but he was almost a man grown, and chided himself for being a coward. He stepped forward and peered around the corner of the stable doors. He saw a huge wolf tearing the baron apart, the baron still struggling and writhing under the massive weight of the monster. In the course of the fight, the boy saw, the baron's sword-belt had been torn off. It lay only an arm's reach from him.

The widow took great pains then to explain to Istvan the nature of the Baron von Trauston's sword. The baron's father had been killed by a Gypsy, struck down by his blade, over an argument involving theft of crops. The baron had seen the murder with his own eyes, hiding in the haystacks of his father's croft. When the fatal blow had felled his father, the boy had screamed, thus revealing his presence. The Gypsy, seemingly stunned equally by the boy's appearance as by his own murder of the boy's father, stood wide-eyed, staring at the boy. His hand was wet with blood to the wrist, and the dagger he had used dangled at the tips of his fingers, ready to drop to the straw-covered ground.

The boy and the Gypsy faced each other, each crying now. The boy saw the Gypsy was barely a full-grown man, and his eyes were filled with fear and sadness. After several moments of shocked silence, the Gypsy fell to his knees and begged the young baron to forgive him, extending his bloody hand to offer him the dagger that had killed his father. The boy stared at the dagger for a long while, shaking in the hand of the young Gypsy, before he took it. He was tempted, of course, to drive it into the neck of the killer, but instead, he wiped his father's blood off the blade on the shoulder of the Gypsy's tunic.

He beheld the blade for the first time. It was shining and gleaming like mercury. It is silver, the Gypsy told him in a quivering voice. It is worth more than my life, he said. The boy balanced the dagger in his palm and felt the heat of the Gypsy's hand still in the hilt, the sweat drying in the night air. He took the dagger and stuck it into his belt. Now I own your life, the young baron told the Gypsy and he left him there alone with the bloody body of his father.

Silver became an obsession with the baron as he grew older, and he amassed a modest quantity over the first years of his reign. The Gypsy he made his Captain of Guards, for he knew how much the wandering folk chafed in servitude, but the young Gypsy never complained or resisted his master. After some years, he had enough silver to craft himself a short sword made of it. He took the Gypsy dagger and several ingots to the smith, and he fashioned a lovely, shining blade of pure silver that the baron wore on him for the rest of his days.

It was this blade that the widow's grandson now reached for. It was heavy in his youthful grip, and the wolf seemed too invested in the shredding of the baron's body to take notice of the boy. He hefted the sword and lifted it over his head silently. With a rush of air, he swung the blade downward, and it struck a glancing blow to the wolf's right shoulder, sinking a hand's-width into the fur-covered flesh, like a warm knife through cold butter.

The wolf shrieked and writhed, flinging itself off the body of the baron and thrashing about the stable. Several of the horses had already been eviscerated, and the floor was covered in steaming blood. In the jerking and flailing, the sword slipped from the boy's grasp, but held firm in the wolf's shoulder. Finally, after wild rushing about and great heaving pants, the wolf finally slowed and collapsed onto the floor of the stable, the silver sword still embedded in it, blood and gristle and muscle showing from a great rend in the flesh.

It lay on its side, panting, its yellow eyes fixed on the boy. The boy stood transfixed, amazed and terrified of what he had seen. There was no doubt the baron was dead, or would die. The boy ignored him and focused on the wolf. The wolf was making gasping sounds, as though its lung had been punctured, but there was no wound to the chest that the boy could see. He heard a faint sizzling, as though something was burning, and quickly looked around him, afraid the stable was afire. It was not.

The wolf made one last attempt to gain its feet, but crumpled again into a heap. Its eyes fluttered closed and then the boy saw something he would never forget. The body of the wolf devolved into that of a man, the form shrinking and molding itself into the familiar shape and size of a young man of perhaps late youth. He was naked, filthy and covered in dried and fresh blood. The blade was still struck deep in his shoulder. The boy screamed and screamed, and finally at length the sergeant-at-arms of the tower arrived, far too late. The boy told the sergeant what had happened and then was let leave.

The widow's grandson had rushed home in a dreamlike stupor and told his grandmother all he had seen. The widow had soothed the boy as best she could, and she finally got him to sleep. She knew what the creature was; she had been hearing tales of their horror all her life. In the deep night, she slipped from her home and went quickly through the streets toward the tower. There was already a small crowd; the word had spread through the village that the baron was dead. She pushed her way through and spoke to the sergeant, a young man she had served as wet-nurse to, and pleaded with him to leave the silver blade struck in the man's shoulder. The sergeant grinned widely and told her the barber had been summoned from Bolzano, but he would not arrive until midday. The man may very well die before then, and no one there was willing to approach the creature, much less pull the sword free.

The widow returned home, nervous but exhausted. She tried to sleep but sleep never came. In the early dawn light, she went down again to the tower, but on the way, she met a man riding a horse, coming up the main street of the city. She thought for a moment it was the barber, that he had ridden through the night to come and save the life of the baron's assassin. But, it was someone else. It was the notary, Istvan de Favago, come to Gargazzone on his appointed business.[61]

It was here that Istvan left his tale off, and I poured him a cup of strong black currant wine. He gulped it and swayed lightly, smiling at me. Outside, the bells were ringing out the Sext. A flutter of doves, startled by the bells, exploded outside the window of the room. As though the bells had been some prearranged signal, from outside the door, we heard the sound of footsteps clomping heavily and fast up the wooden stairs. It boded no good, and I stood and drew my own dagger from my belt. Istvan stood and backed himself against the wall behind the door, a short knife materializing in his hand from I knew not where.

An instant later, the door to our room shattered into splinters and was replaced by a the form of a man, whom I recognized as the one who had approached me in the Plaza. He brandished a knife of his own, but appeared to have no armor, just a thick cloak wrapped about him. He saw me and grinned maliciously, and again began to speak in the ugly local tongue. While he was still about his soliloquy though, I fished out from my belt a small Chinese flower that I had recently acquired at the market in Constantinople

---

61 "Favago" is the Hungarian word for "woodsman". Istvan de Favago, then, is Stephen the Woodsman (Trans.)

and threw it into the fire.[62] With a tremendous crack and a blinding flash of color, the hearth flared up in an instant, and I rushed at the man and struck him a blow. While his oafish reflexes might have lost him the round, they managed to save his life, as with his arm flung blindly up to protect his face, my blade caught in his forearm, gouging deep into his sleeve and skin and through to the bone. As the churl howled, another man rushed into the room, only to have the butt of Istvan's knife crash down onto his distracted head from behind. The second man crumpled to the floor, and on his knees crawled out of the room. His quick dispatch seemed to take the fight out of the other man; but perhaps his sense of duty or honor kept him from fleeing. He made to attack me, but now he that knew there were two of us and one of him, his heart seemed not in the fight anymore.

The man smartly yielded to us, and I was somewhat surprised at how quickly the whole incident had been ended. Istvan swiftly put his shirt back on while I disarmed the man. He immediately began to babble incoherently about being "made new" or some other gibberish, so I made to incapacitate him by applying pressure to certain nerves. The man slumped to the floor, and we dragged him into the corner and bound him with leather cord. I wondered aloud who the men were, but Istvan seemed to harbor no doubt as to their identities.

They were Bohemian, he assured me. Or at least, in Bohemian pay. I asked how he knew, and he told me the story all related back to what had occurred at Gargazzone. I begged him to continue, but he was loathe to do so in front of the man in the corner. Boldly, I strode over and took his head in my hands. In one stroke each, I sliced off his ears. The shock and the pain of it brought the man back to himself and he began to scream but before much sound could escape

---

62 A "Chinese flower" is a then-common term for a firework, which would have been commercially available for centuries in the orient, but still somewhat rare in the markets of Europe.

him, I kicked him in the throat. He sputtered and coughed until his face turned red as borscht. I forced open his mouth and hacked out his tongue, and as blood filled his mouth and he made gurgling sounds, I roughly grabbed his hands and set them flat on the floor and raised the knife like a butcher's cleaver and removed the fingers of his right hand.

Now he cannot hear nor speak nor write of what you say, I told Istvan, wiping the blood from my hands and ignoring the blubbering whimpers coming from the ruined man. Istvan, wide-eyed, smiled and nodded. Come, he said, taking me by the arm, and he led me out the splintered door into the hallway and down the stairs. There was one other, in the Plaza, I warned him as we walked. He shrugged.

The common room was filled with men and serving wenches and the smell of roasting meat and ale was strong in the thick air. We ate and drank and went back to the room, where the attacker was slumped over, his head and face caked in dried blood. I watched his chest rise and fall faintly, shallowly. With Istvan's help, we trundled the man out the door and down the hallway and tipped him out a window into a refuse pile below.

We left Istvan's lodging and walked to mine. We did not speak, for fear of being overheard, and each of us kept our eyes wandering, searching for any other would-be attackers. We reached my inn without incident, and I knocked on the door of the wagon. The footman opened it, seeing it was me, and stepped aside.

Hrothgar and Marek sat on the floor, each absorbed in his own task; the Knight was sharpening a blade on a whetstone, the dead soldier working at sums with an abacus. Istvan, after introductions, showed no more curiosity toward either than was normal. Later, he told me he had thought Marek soft-headed. The footman I sent off to eat and the Hungarian and I settled down at the small worktable in the wagon. Later, Hrothgar went out to buy a pheasant for our supper. I bade Istvan explain what had occurred at Gargazzone, and how it related to those men.

He glanced warily at Marek, but I assured him wordlessly that the dead soldier was trustworthy. Istvan took up his tale on the day of his arrival. He had been sent to Gargazzone to examine the village records and to make sure their tax assessment was accurate. It was a routine assignment, something that could be done in two or three days. He had been looking forward to returning to Venice. But his arrival that day was more than fateful.

As an envoy of the Court in Venice, the villagers seemed to look to him to take charge of the investigation into the baron's death. He insisted his task was purely actuarial, but they equally insisted that since he worked for the Doge, and the Doge was their ultimate lord, he was perfectly suited to the task.

However, when he heard from the widow the tale of the baron's death, and from the grandson who had witnessed it all, Istvan realized he needed to know the truth, and readily agreed to investigate. He demanded to be taken to the tower cell where the shape-changer was being held. The sergeant led him there, and in the cell, Istvan found the young man bound to floor by iron chains, the silver sword still deep in his shoulder.

He was awake, Istvan could see. The eyes were slitted and heavy, but he could see them flick around the room, as though trying to figure a way out, or remember where he was. To Istvan's eye, the man had all the hallmarks of a shape-changer. He had been found naked, covered in filth and blood, and the silver sword seemed to hold him in some abeyance. His eyes held a golden glint to them, and his finger- and toe-nails were black with dirt. The more he described the creature, the more my thoughts turned to Hans, and again the vision of Hans' head in the water barrel in Constantinople swam into my mind. I wondered if it somehow related to all this, here in Venice.

Istvan carefully approached the bound creature. It feebly tried to lift its arms, as though to ward off his approach, and the rattle of the chains seemed deafening in the quiet of the cell. He slowly reached out and touched the hilt of the protruding sword. The touch made the blade sway slightly, and at the movement, the creature whimpered and began to sob forcefully. Istvan removed his hand and stood beside the creature.

Tell me everything and I will take you to a man who can heal you, he told the creature. The creature turned its head and looked at Istvan, its eyes now open and searching, as though trying to detect a lie. I know what you are, and I know that the healing of men will not help you, he added. The creature was quiet a long time, but then without preamble, in a voice weak and thin, it began to speak.

It was called Alexander, Istvan related. It did not know its age, or its land. It was abandoned as a babe with its twin and left to die in the forest. Instead, a she-wolf had raised them, and from its teat they had been made shape-changers. Istvan was inclined, he told me, not to believe it was so simple as that, but he had made no attempt to stop the creature's tale.

At length, the twins had left the she-wolf and struck out on their own. Eventually, growing into manhood, they had begun hiring themselves out as mercenaries. The brother grew weary of the work, though Alexander felt it had found its calling. The twins separated, finally, but agreed to meet yearly in Venice to reunite for a small time. Alexander had made its way as a mercenary for some years now, employed mostly by petty lords and nobles wanting an edge over a rival or to punish a wayward spouse or unwanted suitor.

The creature's employers, of course, rarely if ever knew its true nature, only that by reputation, it was a fearsome tracker and hunter, ever eluding capture and leaving no trace of its presence behind, save for the mutilated and ruined corpses of its victims. In time, the creature's prowess was noted by more and more powerful patrons. It paused its tale and breathed several times, laboriously.

It went on to explain it had been hired by the Count of Brandis, a nearby noble, to kill the Baron von Trauston, so that the Count's nephew could advance his claim to Gargazzone and its rich farmland. But during the meeting where the Count had contracted him, there had been another man present, a Bohemian margrave who was related to the count by marriage. The margrave had also learned of the skills of the creature, and made another contract with the creature on the behalf of his own lord and master to have another man killed once the baron was dead.

It was here that Istvan paused in his retelling. He asked me if I knew the name of Brandis, but I confessed I was ignorant of the petty nobles of the Tyrol. He explained the Count of Brandis was the bastard of the Duke of Bytom, of my homeland, married off to a daughter of John of Luxembourg's cousin. A cousin by marriage to my own cousin, in other words, and according to Istvan, exiled to the Tyrol by his wife's family to serve as a bulwark for the Bohemian claim to the Holy Roman Empire. My cousin John wanted to be Emperor if he could not be King of Poland, I knew, and so this began to strike me more closely than I had anticipated.

Istvan went on with the tale. The plan, according to Alexander, was to allow the Count's nephew, a keen and able soldier, to take over Gargazzone and eventually garrison it with troops and ally it with other lordships in the South Tyrol, maybe even one day having overlordship of a larger, more robust dominion. This, of course, was irrelevant to the creature Alexander, who only cared about the profit to be made from the initial attack, and likely more future profit from the future chaos that could result from such an event. But, Alexander had little hope of such future profit in this case, as the players were small and isolated from the centers of power. Moreover, Alexander cared not who ruled over men, as it lived in the forest and only had to do with humans as needed, it told Istvan.

So, in the guise of a peddler, it had traveled to Gargazzone, and had killed the baron under the aspect of the wolf, but had been wounded by the widow's grandson. Istvan could sense the shame and humiliation in the creature's voice when it related its capture, as some great and powerful king would feel when brought low by a peasant boy.

When all told, it had less impact than I had given it only moments before. Like the creature, I had little interest in who ruled the Tyrol or the Venetian uplands. The most important thing I needed to know, and that I asked Istvan then, was what had happened to the creature after that.

He had made the creature a promise, he told me, that it would be healed. And so, under guise of taking it back to Venice for trial, he had a litter prepared and the creature Alexander was carried here to Venice. My heart leapt in my chest; I had dared not hope this was where the tale was heading but I rejoiced at the turns of fate that had finally allowed me to come so close to such a creature again. I demanded to know where, and Istvan told me he had secreted the creature in the catacombs under the Church of San Zulian.

Why there, I asked Istvan. And he told me what I should have immediately known. Zulian was the local version of the name Julian, and I knew Saint Julian was the patron of Flanders. It was the Flemish church here in Venice. I marveled silently at the breadth and reach of science, able to touch seemingly all places at once, all lives linked by its mysteries. The Fleming and Istvan, my cousin, myself,

Hans. All of them were now part of the same tapestry. And although I knew the answer, I made Istvan tell me the name of the other man Alexander had been contracted to kill, and there was merely the slightest hesitation as he told me my own name.

I had long expected such a thing from my cousin, and yet hearing it confirmed now sent a sudden shiver down my spine. I had much left to accomplish; I could not let such vile and small things as human politics allow me to be incapacitated. I resolved John of Luxembourg must die. But first, I had to meet the creature Alexander.

I was anxious to be on our way and cross the city to the church, as it was getting on toward evening. Aloud, I wondered at how the Bohemians had known I was in Venice, and the idea that I had been betrayed crossed my mind for the first time. Istvan sought to calm me, as I confess to having become mildly agitated. He suggested we take a cup of ale at the inn and wait until dark to make our way to San Zulian.

Reluctantly, I agreed. We sat in the common room mostly in silence. I brooded over the game that was being played by my cousin at my expense. Long ago I had forsworn the Polish crown, but now it seemed events back home in my absence had conspired to place my name back into contention, against my will.[63] My friendship and alliance with the Knights was mostly for my own benefit, and although I held them in high regard, especially certain of their members, I was able to discern in them a staleness, a

---

63 Although not touched upon in his memoirs, Siemowit's loyalty to the Elbow-High went back and forth in the late-1320's. In 1326, he abandoned the fealty he had sworn and sided with the Knights in their contest against the Elbow-High's consolidation of power. In 1329, he switched back, infuriating John of Luxembourg, who had counted on Siemowit's absence to promote his own claim to Poland. The events of this part of the memoir, however, may shed light on the Duke's decision to goad John.

torpor that came not from laziness or cowardice, but from the constant need for vigilance and proving themselves. They were suspicious, and saw enemies everywhere. Perhaps they were right, but I already had my Knights, and I needed none of the rest.

The ale calmed me, and we stepped into the cool of the winter evening air. Suddenly, I realized my obsessions were over the wrong things. What matter to me were the plots of John and the Knights and all of Europe, when I was merely a short walk from one of the greatest mysteries of all? Inwardly I raged at the smallness of my vision, at how quickly I had been led down the too-human paths of vengeance and counterplotting. Nothing mattered to me but science, and now here I was, about to come face to face with science in its ultimate, most animal form.

I hurried us along. The streets were mostly empty, as the weather was cold. Eventually, Istvan led me to the San Zulian. We went around to the rear of the church, where the priest's quarters were. Istvan knocked loudly on the door and some moments later a man answered, wearing a brown robe tied at the waist with a tan rope. The low light did not allow me to make out his face, but this was apparently the man Istvan sought, for they greeted each other warmly and the man stood aside to let us in.

The room was small and dirt-floored, and furnished humbly with a straw mattress on the floor and a small writing table beneath a shuttered window. A candle sputtered on the table and the priest went and fetched another and lit it, holding it in his hand. His face illuminated, I peered close to look at him.

The priest's face was terribly scarred, the skin mottled in fiery red and snowy white blisters. Some of the hair on the left side of his head was missing and the scalp beneath it was smooth as silk, shining in the candlelight like the yolk of an egg. His left eye drooped down at the edge, and when he breathed it was through his mouth and an ugly rattle accompanied each intake. I made him out a failed scientist in that instant.

Father Willem, as he was, had traveled to Venice after a long career in Flanders to minister to the souls of the Flemish traders in the city. Here, he had met Petrus Lombardus, the famous scientist, and under his quiet tutelage had made subtle enquiries of his own, attempting to reconcile what God had made and revealed to man with what man could reveal to himself through science. An accident at the Athanor had disfigured him, and he now devoted his scientific inquiries solely to those in manuscript and pamphlet.

I asked him in a low voice if he knew a Fleming called Nicolas and described a likeness. The priest looked at me, puzzled, and answered that of course he did, he had been the abbot at the monastery where the Fleming had grown up. He spoke in a way that told me he was surprised I did not know this, and I began to question him further, but he was eager to show us what he had been bidden to keep.

Willem led us out and into the crypt of his church. Below the ground, it was very cold and from down the dark corridor I could hear moaning and a faint rattle of chain. The creature awaited. The priest and Istvan and I all held candles, and they flickered in the wind of the underground passage, casting on the rock walls gloomy and eerie shadows. Dead priests and wealthy patrons were sealed up in these walls, I knew. I wondered absently if the priest had ever entertained the notion of resurrecting one of them.[64]

The priest was nervous and made to leave us to our task. Before he did, I seized his arm and asked him why he thought I should have known his association with the Fleming. The same look of surprise came onto this face, shock at my ignorance, and he answered plainly, as though it should have been obvious, that the Fleming had commended to his care a shipment for me in Constantinople, two barrels delivered from Poland, and that I should, upon receiving them, know to come to Venice.

Now, the shock was mine. Obviously, some of my retainers had made it back to Wiskitki with the news I was going on to Constantinople, and their arrival had somehow coincided with that of the Fleming, who stayed at my lodge whenever he passed through. But who had been the man in Constantinople who had taken possession of the barrels, to whom the boy had been bringing them? The questions were mounting, and again I was losing sight of what was truly important: only steps away was a shape-changer.

It seemed I had as many questions for Istvan as I had for the creature Alexander, but as we began to walk down the cold corridor of the catacomb, drawing closer to the cell where the creature was kept, I pushed from mind all the worry and speculation that had run rampant in my head since that afternoon.

The cell had been carved from the wall, whether by design or by nature I could not tell. It was little more than an alcove that had had its mouth barred off. There was a torch

---

64 In a letter addressed to the Editor and representatives of the Publisher, the rector of the church of San Zulian in Venice strenuously denied that "any servant of (his) church, throughout history, would have been involved in such nefarious and satanic deeds." A search of the parish records, which date back nearly a thousand years, does show a "Gulielmus", the Latin form of Willem's name, as head priest during this time period. His cause of death, some three years later, was noted as "veneno", or poisoned.

burning in a sconce on the wall of the cell, casting enough light to see clearly the wretched thing that lay hunkered and whimpering on the floor.

I saw it was fastened with chains at its feet, hands and neck to rings mounted also in the walls and floor. It was still naked, and still filthy and blood-caked. The sword, however, had been removed, or at least part of it, for as I looked closer, I could see a shard of the blade still left inside the wound. I looked inquiringly at Istvan, who explained in a hushed voice that it had been done by the smith at Gargazzone, the one who had made the sword to begin with. He had left the shard inside the wound so the creature could continue to be subdued, as Istvan had instructed. It was well known that silver was a poison to the shape-changers.

Istvan now spoke to the creature, who had become warily alert at our coming. He explained that he had brought the man he had promised, the one who could cure him of the silver sickness. The creature Alexander's eyes flashed over to me, looking at me hungrily, desperately.

I came forward and knelt beside the creature's head and bent to look at the wound in the shoulder. As I did, I spoke, asking the creature questions about the wound, and then abruptly changing subject, wanting different answers. Calmly I probed the wound, causing the creature to gasp and whine and sob. It confirmed much of what Istvan had already told me of its history. I sent Istvan out, and he reluctantly left the cell and waited in the corridor, within voice's reach if needed, although I had a silver knife on my person at all times, in addition to other tools.

Alone with the creature, I sat myself down on the floor beside it. An idea had been forming in my head from the moment I had learned the creature was here in Venice. I spoke now, clear and insistent to the creature, telling it I could not cure it here, for this was a prison and I needed my tools and laboratory to cure it. It began to protest but I cut it off, saying I would take it from here forthwith and back to Poland with me, where I would heal it and make it immune to the silver sickness. At this, it became awestruck, for such a thing was unknown to it, that one of its kind could be made impervious to the silver. I assured it I could keep it alive and dull its pain on the journey, so that it would not suffer unduly, but I made clear to the creature that the price of my service was his servitude in my employ for a period of one year.

I made clear to the creature that without treatment, the silver sickness would continue to weaken it further and further until it drained the very life force from it, killing it. The shard that had been left in the creature's shoulder was enough to allow a slow but steady stream of the poison into its blood, a little every moment, adding up and making it more and more ill.

The picture I painted of the prospects of its pain and suffering made the creature all the more eager to be gone, on the road to its cure. But I lingered, wanting to know more. I admit, I was greedy for knowledge, and here I had a captive font of wisdom. I could not pass up the chance to learn what I could while I could. Who knew if the creature would turn on me during the journey back to Poland? Or even as we walked up the stairs of the crypt and out into the night?

I asked if it knew me, and the creature answered in a rough and pale voice that it reasoned I was the Duke of Masovia, whom it had been charged to kill. I asked how it had reasoned such, and it replied that it had been told my likeness and a fearsome report of my aspect and ability. I had no reason to inquire as to whom had hired it, for I knew already who would ultimately benefit, and it seemed to confuse the creature that I did in fact not ask the identity of its employer. Instead, I demanded of it to tell me what it knew of its twin's whereabouts, but the creature could not, only stating that their scheduled rendezvous was still some months off, and they had no way of contacting one another in the meantime.

Next, I asked if it knew another of its kind, one called Hans, and I spoke a likeness, and said there was a chance the creature had met Hans when it was young. The description, it said, could apply to many of its own kind that it had known; it could not say for certain whether it had known Hans. I nodded and stood, the creature's eyes following me up. I stepped back away, toward the door of the cell, and instructed Istvan, who waited outside, to pass the key to the creature's chains through the bars. The priest had left them with Istvan, and now he handed them to me.

I bent again, taking the shackle of Alexander's right foot in my hand. If you try to escape me, I told it, now or any time in the future, I will kill you. The creature nodded in understanding and acceptance. I unfettered it, and helped it to rise. It was appallingly weak; I had to support near all its weight as we walked from the cell down the corridor, up the stairs and back up into the small rear courtyard of the church. At our coming, Father Willem again emerged from his quarters.

The priest approached with a small brocade bag, and held it out; Istvan took it, as I was burdened by the creature. I gave the priest an inquiring look, and nodded to Istvan, who opened the bag. He reached in and withdrew a chain of thinly-beaten silver links. Lombardus, he told us, had forged it so as to cast it about the ankle of the Angel Jershom, with whom he had commerce and wished to enslave, but who in the end killed him. It was, the priest said, one of the few artifacts he had left of his former master, and he gifted it to us, to aid us in the captivity of the creature.

The creature Alexander, weak and leaning heavily against me the entire time, seemed to revive very slightly as the silver chain was held up by Istvan for inspection. The creature seemed to moan deep within itself, and a shudder rippled through its body. It began to sweat and shiver, and did so until Istvan placed the chain back into the bag.

Willem also gave us a ragged cloak, which we put over the creature. Thanking the priest and bidding him farewell, gifting him and his church handsomely, we took our leave, and under the guise of guiding home a drunken friend, we stumbled our way through the night time streets back to the inn, and into the wagon, which was admittedly becoming more crowded than was strictly comfortable.

Istvan took a room at the inn, and I bade Hrothgar join him, for there was not enough room in the wagon to accommodate us all. The dead soldier I made help me to fasten the slumped and weakened body of the creature Alexander to the iron rings set into the floor of the wagon. A slight nervousness overtook me as we fastened it, and I resolved to begin the return to Wiskitki as soon as possible, where the power of stone would help to hold the creature, rather than mere wood, thick and enchanted as it may be.[65]

But the captive creature gave no sign of stirring as it lay there in chains. It seemed deep asleep, or perhaps out of itself. While I had the chance, alone with the creature but for the dead soldier, I quickly worked some bindings onto the creature, incants that of course would not hold over the long term but would serve to allow me some measure of control over the creature, should the silver sickness ever begin to wane or its effects weaken.

I needed to return to Poland. The sooner we were back in my laboratory, the sooner I could perfect and complete the process, binding the creature to my will. I had been gone far too long, in any event, far longer than I had had any intention of being away. And in my absence, unthinkable things had obviously occurred. The Elbow-High had warred

---

65 According to contemporary sources, the Duke's wagon was carved and painted with protective runes and symbols on near its entire surface.

against the Knights, somehow. And yet, the Knights, or one of them at least, still held commerce with me, a sworn liege of the Elbow-High. The Fleming's interest was not political, though, but scientific, and it seemed it would take far more than a petty noble's war to keep him from helping me.

Another reason for returning so soon was indeed the Fleming. Seeing him again was paramount in my mind, to show him the creature Alexander I had gained through no small effort of his own. And the questions I had for him seemed to grow by the day, most especially the ones regarding the head of Hans.

Too many plans, too many questions, too many theories all clattered around in my head, so that there seemed an endless cacophony of noise that I could never still, the sound of all my worry and hope and intrigue colliding. I had been too long away from the instruments of my science, and aside from meeting the Jew and his golem, I was starved for the kind of learning I could only find in my laboratory. The creature Alexander was, of course, a treasure trove of research and experimentation, but the amount and quality of work I could do with and upon him was severely limited by the crudeness and secularity of my surroundings.

The idea occurred to me that I could detour and visit Vermundr Karl's estate; Zurich was far closer than Wiskitki. But the more I thought on it, the more I suspected Vermundr Karl would covet the creature Alexander with all his scientific heart, and I had no intention of losing it to him, for I had gone across much of Europe to gain it, and I would hate to part in animosity and bitterness from Karl, as he was the closest thing to a colleague I had.

To Poland, I decided, we must go. Back home, into the den of plots and counterplots that seemed to be reproducing almost daily. From there, in addition, I could again renounce whatever claim to the Crown had been put forward in my absence that had so inflamed John, and thereupon devote all my energies to Alexander, to unlocking his secrets and using them to better all mankind.

Next morning, I settled with the innkeeper and bought from a nearby hostler two sturdy, if not young, packhorses to draw the wagon. I sent off a series of letters, one to Wiskitki to inform them of my pending return, and several to the banking houses in the large cities we would pass through on the return. Others were of a more personal nature.

Istvan and I parted warmly, and I paid him several times over his normal rate, for he had performed for me a service that could never be fully repaid. In preparation for the journey, I immobilized the creature Alexander in bondage in the wagon, and about his neck I encircled the link of thin chain given us by the priest. Each time I looked upon him, my heart began to race and my hands tremble, in anticipation of the great work I could perform once we returned.

In the afternoon, we crossed to the mainland and then traveled northwest along the road that led to the Alps, to Gargazzone, to home. Once, I turned and looked behind me, but Venice was too far off, a faint smear on the horizon, an ugly fleck of jet floating upon the sea.

The horses I had purchased in Venice tired often on the slow, uprising road. To lighten their load, I often made Hrothgar and the footman walk beside the wagon, but eventually it came clear to me that I would need to replace the horses with a sturdier breed if we were to cross the formidable curtain of stone and ice that was the looming Alps.

The weather was in our favor for the first part of the journey. The rains had been light or nonexistent, and so the roads were not the muddy soup they could have been, so luckily we made good progress. At any moment, though, the skies could turn against us. I wanted to at least be on the downslope of the Alps before the snows and bitter cold grew terrible. I had no desire to be stranded atop the mountains for the remainder of the winter.

In the wagon, the creature Alexander still lay bound, and only rarely would he stir. I would wake it from deep sleep to feed it broth and vegetables from the cooking pot. I was depriving it of meat deliberately, hoping that too would serve to make it more docile and pliable. Early in the journey, I had washed the creature and shorn its hair off, and often during the slow, wending way of the day, I would enter the wagon while it slept and tattoo upon it in the proper places more binding sigils. But, of course, it would not be enough. Such decoration would suffice for a man, such as Hrothgar, but this was a shape-changer, and for the full control I wanted, I needed it in my laboratory where I could work will all complete access to my tools and ingredients.

---

66   The Duke's memoir resumes at the point it left off. He and his entourage are traveling north, returning to Poland, with the shape-changer Alexander in tow. Much of the manuscript at this point is weather-damaged, but still completely legible. The road to the Alps leads initially northwest, then curves to run north-northeast.

Each day we spent rising upward and upward, scaling the roof of Europe. We had crossed from Venetian territory into Aquileia.[67] The spires of the Dolomite Alps soared above us on all sides and we came to a small village where I was able to sell the horses and for a modest sum more purchase two powerful draught horses of the local breed and temperament. We elected to stay the night in the village, and that evening Hrothgar, the footman and I went out with some village boys to hunt in the rocky forest that surrounded the town. We caught numerous marmots and hares, and the footman was skilled enough with bow and arrow to fell a fawn. When we returned to the village, there was a great feast and most of the folk stayed up well into the night.

I had aided in the skinning and dressing of the fawn, partly to be helpful and partly as a an experiment, for after I had done it, I went without washing myself into the wagon where the creature Alexander was. I was curious to see what effect the smell of offal and blood would have upon it. Surely enough, though it had been asleep when I came in, it soon began to stir and finally awakened, its body tense, its muscles ready to spring, although it was bound.

I watched it, standing out of its reach. I saw the lust kindle in its eye, the slaver begin to drip from its mouth. Underneath its skin I thought I could sense a faint ripple, as though its very skin was a fabric caught in a light breeze. It began to snarl, just like a wolf, even though its aspect was still that of a man. It bared its teeth and growled at me. I paid especial attention to its hands and feet; it flexed them over and over, as though trying to work out some stiffness in them. I could see the skin of its neck beneath the thin chain was raw and chafed, and this seemed to prevent the creature

67   The Patriarchate of Aquileia was ruled by a Catholic bishop who was also ennobled as a prince of the Holy Roman Empire. At this time, the patriarch of Aquileia was Pagano della Torre. Much of his rule was spent infuriating his subjects by raising their taxes egregiously and sacking the business interests of his enemies.

from moving its head in a natural motion.

The creature was trying, I could tell, to devolve into a wolf. It began to moan and whimper, though, the more it found it could not. The silver shard in its shoulder and the chain about its neck, coupled with the tattoos and binding I had done upon it already were holding—were keeping the creature in its human aspect—despite its patent lust to devolve into a beast triggered by the scent of the blood upon me.

I walked about and about it, and each time, it followed me with its eyes, turning its head when it could. I drew close, to gauge its reaction, to study the dilation of its pupils. I pulled away, to examine the frenzy into which it fell when the stimuli of the blood was taken from its potential grasp. For nearly half of an hour, I examined the creature thus, driving it into a fit of near-insanity, though at no time did it ever stir from its chains to reach out to me, or make any effort of an attacking kind. I gathered that the binding work I had done was sufficient for the moment, but that another session such as this may be enough to undo what had been done. I did not endeavor to repeat the experiment on the continuation of the journey.

The road climbed higher and higher, and on all sides great fortresses and towers of stone piled atop one another, their jagged peaks like serrated knives ready to carve the very sky into ribbons. In most places, the road was barely wide enough for our wagon, and so we rode in file. Sometimes, though, the road widened, often as we neared a small town or smallholding. Often, we would pass a young shepherd tending his flock in a tiny green patch high up on a rocky slope. Once, we passed, coming in the opposite direction, a small procession of pilgrims, who were on their way from Prague to Rome to seek a blessing from the pretender there.[68]

One of this group was a young girl, still a child. She had the olive complexion, the bright green eyes and the black silk-like hair of the Gypsies. The family she traveling with was apparently not her own, for they had nothing in common, and I supposed she was their servant. Seeing her put me mind of the Gypsy seeress who had cast my fortune as a youth at the fair in Wiskitki. She had proved so far so correct, it sent a brief shiver through my person. Had not she predicted so much of my success thus far, although tempered it also with premonitions of failure? Years had gone past since I had given any real thought to her prophecy, but now that I did, I could see clearly how all my life seemed to fit into the pattern she had seen, as though I was merely acting out a role in some mummer's show she had written.

Eventually we reached what was called the Valle de Cofanetto, or the Jewel-box Valley. It was an excellent name, for the shape of the bowl was indeed irregular and almost square. Steep fingers of mountain surrounded the valley, and green carpeted the floor and crept some ways up the slopes of the peaks, but giant boulders and rocky scree littered the fields as well, and we saw several sheep and cows grazing in the shade of a house-sized boulder beside the road as we came upon the village of Ampezzo.

The snows of winter had barely descended to the floor of the valley, although the higher slopes of the mountains were white and sparkling. The day was clear and bright and cold, and we entered the town past midday, and found the streets all bustling and the folk of the town animated and seemingly on edge, although none were rude to us.

We found an inn, for there was no place else that could accommodate us within a day's ride, and none of us relished the idea of sleeping on the cold ground. At the inn, the

68 "The pretender" is Nicholas V, installed as Pope by the Holy Roman Emperor in 1328, in opposition to the "true" Pope at Avignon, John XXII.

keeper asked if I was in the retinue of the Patriarch, and I answered negatively. That explained the mood of the town, then: the ruler of the country was visiting, and had set himself up in the Palazzo Bigontina, near the river. I felt it incumbent upon me to pay him a visit, as among the confraternity of nobles such things were expected.

I brought the footman with me to the Palazzo and we were received almost at once. The Patriarch of Aquileia was a small, rat-faced man, with long greasy hair and protuberant yellow teeth. His face was pockmarked and scarred, and he had a slight hunchback. He wore his bishop's robe, although it had been modified somewhat to allow for a tunic of deep red and a black belt about his thin waist. He wore high leather boots, his fingers were heavy with rings, and his wrists weighed down with bracelets. I bowed to him, though I made no effort to kneel and kiss his ring, as I am sure he was expecting.

The Patriarch was attended by several cupbearers and pages, all of whom bore markings on their skin; one boy had been plainly branded on the back of his neck, and though I could not make out the design, the mark was red and bright. He served a meal of cold meat, bread, and watered ale. As I knew nothing of the local politics or factions, I had few answers to his probing questions. He seemed to take me for some kind of spy or informant. The man was preternaturally paranoid, and wished to bring the audience to quick conclusion and leave the town.

However, the subject of my travels inevitable came up, and when he learned I had recently been in Venice, his suspicion and wariness of me moved from the guarded to the blatant. He became abruptly rude and insulting, and in the midst of the meal, I stood and took my leave. As I made to go, however, I was stopped by two of the Patriarch's guards. One I easily incapacitated by applying fast and accurate pressure to the nerve cluster of his neck, but the other took his initiative while I was so occupied. He struck me with his staff across the back, and I fell to my knees. However, before he could strike me again, I grasped his ankle and pulled him off his feet, and the man crashed to the floor, striking his head loudly on the flagstone. He did not move to rise and so I stood and turned to face the Patriarch, who now stood trembling at his table, a blunt knife in his quaking hand.

I strode purposefully to him, and though his pages and cupbearers stood all about the room, none of them made to stop me or aid their master. From the table I took up a pewter flagon filled with watered wine and as I neared him I threw the wine into his face and he stumbled backward. Losing his footing, he collided with an iron brazier, sending it toppling to the floor with a ringing crash and scattering coals and embers over the stones. Finally, he slumped back into his chair, dazed.

I was far taller and broader than he, and as I stood before him, he seemed to shrink from me. He fell back into his chair, staring up at me in fear. I caught a movement from the corner of my eye, and saw several of the pages scurrying from the room. He took advantage of my distraction and struck at my leg with the knife. The point of the knife passed through the leather riding leggings I was wearing, and I felt a slight prick as it bit into my skin.

Anger bloomed in my heart like a fiery rose. Trembling with rage, I stood over him, glaring; hidden from his view, my fingers in my cloak pocket had fastened upon what I needed. With a swift and fluid motion, I drew my arm outward, extending toward him my flared hand, throwing into his face the granules of the burning sand I always carried on me. Contact with my target had the intended effect: the sands hit his face, and instantly he cried out, his skin beginning to bubble and scald.

I had created the burning sand years ago, while trying

to perfect a scouring agent. Made of the ash scrapings that lined the Athanor after the obliterating fire had cooled, and then admixed with various other salts and left to crystallize in a solution of mercury and vitriol, it formed into fine grains, hence the name I gave it, the burning sand. The most minimal contact resulted in blisters and painful burns. If thrust at the eyes, it would blind. I had protected my own flesh through science, but there was no resisting the effect of the sands for the Patriarch.

He screeched and clawed at his red, bubbling face and then slumped over, and released the knife, which stuck in my leg. I withdrew the knife and quickly poured wine onto the small puncture. I hefted the Patriarch from his chair and threw him over my shoulder and carried him from the room, deeper into his suite. I found his chamber and dumped him onto the floor; a page boy was there, and watched unmoving.

My own footman rushed up to my side, carrying a small leather pack; he had anticipated me well, as he should have, for he was one of the children who had been born at Wiskitki into my service. I knelt beside the Patriarch and tore the sleeve of his tunic off, exposing his right arm. I ordered my footman to bind the man's mouth shut with rags and told the page boy to leave if he did not want to see a vile thing; but he elected to stay.

The Patriarch's hatred of the Venetians had spurred his rage at me, and so I effected his ruin at their hand. Onto his arm, with a finely-wrought knife inscribed with Arab script, I wrote a curse that his hubris should be his fall, that the waters of Venice should spill over his land and drown him, and added some small refinements that would protect his servants from his wrath. I bound up the bleeding words in a strip of linen taken from the death shroud of a virgin and soaked in camphor, and when the linen had soaked up the bloody script, I opened his slack jaw and forced the strip down his throat. The involuntary choking revived him, and in his sputtering, he swallowed the linen, as I had pushed it far enough back as to effect it.

As he coughed and spat and wretched, I delivered him a kick to his head and sent him sprawling again to the floor; his face was now blotched red and ugly white blisters had appeared on his cheeks and forehead. The footman and I promptly bundled the tools back into the bag, and I told the page boy he was free to leave, and to never speak of what he had seen. He rushed out the door and was gone. The footman and I left the Patriarch on his floor and returned to the inn. I knew a man of his arrogance and weak-heartedness would be loath to pursue a vendetta against me, though I made sure we had left Ampezzo before dawn and were well on the road by the time the sun came up.[69]

Heavy snow began to fall as we made the down slope of the Dolomite Alps. We were now in Austria, the heart of the Holy Roman Empire. Vienna was the de facto capital, perhaps a fortnight or more away. The country all about was dotted with castles and fortified keeps, petty lords and nobles holding tightly to their little fiefs. The deeper we went into the land, the more I rankled at the presumption and arrogance of John. He wished all this land to be his, from the Alps to the North Sea. I cared not for worldly power, only the power that came from knowledge and science, the power that was given to me through discovery and experimentation. John had no such lofty ambition; he was firmly grounded in the profane, in the filth of human mire, the feeble squabbles and quarrels of an endless array of pompous popinjays constantly begging for his favor and patronage. To me, this was as appealing as wading neck deep in excrement. I had renounced the Crown to be done with that life, to devote my energies to science instead.

But John had no inner light burning within him, no

---

69   Pagano della Torre met his fate in 1332, when he invaded Venetian territory in Istria, and was captured by Giovanni Cornaro, who was half-brother of the bailie of Budua, in whose chapel rested the Altar of Bones.

longing to discover the endless mysteries of creation. The only mystery that appealed to him was when would he finally become overlord of Europe. I knew him somewhat, and had found him vain and small-minded, just the sort of man I would loathe even were he not such an incomparable ass and conniving shit-eater. In addition, he was actively attempting to have me killed.

We drew nearer and nearer to Vienna, wending and winding through the twisting mountain roads, slowly leveling, then rising again briefly, then falling, then turning about on itself so dramatically that several times a day we traveled in opposing directions, seeming to make no progress at all. An endless parade of pastureland and forest presented itself beside the roads, all dusted with a light snow now that we had reached lower elevation. We had been lucky in the high country; the draught horses had been born and bred to such weather and performed marvelously, and we had incredible luck when it came to hunting, so that there were only a few nights where we were forced to eat meagerly.

Often at night, I had the footman and Hrothgar sleep in the wagon and drove the horses myself, for I had no need of sleep, and we pushed on and on through the night, the way ahead lit by burning brands affixed to the top of the wagon. As such, we neared our final destination that much faster.

We neared the village of Gutenstein, where the King of the Germans, Frederick called the Fair, held his winter court. He had been passed over as Holy Roman Emperor some years before, but remained the presumptive heir. The castle high was built on a rock outcrop, glowering down at the village like a haughty dowager, and from its towers fluttered the king's standards, announcing to all that he was in residence.

The currents of politics and intrigue had been blowing like a storm through my mind since Constantinople, and even in my moments of relaxation, some small part of me was still plotting, still developing ways in which I could secure my own future free from the harassment of outside forces and in the process exact a fitting revenge on those that would seek to eliminate me.

That several of the heads of Europe saw me either as a threat or a pawn was not unknown to me. I had thought that swearing Masovian loyalty to the Elbow-High would have put an end to the basest intrigues, for in my youth I was foolish enough to think that the world's politics encompassed merely Poland. But circumstance forced my worldview to expand, despite my desire to shut myself off from it.

The Elbow-High had turned on the Knights, and so my loyalty to him was a liability with them. John of Luxembourg had long wanted rid of me. Despite my blood ties, I had fought Lithuania.[70] Even my brothers and I had warred several times in our lives. The Czechs and Bohemians, I also knew, harbored a desire to see me dispatched, so they could then advance their own claims to Masovia. In short, my enemies seemed legion. Yet there was only one for whom the fires of vengeance burned strongest.

As we neared Gutenstein and its storybook castle, the threads and tendrils of my revenge began to coalesce. My cousin John's relationship with Frederick the Fair was contentious. John had been passed over by the electors for the Holy Roman crown; they had rightly seen him as too powerful. John had accepted their decision with ill-grace, of course, but had eventually supported the eventual and current monarch Louis, who was elected on two ballots, defeating Frederick.

Louis then consolidated his power through alliances and warfare, with the support of John. Rumors abounded

---

70   One of the consequences of the Duke's abandonment of the Elbow-High was an invasion by the Elbow-High's Lithuanian allies.

that John was the puppet master who pulled the strings of the marionette Emperor. But, of course, ruling behind the scenes was never what my cousin wanted; he desired the trappings and blatant naked power of being the acknowledged master.

Frederick, though, was still the presumptive heir. He was a good man, by all accounts, fair and just and even-handed, all the hallmarks that would make a beloved sovereign and the antithesis of John of Luxembourg. He had wide-ranging support in the courts of central Europe that made up the voting electorate. There was little doubt anywhere that when Louis died, Frederick would become the Emperor.

And here my plans for my own life and work dovetailed with the plans and schemes that drove European politics. I admit now that it was merely the whims of chance and opportunity that allowed what was to happen next to occur. Had I been traveling through Aachen or Prague at that moment, truly the outcomes would have been different. But fate had sent me to Gutenstein, and as such, sadly for most, a good man must die.

If Frederick were dead, John would of course become the presumptive heir. John was now even more powerful than he had been before, when he had been rejected, and the Empire had suffered from the weakness of Louis. But John was dreadfully unpopular; even in his own Bohemia, he was hated and spent most of his time away from court, plotting in Poland and Tyrol. If he wanted to assume his role as heir, he would have to fight for it, drawing his armies from all over central Europe to protect his chances of becoming the Emperor. There would be a war to stop him. And a war in which John fought was a war in which John might die.

I spared no thought for anything other than John's ultimate demise. We entered the town and I halted the wagon at an inn. It was late in the night, and so I let the others sleep while I worked out the details of my plans.

Eventually satisfied, toward dawn I woke the creature Alexander from its sleep. I told it that I wished it to perform a service for me, and in return I would recompense it in gold equal to its own weight when we gained Poland. I could not tell which appealed to it more: the prospect of being healed from the silver sickness, or the promise of eternal riches.

However, the creature acceded to my wishes and I laid out what I needed it to do. To accomplish my ends, though, I needed to remove the silver shard from its shoulder and the chain from its neck. I was wary, for although I had used minor bindings on the creature, and had appealed to its lust for wealth and a cure for its ill, I did not trust the creature.

What did I want more, though? The fall of John or the opportunity that would likely never come again, to possess a shape-changer? Without John's preoccupation with holding onto his power, or his eventual demise, I could never truly be free to advance my science, and although it may seem a worldly concern, and one that is out of character for a man who has devoted himself solely to the work of investigation and human betterment, I elected that I would be better served if John were neutralized as a threat.

That said, there were precautions I could take to ensure, or at least make more probable, the loyalty of the creature Alexander. While the creature was still bound, I tattooed the symbol of the carcer upon the back of its neck and my own sigil within, invoking the angels Agiel and Zazel.[71] Without access to my laboratory, it was the best I could do, and with a sigh, one of hope mixed with trepidation, I sat back and allowed the creature some modest quantity of raw meat, while I removed the shard and the chain.

For all that day, I kept the creature enchained in the wagon. I went up to the castle, to pay my respects to the

---

71   A "carcer" is a geomantic rune that serves to bind one person or creature to another; the rune is associated with and governed by the angels Agiel and Zazel, according to Jewish mysticism.

King of the Germans, and although the audience was brief, I found Frederick to be all I had heard: kind-hearted, easy to like, an excellent conversationalist. He asked intelligent questions about Poland and Masovia, about the politics of my home country. I felt a keen sense, as I was leaving his presence, that what was about to occur was unfortunate.

I spent much of the rest of that day in the town, walking its streets and markets. It was a cold and overcast day, and most of the folk were bundled warmly. I bought several hares and foxes and fowl and had them delivered to my inn. Toward evening, I returned to the wagon and again allowed the creature to eat its fill of the meat. Finally, night drew about the town, and I knew the time had come for me to put my plan into action.

I unfettered the creature Alexander, after reiterating my promise of reward and obtaining an oath of loyalty. Over and over, we went through the particulars of the plan; I described for it that part of the castle I had seen, the strength of the guardsmen in each area. The plan called for the creature to enter the castle under the guise of a jongleur, and gain access to the king's apartment once inside, ostensibly to give him a recitation of a long poem composed in his honor. It was known that Frederick was a great patron of the arts and especially of spoken poetry.

We arranged our rendezvous, a ruined church in the forest some distance out of town, where we agreed to meet at dawn. Just before parting, I told it, Do not forget what I have promised you, and what you have sworn to me. Then, from my cloak I withdrew the shard of silver sword I had removed from him and held it in the palm of my hand where he could look upon it. I said to him that while he was gone, I would burn the shard until it was liquid, and admix it with certain humors and salts to prepare it as the first part of the cure, and when we met at the dawn, I would administer it to him, as a sign of good faith.

The creature went off, attired as a jongleur. I waited in the wagon for a few moments, then set to work, Hrothgar and the dead soldier assisting me in setting up the small brazier where I would melt down the silver shard.

It took much of the night to gain a blazing heat fine enough for the task, and I had but small quantities of that which I needed, so the final product would be of lesser strength than I had led the creature to believe. Birch wood and ash wood I laid in the brazier, crossed with green shoots of yew. The smoke was fragrant and thin, and floated up like mist through the grate in the wagon's roof.

On small pieces of old parchment, I wrote the proper words of Latin and then tossed them one by one into the flames, chanting the incants as the flames grew hotter and more deeply red. Handfuls of rose thorns and a droplet of oil of pasque and six granules of vulcan salt went into the brazier.[72] With tongs of cold iron, I held the silver shard over the now-roiling flames, catching the liquefaction into a retort whose bottom had already been lined with bone ash and milk flower petals.

The tonic was completed in the deep of the night. We made ready and left the courtyard of the inn, moving slowly so as not to make much noise and not to arouse any suspicion other than that we were travelers who wanted an early start on the road.

After an hour or so, we gained the ruined church. There, we stopped and waited. There were still some hours before dawn. The others slept, and I sat up, nervous and wondering. Was Frederick already dead? Had the creature found its way to the apartment, or had it been caught? Had it been captured trying to escape? I realized there was no way of knowing anything until and if the creature arrived.

---

72   Pasque, also called fireweed, is a wildflower. It is often the first flower to grow after a forest fire. Vulcan salt is the alchemical name for obsidian that has been crushed and granulated.

I settled back to wait, but my mind was reeling with all the possibilities. So much could have gone wrong, and I was still not entirely sure I could trust the creature Alexander. I began to wonder, as dawn crept closer, whether I had made a terrible mistake.

The dawn seemed never to come. I found myself looking out the window every minute or so, and seeing the same purpled black sky, wisps of cloud like torn linen dragging across the face of the moon. I waited, trying to occupy my mind with other thoughts, other plans and theories. But there was no ignoring the constant worm of worry that burrowed into my thoughts.

I swirled the flask, watching the thick, viscous syrup coat the sides. The first part of my promise to the shape-changer. I had written back and forth to Vermundr Karl for years, on a variety of subjects, but as time and our acquaintance went on, more and more the subject turned to shape-changers. He had come across credible information that silver was a poison to them, and now that I had seen the creature Alexander suffering under its curse with my own eyes, I could confirm it. In one of our letters, I had inquired as to whether there was a way to neutralize the effects of the silver poison. He had written back several pages of theory and speculation, and it was from this that I distilled the syrup which I now watched swirling in the glass flask.

Hrothgar and the footman were sleeping; the dead soldier was like myself and needed none. He sat up at the desk, writing the Roman emperors in succession from memory upon a slate. I checked his work, absently; he had worked from Augustus Caesar through to Vitellius, not a very impressive list. I chided him, but my heart was not in it. I sat back again and continued to wait.

Finally, I felt I could not sit in that wagon a moment longer, and so I stood and went out into the cool of the predawn dark, taking a lantern. I walked through the ruins of the church. Grass and moss and saplings now sprouted up where the flagstones had once been; these had been carted off decades ago by enterprising builders. The walls of the church, too, were gone, and now only a shin-high foundation wall described the squared cross-shape the building had once had, but even in places these had been pried from the earth, and there were large gaps. Of the interior, there was nothing; no rotting pews or any sign of what could have served as an altar. I walked to where I supposed the altar would have been, at the rear of the ruin, straight down from where the doors had been.

I wondered at what manner of church it had been, out here in the forest, hidden away. I sat on the ground, on a large flat slab of stone overgrown with moss and weeds. It had probably once been the base stone of the altar, I guessed. If all had gone according to plan, Frederick was by now dead, and wheels had been set in motion that would send shudders all throughout Europe. I confess that in that moment, sitting alone in the ruins of the church, a feeling of momentousness swept over me, that I should have been the cause of such an upheaval that would affect countless lives across this continent. It was, of course, only fitting.

Overhead, the sky began to turn from black to purple, then bruised pink and orange. The day was coming on, the sun clawing its way up from below the earth. I stood and listened, straining my ears, hoping to hear the sound of footfalls. Or would it be wolf's paws I heard padding through the forest? Would the creature kill me too?

The sun came up. Birds began to twitter in the trees, flitting from branch to branch and swooping in the early morning light. A wary fox peeped its head around a break in the wall and looked about. It spied me suddenly and jolted away. From the wagon, the footman emerged to make his water. A growing sense of despair settled over me.

It was no long time before I heard the sound of

something crashing through the branches and underbrush of the forest. I sprang to my feet, knife in hand. The noise was coming from before me, and to the left, from the direction of town. The sound was getting closer and closer; startled birds angrily burst into the air, speeding above me like arrows.

It emerged from the forest, a huge hulking wolf, yellow-eyed, its maw and teeth stained with fresh blood. Its fur was black and had bits of tree branch and fern in it. It had burst from the forest on all fours, but when it saw me, it stood upright like a man and walked toward me on its back legs. As it neared, the smell of it overpowered me. It had an animal stink of unwashed fur and earth and blood. It loped toward me on its back legs, covering two strides for every one of a normal man's. Finally, it stood before me. It was taller than I, by perhaps a head and a half. It was very broad across, the chest heavily muscular, as were the arms. The legs were incredible, the muscles seemed fit to burst through the skin.

It breathed heavily, and the stink of its breath now added itself to the other smells of it. I nearly wretched. The muzzle of the creature was crusted with dried blood and bits of meat. The forepaws of the creature were muddy and the whole body was likewise covered in dirt and filth and more blood. I looked it over closely. It stood panting, its chest heaving. We stared at one another for some moments, and I finally asked it if it was hurt, and it shook its head.

It held out to me one of its forepaws. In the great, furry palm of it was a golden chain, from which hung a pendant, a circular disc the size of a large coin, also of gold. Inscribed onto the disc were the arms of Frederick; it was his seal. I had seen it about his neck when I had met him the day before.

I took it from the proffered paw. Frederick was dead. My plan had worked. I felt an invisible weight slide from my gut down to the soles of my feet. I looked up into the face of the wolf. We were now linked together in a way that I had never imagined I would be to any creature. For a long moment, I did not speak. I stared into its yellow eyes for what seemed hours. Finally, I looked up. The sky was clear and blue; the morning was full upon us.

It came back to me. The realization had been slowly sinking in, but at that moment, looking up at the sky, it hit me fully. It had come back to me, and now it was mine. We needed to get out of there, onto the road, as far away from Gutenstein as quickly as we could go. I said something of that nature to the creature, and it nodded. It turned and loped into the forest again. I called after it, but it had disappeared into the trees, only to emerge only a moment later, in the aspect of a man, naked and covered in blood and filth.

We entered the wagon and I washed the creature and gave it some quantity of water and food, but it was listless and soon fell into deep slumber. The wagon was hitched to the team and we were back on the road shortly. I drove the horses hard through the forest, and by midday we had left Gutenstein far behind us.

The first time the creature Alexander woke, nearly a full day out on the road, I made it to drink the syrup. It drank, in gulps, and fell into a convulsion that made it thrash about the floor for some short time, and then again it fell into sleep. It woke again, some hours later, coughing and sputtering, but it ate and drank meat and ale without difficulty. It did not speak to me of what had occurred, nor of much anything else.

Over the next weeks, very little of import occurred. We crossed the Danube into Bohemia during the night, unchallenged by sleepy sentries at the remote crossing in the forest. In a small village two days inside the border, we heard the news that the King of Germans was dead. Hrothgar and I had taken our supper at the local inn, and all the talk of the place was of Frederick's death. I listened closely to the townsfolk, listening for any mention of how the King had died, or for any mention of John's name.

The word 'murder' was commonly heard, but none there had any details, nor was there any mention of a wolf or of any especial brutality to the crime. At length, several of the more inebriated openly, and with evident happiness, speculated that their own sovereign John should now attempt the Roman throne. The subject, however, was quickly overshadowed by the local gossip involving a brewer's daughter and a stable boy.

By day and night, we crossed the Bohemian frontier. We skirted the smaller villages and only once did we stop in a larger city. Olomouc was the place where the Elbow-High's rival had been murdered years before, assuring his hold over Poland. It was a thriving city, full of Jews and merchants. The great cathedral of Saint Wenceslaus drew every eye to its spires, and the squares and markets of the city were thronged with hawkers and sellers, the bargaining and arguing ringing off the stone walls of the shops and halls.

There was a banking house there, also, and it was there that I went. I conducted my business, exchanging the sheaf of yellowed notes given me by Istvan in Venice for a large quantity of gold and silver. I stayed long enough in the town to re-provision my wagon of the supplies most readily available, but since we were so near to home, I thought it wiser not to waste time and gold hunting down the exotic. Mere hours after we had rolled through the city's gates, we were trundling back out again, northeast toward Poland.

I was driving the wagon through the first light of morning, when we first came within sight of the river and flatland that surrounded my beloved Wiskitki. I had been away for a very long time, and I could see all around me, in the dawning light, that little had changed. At least, outwardly. I drove up to the gates of my lodge, and there was a great rejoicing in the place, that the master was returned.

The steward came down to greet me in the courtyard as I was having the wagon unhitched from the team. He embraced me warmly; he was an old man, and I was glad he had not perished in my absence. Yet his face wore a mask of worry and trepidation. He had news, he told me. News of a grim and distressing sort. I told him to await me in the great hall. I went to the carters who were tending to the wagon, ordering them aside.

I went in, and with the aid of Hrothgar, unfettered the creature Alexander. It had long since been dressed in the clothing of a servant, and under Hrothgar's direction, it was led out the wagon and into the courtyard. I took the dead soldier Marek up from the floor where he was scratching the Hebrew letters in the dust and led him out also. The four of us went up into the lodge; I led them all up the stairs into the large quarters I had at the top of the keep. I left them there, after again fettering the creature to the floor, under Hrothgar's eye, and went down to find the steward.

His news was indeed grave, but not unexpected. The Elbow-High's war, which had begun in years gone against his northern rivals, had boiled over in my absence. Indeed, he was now warring with the Knights. For good cause, the steward told me, were the Knights aggrieved: the Elbow-High had begged for their aid in subduing his northern rivals, and when the Knights had slaughtered the northmen, the Elbow-High had reneged on his reward and repaid the Knights with contempt. The war now was raging all across the land, and the Elbow-High had sent out a call to his subject lords to send men and aid to his cause.

The steward said he had responded, in my absence, by sending a token force of some hundred men, but they had not fared well, and in the event, the small number of men had incurred the Elbow-High's wrath, as he took it an insult that Masovia was unwilling to aid in his protection.

Up in my quarters, there was fettered a shape-changer, a reanimated Russian soldier, and a bonded Knight. And yet, here I was, again enslaved by the ugly mechanisms of man's desire to rule. I had foolishly hoped that by returning home to Wiskitki, I would have been able to put all the whims and plots of others firmly away from me and to lock myself up in my laboratory to explore the realms of the unknown and to perfect the union of science and man. Yet, as soon as I set foot back in my own lodge, I was besieged by the outside world again. Not even the death of the King of the Germans had kept a worldly fate from my doors.

There was no escape, it seemed. I could not back out of my leal pledge to the Elbow-High without drawing his own force and armies upon me. I would have to go to war at his side, but I was loathe to incur the wrath of the Knights, whom I had always felt a respect for and who had done nothing to me.

That first night at Wiskitki, I sat up in thought at my writing table. I drafted several letters to the Elbow-High declining to support him, but I threw each of them into the fire. I could not survive his revenge upon me, nor could I afford to die at his hand or design. And just as dreadfully, if I were to ride at his side in war against the Knights, I may be slain in battle. I had no desire to give up this life, when so much of it remained to be discovered. Toward the dawn, an idea so momentous and beautiful crystallized in my mind, a method of defeating even the power of death.

A phylactery. A way of keeping my mind and work and spirit forever in the world. I had read of them many times, and yet the idea only solidified for me that night, worrying at my fate, seeing my own death in horrid battle. The learned Jews, I had found, knew most of such things; most of what I had read and studied had come from them.

There was too much for me to accomplish, I thought as the sun came up. The shape-changer awaited my investigations. The dead soldier and his potential remained largely unstudied. The binding of Hrothgar and Marek needed to be perfected and completed. In addition, I had set myself the task, and already undertaken several experiments on the subject, of eradicating man's capacity for feeling pain. I had several numbers of twins in my employ at the lodge upon whom I wished to test the power of the insuperable tension. Too, there was the dragon and the boy Lukasz, and also all the mundane potions and tinctures and cures I constantly needed to create. Upon all that, the phylactery.

I commended myself on the foresight I had showed in conquering sleep, yet still I wondered how I could accomplish so much, and complete my researches as well. Even were I unmolested by the tides of war and politics, it seemed too much.

I had worked many spells and done much nefarious work in the effort of extending my own life, filling my veins and blood with such magics as could be untangled from the hidden webs of science. Many of these, I feared, had been the work of charlatan scientists, and had made me wretchedly ill for days after. But there was one scroll, from the hand of the Arab Alhazred, which I had painstakingly copied out on my visit to the Hall of Wisdom in Constantinople. It was, to most eyes, even those trained in science, a jumble of meaningless phrase and symbol. But the moment I had laid eyes upon it I knew its worth.

It had been collected and stored with hundreds of other scrolls from the conquered Arab lands, sitting loose alongside such mundane and worthless scribblings as cooking recipes and town census records. The librarian, who had no inkling of the dark power written on the scroll, happily chatted to me as I copied it down, as I had presented myself as a scholar of Arab antiquity. I had packed my scroll away carefully and carried it close to my person all through the sea voyage to Venice, and overland to Poland.

The idea contained in the scroll had been resting in my mind for years, but now I had the words of the Arab to hand, I could little more resist them. The Stilling of the Sun, it was called, and it showed how to stall in its courses the labor of time. I could work it concurrently with the phylactery. Even if one failed, there would be the other to collect and suspend my soul and life and keep it for always.

That day, I went and unfettered the creature Alexander from its shackle and led it to the laboratory. I set it upon the great stone table and again chained it down. It made a great anger of this, and as it had indeed come back to me after its task, I relented and unchained it; I left about its neck, however, the thin silver chain which I had replaced upon it before leading it from the wagon. It sat placidly on the table while I collected my tools.

From its arm, I took several phials of its blood; it was not the red of man, though, but rather it had a deeper, richer color, more to black, and within the liquid there seemed to glisten and sparkle tiny bits of silver light, as though somehow starlight had gotten into its veins. As I worked, I spoke to it, explaining what I was doing, asking it questions, attempting to allay its fears. At one point, it asked me about the gold I had promised, and I told it I would give him it that evening. Then I made it to drink the incapacitating potion I had given so many others who sat upon my table.

As it slept, I worked one of the most powerful bindings I had yet accomplished. I inked the binding tattoos with a solution of liquefied gold admixed with a droplet of melted silver and grains of iron salt. The runes and sigils I made glowed a faint red when I etched them into its skin; the incants I chanted seemed to echo in the still of the room.

It slept on, and I separated from one of the phials of its blood a small droplet and heated it over the silver brazier until it bubbled. Eventually, into the heating flask I threw crystal of mercury and several granules of jet and a droplet of oil of vitriol. Swirling the flask with iron tongs, it bubbled and sent up an acrid smoke that burned my eyes; I took it off the fire and, still boiling, I poured it directly onto the creature Alexander's chest, scalding into its flesh the final rune that would keep it mine always.

The creature did not stir once during the whole process, and when it was done it still slept on. I sent for food and drink and ate while watching the creature's chest rise and fall in rhythm. The smell of its burnt skin had faded from the room and finally I stood and removed the thin sliver chain from about its neck. I waited, but it was many hours before the creature finally awoke.

It was docile and confused when it awakened. It recognized me at once, though, although I could tell it did not know where it was. It ate ravenously of several dead fowl I had had brought up. It was gruesome to see a man, or at least this creature in man's aspect, devour the meat of a fowl raw as an animal would. Soon enough, its face and chest were covered in blood, the thin blood of a bird rather than the thicker, congealed redness I had seen it covered with when it emerged from the forest.

In time, I led it out of the laboratory to its quarters. I locked it inside, but made no use of the heavy chains. I made to visit it near every day, and after a fortnight or so, I allowed it free rein of the lodge; the binding had confined it to the lodge unless by my express will: it could not leave the grounds. I had already, over the course of that fortnight, completed the binding of Hrothgar and Marek. They were simple tasks compared to the shape-changer, and as I worked them, I realized that men were by and large merely lumps of soft clay, able to be molded by the right hands into whatever shape and design was needed. I barely exerted myself, whereas with Alexander, I had sweated and felt the strain of each incant.

Weeks and months went on, and I locked myself in my

laboratory, performing experiments and filling volumes of vellum with my findings and theories. Countless vagrants came through the hidden stairs of the lodge and ended up on my stone table. Phials were filled and emptied, bones were sawed open and scraped clean, their marrows then distilled into tinctures or potions. Soon, my storeroom was near-overfull with glittering phials full of liquid, chests of powders and herbs and salts. Everything I had spent and used on my journey was replaced, or improved. I felt rekindled, more alive than I had been in months; I was active in the sciences again.

But even science could not shield me from the events of the outside world, as I so hoped. The Elbow-High's war raged on, and in time it grew closer and closer to me and all my work. I came down one morning to find the household in titters and mutters and trepidation. I called one of the servants to me to explain what was afoot.

The Elbow-High's men were near; they had been sighted some small distance away. I was enraged. The little fool had come to me, ridden his army to my step and intended to shame me into helping his war. With stiffness and barely hidden anger, I ordered the lodge to be made ready to receive the Elbow-High, then stormed back up to my quarters. I dressed in my finest garments, and buckled on my sword.

I stood in the courtyard, awaiting my sovereign. Behind me was a line of my household guard, many of whom I had enhanced with potions and magics to create a more vicious fighting force. Far off, I heard horse hooves pounding upon the ground. Closer and closer they came, until finally they reared to a stop at my gates. At their head was, resplendent even in his shortness, the Elbow-High.

He dismounted awkwardly and strode powerfully forward. I bowed my head at his approach. We had long since made peace over my brief defection, but now the time had come to see whether all had been forgiven, as I suspected it indeed had not. He wore a richly-decorated robe of burgundy and gold over a black tunic and leather riding pants. His boots came up to his knees and upon his head was a circlet of jeweled gold. A sword, a short sword it should be noted, hung from his hip. He stopped before me, waiting.

I welcomed him to my hall and bade him enter. He and several retainers, one of whom I recognized as the Duke of Bytom, swept into the main hall of the lodge. Inside I seethed with anger at the presumptuousness of this little pompous fool, but even as I did, I knew I was in the wrong. I had sworn fealty to him, once in my youth and again after I had turned on him. I was pledged to his service, as ill-disposed to it as I was. I sat and awaited the control of another to weigh down upon me.

His manner was stiff and formal, with none of his previous gregariousness and warmth. Over a flagon of my own vineyard's wine, he chastised me for the meagerness of my earlier contribution to his war, the one my steward had arranged in my absence. I listened and absorbed his criticism without comment, all the while flaying him alive in my mind.

I served him a cold meal of pheasant and bread and ale, fish and potatoes. After the meal, he came down to it. I was to provide him with five-hundred men, upon his request. He ordered me to post levies around Masovia to raise the needed men. I protested at last: five-hundred able-bodied men could not be taken from my fields and workshops without a dreadful impact upon my economy. He brushed aside my concern and repeated his demand. As though to sweeten a bitter draught, he deigned to offer that he would not need the men for some months yet.

The Elbow-High was my liege lord and sovereign of Poland, and thus I was obliged to offer him quarters for the night. He stated he was moving his army to the east, closer to the allied armies of his other vassals. His next campaign, he thought, would not commence until the summer. I avoided him as best I could for the rest of that day and most of the night he was my guest. The evening meal was eaten in near-silence, and after he forwent the customary socializing.

I had cause, however, to have small words with the Duke of Bytom. He was an aged man, older than myself, in the full bloom of his elder years. We had met several times before, always at court, and had a merely passing acquaintance. Now, however, I had some marginal connection to the man: the Count of Brandis, in the Tyrol, was his bastard.

Bytom, I knew, over the years had traded hands between Poland and Bohemia dozens of times. In fact, even at the moment, the only reason I was sure it was in Polish hands was that he was here in the Elbow-High's retinue. But, I also knew his bastard had wed John of Luxembourg's cousin's daughter. It may sound tenuous and ethereal to the outsider, but allow me to assure you that even in the backwater courts of Poland and Bohemia, such connections, however remote, counted for much. The old Duke was taking no chances, it seemed, and so in the guise of speaking of the current state of politics, asked him if he had heard of the death of the King of the Germans.

From his own mouth, he told me he had heard it from the King himself. Which king, I was left to wonder, as surely was his intent. He had been grudging as well in his loyalty to the Elbow-High, at least in the early days. Now, though, I wondered if he was beginning to swing back toward Bohemia. Brandis was surely sworn to John, of that there was no doubt.

We spoke pleasantly if vaguely around the subject and finally the man's age forced him into bed. I saw a small opportunity. I sent a page into the Elbow-High's chambers with a note that stated I wished an audience with him in the morning, before breakfast.

I stayed up the night working on several experiments at once. Several hours I devoted to pain research, and the rest of the time I spent examining the connectivity of twins. At last, day broke, and I went downstairs to await the Elbow-High.

When he came down, I suggested a walk in the orchard, so that we could not be overheard. There, I laid before him a supposition I had crafted, one that would put me back into his good graces and perhaps earn me a small reprieve from his demand, and would also knock down another piece of the vast chessboard that John of Luxembourg had made of central and east Europe.

Under the early, globule fruits of the plum trees, I warned him that the evening before, the Duke of Bytom had attempted to recruit me into a betrayal, wherein his army and mine would defect and join with the Bohemians on the western front. Now, I knew the Elbow-High's fear and hatred of John was every bit as large and vehement as my own. His eyes flared and he demanded details. Hesitatingly, feigning reluctance and shame, I made that the Duke had told me his bastard, an Alpine count, was wed to John's kinswoman, and had been making strong allies all through the Tyrol and Austria, a fact that was not strictly untrue. I embellished what I knew to be so, and allowed the Elbow-High's natural fear and suspicion take hold. John was making ready an assault on Poland's weak west, I told, a plausible untruth that played into the little man's fears: while he was off warring with the Knights, the rest of his realm lay ready for attack. Bytom and John together, enlisting me into their plot, would move in from the west and overrun Warsaw and put John on the throne.

I began to expound on the errors of the plot, hoping my gainsaying would give the whole effort credence. But the Elbow-High's ears were stopped to all reason; I could see anger and suspicion roiling in his face, behind his eyes. I bent my knee and pledged my service to him again; he was distracted by his own thoughts and it was some small time before he gently touched my shoulder and bade me rise. He would think on what I had said, he told me, and thanked me for my vigilance. At the end, he embraced me, not with the warmth of a brother, of course, but rather the generosity of an enlightened monarch, rewarding a subject.

He and his retinue left that day. I was pleased to note that the Duke of Bytom's place in the procession was significantly further down the line than when they had arrived. With them gone, I resolved to make up for the wasted day by devoting all my energies to solving my most pressing scientific conundrums.[73]

Up into my laboratory I went, having sent up from my household two strong youths whom I had purchased as boys, and were now in their early manhood. They worked the fields and were housed in barracks I had built for my farm workers many years before. They were hale and healthy, and had served as scientific subjects before. This time I needed them for their pain receptors.

My experiments into pain, up to that point, had been mostly failures, as I had not found subjects whose strength was commensurate with the infliction I needed to apply in order to study it effectively. Several test subjects had died, well before the thresholds I had predicted. I had had my eye on these two field hands for years, and even before I had left for my journey I had made plans that they should be the next subjects used in the pain experiments.

All my experiments over the years, from the most basic ones using birds and animals in my youth, to the reanimation of the dead and binding of demons, had contributed to my evolving theories about the nature of

73   Several months later, just prior to the Elbow-High's summer campaign against the Knights, the Duke of Bytom was arrested and later executed for attempted treason.

mankind and his relationship to the scientific realm. I had spent many years working on my magnum opus, in which I would elaborate on these theories and attempt to teach the minds of the willing to know the darkest shadows of human existence alongside the bright pinnacles. In particular, I had developed a theory regarding the stages of life, which I called the Planes of Anima. I enumerated Five such.

These were, giving their Latin names: Vitale, or vitality, the truest and most robust health; Labore, or fatigue, the time when the body and its mechanisms tire from use; Torpor, torpor also in our tongue, in which the body and its mechanisms begin the descent into failure, and severe malaise and weakness sets in; Tabes, or decay, in which the body, long now freed from the quickening spirits and impulses of life, begins to wither and rot; and finally, Mortem, or death, where the functions of the body cease.

I had brought several subjects through the first three Planes. But, it was there, in the throes of Torpor, that they expired, as though giving up, refusing to fight for their life. I knew that the only way to confront and destroy pain, and even death as was my ultimate goal, was to bring a man successfully through the third and fourth Planes, into the final Plane, and yet not to the brink, not over the edge of that final Plane.

My greatest error, time after time, has been in failing to find subjects strong enough to withstand being drawn down to the fourth and fifth Planes. I had hoped, that in these two field hands, I had found perhaps the sturdiest and healthiest humans I had yet studied. Yet, it was not to be. Both of them passed through the first and second Planes, enduring the slowly-increasing infliction of pain and then its cessation, the push-and-pull-back method I had been perfecting for years. One of them, the name escapes me, survived into the late third Plane, longer than any other man had yet. Still and all, in the end, they proved unsatisfactory.

I retired to my laboratory that night, after they had failed. I pored over my notes, especially of the one who had survived longest. Their strength and healthiness was not in doubt, though. Perhaps the failure was in my method? Perhaps I was missing some powerful tool or ingredient in my process, that would allow the final Planes to be conquered. Perhaps I was lacking something that would make a strong man even stronger, some talisman or potion that would buttress his inner power and allow him to break through the final excruciation, to face his pain and stare into its eyes and make it turn away, beaten.

All night I delved deeper into thought, searching and searching all I had knowledge of, for the thing I needed, the missing piece of this enigma. Casting about in desperation, toward the dawn, the thought came to me: I had in my own possession, in my very thrall, a man who also held the strength inside him of a wolf. And also, I had that man's blood and his humors in phials, stored safely away for whatever use I deemed fit.

The dawn lit the room, just as the realization lit my mind. I would make a serum of the creature Alexander's blood, distilling it down to its essence of pure strength and power and ferocity, imbuing it with additional strength and fortitude. I would wed the animal to the man, and make of the man the true master of life and death. Pain would be a memory, a thing overcome and to be laughed at when reminded of it. It would be the greatest breakthrough of science to date, and I would be renowned for all time.

The creature Alexander seemed to sense a purposefulness within me when I came into its rooms later than day. It shrank from me initially, a thing it had never done. I no longer kept it chained, and often allowed it free rein of the grounds. Once, I had allowed it to hunt in the forests around Wiskitki, forcing it to swear it would not feast upon a human without my permission. Each time it left, it came back. I had, as promised, delivered to it its own weight in gold, several large chests' worth, which it kept in the chamber with it. I had not had occasion to see how or if the creature spent its reward, but I knew that at times it went into the village in a man's aspect and mingled with the peoples there.

Those days were done, however. I could not take a single risk of the creature abandoning me, of somehow breaking its binding, of betraying me. And it was this the creature sensed, I think, as I sat across from it and the daylight came in through the high window, making a square patch of brightness on the stone floor between us. It was again to be my prisoner, or rather the prisoner of science. And although I said nothing of my plans for it, as I was leaving, it stood and came to me, head bowed, shoulders slumped, muttering under its breath.

I placed my hand upon its shoulder, as close to a gesture of affection that I had ever bestowed upon anyone, and told it I would deliver the remainder of the cure that evening, in the laboratory. It looked up into my face, tears in its man's eyes, and thanked me. As I left its room I thought about my deception. Even if I could cure the silver sickness, which I could not, for it was not possible, the first thing the creature Alexander would do when I gave it would be to betray or even kill me. It would have nothing to lose, were it not susceptible to the silver sickness. I had held the pretense now for months that I was close to perfecting the cure, to keep the creature in my thrall even more than any binding could have. But now, I had another use for the creature, a use that would draw man up from the slime and waste ground of the animals and into a higher state of being, a species devoid of pain and ache.

And yet, I would need a man to transform. A man far beyond even the heartiest field hand I could have bred and raised at Wiskitki. A natural brute, a born lion amongst men. I resolved to scour all Poland and Europe if needed to find such a man. That afternoon, I sent letters to Istvan, to the Fleming, to Vermundr Karl, to every scientist I knew, to keep an eye open for me, for any man fitting the qualities I needed.

But, as fate and the will of science would have it, the man came to me, and laid himself down nearly at my own door. He was a soldier, a Knight, and I already knew all about him.

13

[pages missing][74]

True to his threat, the Elbow-High sent word to me that my levy was due, that I was to send a force of five-hundred men to his camp at Inowrocław. They were to report to him within the fortnight. Over the past weeks, I had placed the steward in charge of the levy, and his report to me suggested I would be able to meet the Elbow-High's demand, but just barely. I loathed to think what this war would do to my fields and revenue, but the little sovereign was not to be trifled with again. I ordered the steward to have the men ready to march within three days.

I retired to my quarters in a state of resigned fury. As I sat at my desk writing, a sensation of defeat, or failure began to settle over me, slowly, so that at first I was only aware of a heaviness of limb and fogginess of thought. But as the day wore on, the feeling grew and grew, becoming more pointed as a knife the longer it festered in my mind and heart, until by the evening I was seething and morose, and a black dread had fixed itself over me.

What was I afraid of? I had been subjugated to the Elbow-High, a thing that never sits well with a man like myself, humbled by a lesser. The man barely reached my chest, could not mount a horse without a wooden block for him to stand upon, and yet I had bowed my head and kissed his ring. Absently, I dreamt of a day in the far future when such men of feebleness and flawed character were eliminated from the greater human family, science abetting their extinction by targeting those subhuman

---

74   The Duke's manuscript resumes at some small remove from where he left off. Although there is no definitive measure of how much time has elapsed, it is most surely not more than a few weeks, for as the memoir resumes, the war waged by the Elbow-High against the Knights is now fevered and the battle has moved closer to the Duke's door. The best guess of most scholars is that this portion of the diary begins in the early or middle summer of 1331.

traits, perhaps even going so far as to sterilize the present generation so that they could not pass on to their heirs the feebleness of their own makeup. I even went so far as to draw up a rudimentary plan for such a pogrom against these subhumans, but it was merely an exercise in drawing off the anger of my heart, as such a project would be vastly impractical and nigh impossible from a logistic standpoint.[75]

At near to midnight, I went up to the laboratory. The creature Alexander was there, of course, chained to the stone table, insensate from the draughts I continually plied it. I had kept it confined for weeks, incapacitating it two or three times a day to extract more and more of its blood and humors, replacing what I had taken with elixirs and scientific oils of my own creation, all with the intent of charging his already inhuman blood with the power I needed for myself and the new man I would create. It seemed that every precious ingredient I had acquired over the decades of my life went into these potions: a scale and several droplets of blood from the dragon, material from the creature Hans, liquid gold, holy water, all of these and many more. I spent five days distilling oil of vitriol, salt of lemon, gold, silver, copper, clay of Cyprus, and numerous other herbs and salts in the Athanor, solely so I could take a scraping of the ash and blend it into the elixir.

I would have to be more sparing, though, for as that spring had come to a close, a calamity befell me, at least from an experimental viewpoint. The dragon died. It had become

---

75   While no record of this document exists, it may perhaps be of note that the notorious Prussian novelist and anti-Semite Hermann Goedsche listed Siemowit's name in his diary while he was writing his novel Biarritz, which predicted Hitler's Final Solution by some forty years. How Goedsche came across the Duke's name or work remains unknown. It should be noted, for the record, that despite his many flaws, nowhere in any of Siemowit's writing does anything close to anti-Semitism appear. Indeed, for the times, the duke's outlook is actually quite egalitarian; it is only short people who seem, as a group, to have drawn his wrath.

enfeebled and weak while I was away in Constantinople and Venice, sickening and never really recovering. I had tended to it, ministering to its health as well I could in the days since my return, but nothing seemed to bring the beast back into the full bloom of health. Often times, I would not even have to secure it to the examination table in the laboratory, for it was so weak I could prod and prick it for hours and it was all the beast could do to utter the weakest mewl like a dying cat. Finally, one evening, after I had tried to feed it a small quantity of honeyed mare's milk, it gave up its ghost and was still.

Working quickly to preserve the integrity of its constituent parts, I laid it out on the table and took my knives to it. I divided it along its segments, extracting its heart and liver and eyes, draining its blood, harvesting its scales, its claws, its tongue, its wings. Near every piece of that mythic beast was kept and stored. Even its bones were ground into granules and dust. By the end, I had harvested a small but fruitful quantity of irreplaceable, unobtainable items from the carcass of the unfortunate serpent. I felt flush for a brief moment, knowing I now had in my possession more dragon material than most other scientists would ever see if they lived five lifetimes. But the pride was fleeting, for I knew I would have need of nearly all I had just taken, if I were to be successful in the work I was planning, for there were fewer more potent, more powerful base ingredients that can be used in science than those that originate from the dragon.

I had even begun, as a precursor, preparing the way as it were, to the phylactery, placing a small quantity of certain elixirs of dragon's blood and liquid gold into my own veins. The first time I had done this, the violent spasm that racked my body nearly sent me fracturing my skull on the stones of the floor and wall. Luckily, I had had the presence of mind to use the Diacodus before injecting myself, calling upon a protective spirit to watch over me, in addition to the several spells of protection I had cast upon my person. From all I had read in the Jewish tomes of science, there was much preparatory work that needed to be done before a phylactery could be successfully created, much less imbued with one's spirit. As more and more time passed, though, I grew more and more nervous, more afraid that not enough time was left me to complete the work.

The creature Alexander, when its blood improvements were complete, would serve as the fount from which I would delve deep, for my own needs, but more importantly for the needs of the new man. It was imperative, as I saw it, to complete the improvements as soon as I could, for I wanted all in readiness when providence sent the new man to me. Through weeks of experimentation, I had discovered a regimen that forced the creature to devolve into the wolf. Certain levels of pain and deprivation needed to be met, but at will, I could force the creature to assume whatever aspect I required, and I experimented as equally on both forms. I studied what I had taken from each form, finding its wolf's blood a thicker, darker consistency than its human, its human bile more pungent and unpleasant than its wolf's. Separately, or admixed together or with other ingredients, I filled phial after phial with its fluids, readying them for reintroduction into itself or into my person, and should I be so blessed, into the veins of the new man.

Incidentally, shortly after the dragon's death, I had a letter from the Fleming. He was traveling again with the Knights, with their army that was now only a few days from my lodge. I had numerous questions for him, and agreed to host him under a flag of truce at Wiskitki in a day's time. Finally, a palpable relief unclouded my mind, I could get some answers, about Hans, about Venice. I quickly set about attending to his arrival, ordering the kitchens to prepare a feast and to arrange quarters for him in the lodge and for his attendant and mounts in the stables.

All that night, I sat up in the laboratory, making notes and observing various phenomena regarding the creature Alexander. As dawn began to lighten the sky outside the window, I went down to the courtyard and mounted my own charger and rode out into the countryside, hoping to meet the Fleming coming in. I dismounted near the river and let the horse graze at its leisure. There was dew on the tall grass, and the smell of the river brought me back to Constantinople, following those barrels through the narrow streets to the little warehouse. I took a bottle of ale from my saddlebag and drank my fill, a slight unease in my gut. The gnawing feeling that had stung in the back of my mind since Constantinople now throbbed like the bite of a spider. The priest in Venice, Willem, the creature Hans, the warehouseman in Constantinople, the Bohemian assassins. They were all connected somehow, and all the threads led back to the Fleming. I wondered, and worried, whether he was not all he seemed.

I rode up the river slowly, and finally, as the sun was about a hand's width above the horizon, saw ahead of me two riders, the leading one wearing a white plumed helm and his attendant carrying a tall pike with a fluttering white pennon streaming behind it in the breeze. The flag of truce. The Fleming was coming. I spurred my horse on and rode to meet them. I realized, as I closed the distance, that my hand unwittingly had gone to the pommel of my sword.

I hailed him as I neared and he raised a hand in greeting. We dismounted and embraced warmly, although I admit a small shiver of trepidation slid down my spine as I was in his grasp. I had taken precaution of wearing beneath my tunic and cloak leathern armor that a dagger could not pierce, but my face and neck were bared. Was I being unjust? Paranoid? The Fleming had ever been a friend and accomplice, I had no reason to distrust him. My nature, though, is to be on guard, and to never fully trust any man.

We rode abreast along the river back toward the lodge. Once, I looked behind us and noted the face of the attendant. A familiarity there struck me, and in German, which I knew he spoke, asked the Fleming the nature of this. He smiled and told me to look again. I did so, and was struck by an image of the narrow streets of Constantinople, for it was this boy who I had followed, carrying the barrels that bore the waters of my homeland and something stranger. And though it was only a matter of some months, the boy was taller and now had the bearing of a soldier in the making. A thought crossed my mind, whether anyone I had even casually met over the course of the last year had been somehow in this Fleming's employ. The boatman, perhaps? The slave trader from whom I purchased Hrothgar? Nothing seemed to be in my control, the more I followed this reasoning, and I abandoned it as being impractical and ludicrous. No man had such a breadth of reach and power, and certainly not a lay preacher.

At Wiskitki, I left the Fleming to refresh himself after his travel and went instead to the stable where the attendant was brushing the horses. I asked if he recalled me from Constantinople, and he stated that indeed he did. He was called Ioannis, he said, he was Greek by birth and had lived in Constantinople for all of his boyhood. His great-grandsire, he explained, had gone to the Palestine in the entourage of the French King who was captured there, and escaped with his life northward into Greece, where he had settled.[76] His own father had sold him into bondage across the Bosporus into the service of a shipping agency that served most of the eastern Mediterranean, and was operated from Venice.

Ioannis told me he had met the Fleming but once before he had become his squire, several years ago when the

---

76   Louis IX was captured by the Arab forces in what is now called the Seventh Crusade. Many of his own soldiers fled the Battle of Damietta over the Mediterranean to Cyprus and Greece.

Knights had sent a ship carrying Slav prisoners through the Golden Horn on its way to the slave markets of Sicily. He had carried messages to and from the Fleming for several months, endearing himself into the service of the Knights and their lay preacher. And one day, a man had arrived in Constantinople, bearing a small silver coin stamped with the Teutonic cross, a sign to the boy that the Fleming wanted his service again. The man, who spoke in a strange accent Ioannis could not place, told him a ship would be calling soon from Venice, and aboard it were two barrels that were to be conveyed to a warehouse where the Fleming had contracted with its owner to use the place for various purposes. The ship had come in, the boy had taken up the barrels, and the rest we both knew well.

It was what occurred afterward, though, that I did not know. I had dismissed the boy at the warehouse and turned my attention to barrels. The boy, though, had not lingered, but run off again to the docks, where he had been instructed to return once the barrels had been delivered, and went to an inn there that catered to sailors and shipmen. There, he found the man who had earlier approached him, already in drink, gregarious and lively. The man dragged the boy drunkenly through the inn, loudly berating him as a beggar, and once through the door the man's demeanor quickly and abruptly shifted, so the boy knew the man had been playacting. In the dark of the alley, the man demanded a description of the foreigner to whom the barrels had been consigned.

Ioannis gave the man my likeness and the man seemed well pleased. He gave the boy two silver coins, these stamped not with a cross but with the face of a bearded man. The boy could not read the Latin inscription on the coins, though, but he could recognize silver when he saw it. I told the boy to describe the man to me, and as he did so, the picture rose in my mind of the Bohemian assassin I had disfigured in Venice with Istvan. I was confused beyond measure, and now more convinced that the Fleming meant me ill. I left the stables and went up to the Fleming's quarters.

My aspect must have appeared fearsome, for he quailed as I entered his room. Have you sold me to the Bohemians, I demanded. He feigned ignorance for the briefest moment, but when I confronted him with what the boy had told me, and my experience in Venice, he sat quiet and still, staring at the floor, as though awaiting some judgment.

So it is true, he finally muttered. He sighed and settled into an explanation of events. Hans, he said, had left Germany and traveled for years in central Europe, finally settling in the forests near Prague. It reverted to a wilder state, far more animal than it had been while living in the woman's house in the Black Forest. It was now free to live as the wolf, as it saw fit, never reverting to the man unless it needed or willed it. Once, almost a year ago, the Fleming told me, a hunting party came across the creature Hans and drove it from its forest lair, thinking it merely a large and strong wolf. It outran them with the power of ten wolves, though, and the hunters returned to their village with a tale almost unbelievable. Yet, there was one who believed it.

The believer was an old scholar, a certain Manfred Teigart, who also happened to be minor scientist himself but more importantly, a correspondent of Vermundr Karl.[77] He sent a letter to Karl that very night, informing him of what he had heard of the incident in the forests outside Prague. As it happened the letter arrived at Karl's estate while he was entertaining a certain guest, by which the Fleming meant himself. I had given the Fleming a letter of introduction to Vermundr Karl several years ago, and they had become

77 According to the records of the University of Prague, a Manfred Teigart was dismissed as a lecturer there in 1320, some eleven years prior to the events related. The reason listed is "heresy". How Teigart managed not to be tried or burned outright is unclear, and his name appears nowhere else in the parish or civil records of Prague or the surrounding cities.

acquaintances as well, although I knew, or thought I knew, that the Fleming's loyalties lay with me, and that he saw Karl as a scholar more than a scientist.

The Fleming and Karl discussed the letter, and the Fleming divulged the story of the creature Hans, and his and my interaction with it. Karl seemed to equate the creature in the letter with Hans, and the Fleming had to admit there was the possibility. In the event, the Fleming left Karl and returned to his duties as a wandering preacher-Knight. Meanwhile, reports began to reach Karl from rural Bohemia and Poland, reports I had not had from Istvan for his work was focused on the Veneto, of sightings and attacks by a large, voracious wolf.

The signs were clear to the Fleming. I had offered the woman and Hans refuge at Wiskitki, he recalled. To the Fleming's mind, it was coming to find me, whether for sanctuary or for vengeance, there was no way of knowing. The Fleming and his Knights traveled northeastward, toward Poland, all the while in the wake of the creature. Near every place they stopped at night, a villager would tell of some decimation of livestock or a horrific mauling of some townsperson. Closer and closer they all came to Poland, finally crossing into the south and moving northward. To Wiskitki.

The Fleming and his Knights rode hard and through the night, and gained the lodge. I was, of course, away in the Elbow-High's entourage in Russia, but the Fleming was well-known at Wiskitki, and he was not begrudged a few nights rest there. He barely spent an hour in the lodge, though. Mostly, he was riding the countryside, tramping through the underbrush of the forests and lowlands that surrounded my estate. Finally, at evening of the second day, he found signs of tracks, made by large and powerful legs. He tracked the creature to a rocky hollow beside the slow-moving river. The stink that came from the place was unbearable, and he drew his cloak over his nose and mouth, drawing a silver dagger from his belt.

He entered the mouth of the low cavern and saw it was strewn with hunks of rotted meat and broken bones. The moss and underbrush, the blades of the ferns about, were stained with dried blood. The Fleming drew himself out of the cavern and retched, then he concealed himself as best he could, waiting for the creature to emerge or return, for there was no way he could ascertain whether the beast was inside the cavern or not.

Finally, after some long time of waiting, he heard prowling, lumbering feet crunching through the forest. Abruptly, though, they stopped, and the Fleming knew the creature Hans had detected his scent. He heard a faint whimpering, though, and with a resolve that surprised even himself, he stood and revealed himself, brandishing the silver dagger.

It was a wolf, but it was sickly and injured, he could see. There were bald patches on the wolf's back and legs, and deep scratches and cuts all over its sides. And although it bared its teeth to the Fleming, he could see that some of them were missing, and the others were black with rot. The yellow eyes were milky and one was crusted with a grayish film. It stank to pure hell, and again the Fleming brought his cloak up to his face.

He had never seen the creature Hans in the aspect of the wolf, but there was no doubt, he told me, that this was Hans. And so, he told me, he spoke to it. You are called Hans, he said, and the wolf stood, merely watching him. I know what you are, the Fleming spoke again, I saw you in the Black Forest, as a man.

At this, the wolf began to cough, almost to choke, as though some piece of meat had lodged in its throat. And indeed, finally, a morsel of something was ejected and landed on the forest floor between them. The Fleming saw was it was covered in blood, and almost as soon as it hit the ground, it burst open into a bloom of writhing maggots. The creature Hans was dying, he realized. It had eaten something rotted, or poisoned more likely. Perhaps a cunning hunter had after all succeeded in bringing it down somewhere along its way, only the death was to be prolonged and painful.

The Fleming made the assumption that should the wolf devolve to the aspect of a man, the illness would in all likelihood kill it, but the Fleming would recognize the human aspect readily, and could speak to it, to find out what had happened. And so, he spoke again, saying, I know you can assume the aspect of a man. Do so, before you expire, and tell me what has happened to you.

The wolf again began to hack and gag, and its body began to shudder. For a long time, it stood trembling, its legs wobbling so severely that the Fleming lost all fear he had of the creature, and went to its side and eased it to the ground. From his waterskin, he poured water into its panting mouth, though the tongue was black and its breath was vile. As he looked closer, he saw more maggots squirming and slithering in several of the wounds and scratches on the wolf's side.

Finally, a great shudder, a violent thrash went down the wolf's body from its head to its tail, and it shook in a seizure that made the Fleming leap back and renewed the fear in his soul. It let out a groaning scream, hollow-sounding yet filled with misery, and at length, it began to roll and thrash upon the ground for some moments, and when it stopped, the Fleming beheld the aspect of Hans, the man.

It had wounds that corresponded to the wolf's, though they looked more fearsome and ugly on its human body. Its naked flesh was covered in filth and wounds, and the Fleming knew it only had moments to live. What has happened to you, he asked the creature again. The creature's eyes slowly rolled in its head and finally came to rest on the Fleming's face, and recognition dawned slowly there. It remembered him, the Fleming knew. You are here for the scientist, the Fleming stated, not questioning it but rather confirming its intent.

The creature stared blankly at the Fleming. Perhaps its mind has failed it, he thought to himself. And just then, the creature sat up with a massive effort and looked in the direction of the lodge. The Fleming supposed the creature had prowled about the place at night, perhaps looking for me, or for some way inside. The thought occurred that he could take the creature back to the lodge, but he soon abandoned the idea, as the journey, though short, would very likely kill the creature. And so, the Fleming resigned himself to the inevitable and even then began to formulate the plan that would bring me home.

The creature lay on its side, coughing and wheezing, barely able to breathe through the thick, black bile it kept coughing up. Its eyes remained fixed in the direction of Wiskitki, and as I listened to the Fleming's tale, I cursed myself over and over for being gone when the creature had come, dying, begging for my help. After a short while, indeed, the creature Hans had died, and before the final breath had left its chest, the Fleming had already begun to saw the head from its body.

Wrapping the head in his cloak, he dragged the headless body into the cavern and left it there. Then, he rode back to the lodge and bought from the cooper two barrels. Into one he placed the head, and with the aid of one of my servants, went down to the Vistula to fill them with river water. The next day, when the Knights left Wiskitki, the two barrels were part of their train, and wended across Europe with the Fleming and the Knights until they reached Brno. From there, according to the Fleming, he accompanied the barrels and several other crates of supplies and various merchandise to an agent of the Knights' commercial enterprises there, and arranged for their transport to Venice with himself as guarantor.

Eventually, the Fleming and his barrels reached Venice, where he put them into the care of Father Willem at the Zulian. From there, the Fleming commended them to God and fate and turned his back on that floating city and went back over the Alps to meet his brethren at Aachen. The barrels, meanwhile, sailed to Constantinople, where they found me. In turn, I went to Venice where I met the Bohemian.

It was here, in his tale, that the Fleming stopped and looked out of the window for some short time, as though deciding how to continue. It was precisely the point in the story that I wished to know most about, how the assassins had come there, had come to know I would be there. In my mind, the Fleming's pause merely confirmed his guilt, for I took him to be setting his story straight in his mind, the lie that would release him from my suspicion, when in point of fact it merely made my suspicion grow more and more intense. When finally he spoke again, I listened, ready to spring from my chair and slice his throat.

In Brno, he said, there were many unsavory men, many of whom had worked in the past on John's behalf in secret and violent ways. The city was a meeting place for the spy and the assassin, and from there they could branch out all over the east of Europe, or down to Greece and even the Palestine, working the will of their nefarious masters. Some were even said to be former Knights, disgraced and excommunicated. And it was one of these, the Fleming told me, whose hand was behind the attempt on my life in Venice.

Faltzgraff, his name was. A German, from the North Sea coast. The name meant nothing to me, but the Fleming gave me the history of the man. He had joined the Knights as a youth and slaughtered his way across Europe and the Baltic, subjugating the tree-worshippers of the frozen lands with the sword of Christ. Additionally, though, he was also stealing from the coffers of the Order, and was found out. He was excommunicated from the Church and the Knights and sent into exile into the monotony of middle Europe. He wandered for years, making his living as a mercenary for petty barons and oppressed landowners, once even being hired by the folk of a small town in the farmlands of Silesia to murder their vindictive overseer. Finally, as is often the case with such men, he came to Brno, and fell into a brotherhood of men much like himself.

In time, he had surrounded himself with a ring of men, a team of mercenaries. Little by little, murder by murder, they came to the notice of a very powerful man. This was the Baron von Immerholt, one of John's generals and, more importantly, his Lord Treasurer.[78] Faltzgraff made an impression on the Baron, and the assassin became the preferred tool of the subtle diplomacy for which the Baron is now known. And eventually, the man was contracted to take my own life; the Fleming had no doubts that John himself must have known and approved of the plan.

But, it seems Faltzgraff's honor as a hired killer was less than even the guttersnipes he ran with, for nearly as soon as he left the Baron's palace, he found his way to a caravan of traveling Knights, tramping across Europe from Aachen to the Baltics. It was in Pressburg, and the company of Knights was encamped in the forests outside the town, awaiting the arrival of another group.[79] He had hardly been in the camp for an hour when he approached one of the men and said he

---

78   Ignatz Maria von Immerholt was born to German parents who moved to Prague when he was a child. He joined the army at 15 and fought at John's side for decades, being made a Baron and trusted advisor, and finally, at the age of 56, master of the realm's coin.

79   Pressburg is now known as Bratislava.

wished to be shown to the commander of the company.

Faltzgraff was led into the tent of the commander, a tall and wiry Swede called Konig, under whom the assassin had served while still a member of the Knights. The two men reunited warmly, for the Swedish commander recalled well the prowess and might of the wayward man, and even for the most minimally religious, which surely some of the Knights were, the implications surrounding the return of a prodigal son could not be more obvious. And as they talked, it became apparent that Konig was either unaware of the reasons for Faltzgraff's leaving the Order, or simply a forgiving man.

As the night wore on, and the wine flowed, the assassin broached the subject with his former comrade of an alliance against evil. With embellishments here and omissions there, Faltzgraff laid out the plan for which he had been hired by the Bohemian court, namely to travel to Venice and assassinate a Polish noble. However, to the Knight's ears, Faltzgraff named his benefactors as being secretly funded by the Pope himself, and the target as being a known Satanist, an insult that I confess I raged about for some days after hearing the story, as that mythological fraud was no more real than Zeus or Apollo and I certainly would waste none of my valuable mind on praising or advancing him.

Konig was quickly enfolded into the false conspiracy, eager for a chance to assist the Pope in vanquishing a stalwart man of evil, and for a share of the promised reward, lent Faltzgraff one of his own Knights to travel to Venice with him, along with several letters of free passage. At my urging, the Fleming told me a likeness of this other man, and without doubt it was the second man who had burst into the apartment in Venice, whom we had sent scurrying back out on his knees.

And you know the rest, the Fleming concluded. He told me he had the story from Konig's attendant, who had overheard the exchange and who was a devout young soldier whom the Fleming saw from time to time on the travels of his company, crossing paths with other troops. It was this company, the one the Fleming rode in, that Konig's men were encamped and awaiting, and so when they arrived, and the Fleming again made the young soldier's acquaintance, the story came out, and the Fleming was quick enough of mind and presence to know the target was myself. The two barrels, he told me, were a message to call me home, to my work, to my true self, but the path would lead through Venice and possible death.

Faltzgraff, though, had not left forthwith, but had lingered in the camp for unknown reasons; perhaps awaiting someone who was arriving in the train of the other troop. In the event, the Fleming told me, he went to the tent where the assassin was sleeping off his drink, to size the man up and assess the threat he thought was posed to me. The man was drunk and snoring, though it was nearly midday. Outside the tent, the other Knights were going about the work of packing up the camp and readying to strike out that day, but this man, flush with Bohemian gold and Catholic wine, only stirred to snort and gasp in his sleep. The tent was filled with a foul stench, and the Fleming had to cover his mouth and nose when first he came in. He went to the man's bedside and stood over him for some small time, noting the features and aspect of the brutish creature.

Finally, he reached down and tore the blanket from the man's body and roughly shook him awake. Since the fellow was so intoxicated, the Fleming supposed he would be slow and confused in his thought and movement, but it was not so. As soon as the cold air of the day hit his skin, the man bolted upright and lunged outward, catching the Fleming in his gut with a clenched fist and sending him to the dirt floor, doubled over. A swift kick to the head followed, as the assassin leapt from the bed, ready for melee. The Fleming balled himself and cried mercy and the assassin, seemingly finally succumbing to the haze that drink can descend upon a man, slumped to the bed and sat watching the Fleming spit clots of blood onto the floor.

At length, when he could speak, the Fleming said, between painful breaths, I know the man you seek. The assassin looked into the bloody face of the Fleming and waited. You cannot defeat him, the Fleming went on, he will master you. The assassin's face broke into a savage grin and he proceeded to enumerate the horrors he planned to visit upon my person, and when he finally was done, the Fleming, now recovered, merely repeated his warning. He can make you better than what you are, he told Faltzgraff. Invincible.

The assassin spat onto the ground at the Fleming's feet and rose from the bed, drawing a long hunting knife from beneath the pillow. Tell me how to kill him and I will let you live, the man snarled. The Fleming, a preacher rather than a fighter, admitted his fear at that moment, and I supposed I cannot blame him for the milk in his veins.

The point of the knife dug into the soft flesh beneath his chin and the Fleming could smell the stink of stale wine on the assassin's breath as the man's face hovered close to his own. Summoning all the will he could, facing his own death, the Fleming's voice caught in his throat as he began, but as he spoke the words grew clearer and stronger. You must beg him, he told the assassin, beg him to make you one of the new men.

The Fleming saw the assassin's eyes narrow in confusion and rage, felt the tip of the knife poke more harshly into his skin, and he braced himself for the cold rush of the blade up into his brain. But just then, the tent flap was torn open and a Knight, a tall blond, broad man stood in the entrance, barking to Faltzgraff that it was time to saddle his horse and strike his camp and be off. The Knight eyed the situation in the tent and sternly warned that there was to be no bloodshed in the Knight's camp, as it was considered consecrated ground. The assassin flung the Fleming to the ground and spat again, and the Fleming was not too proud to scramble out of the tent, ignoring the calls of the blond Knight. He returned to his own troop, and rode out that evening.

Of course, I had not given the assassin the opportunity to beg me a single thing, but when the Fleming left my company that evening, I felt a calm descend over me, that the mysteries of the recent months had at least been explained away in a somewhat reasonable manner. Whether or not I completely trusted the Fleming as I once had, I could no longer say with certainty; there seemed too many coincidences, too many far-reaching tendrils of fate for his involvement to have been as innocent as he claimed. But I had no proof of deceit, and so I let the years of fraternity between us stand as bond and bade him the farewell of a true and honored friend.

It was next day following his departure that I was to remand my levy of soldiers to the armies of the Elbow-High. Hardly had the dust settled on the road from beneath the tramping hooves of the Fleming's party than did a small entourage of riders come up to the lodge, bearing from a tall pike the fluttering pennon of the sovereign of Poland. It was a group of five men, led by a Count Miecław, whom I knew by name only. He dismounted and bowed with courtesy, for I outranked him, and was by far the stronger and superior man. He presented himself as emissary from the Elbow-High, seeking to know the state of readiness of my men.

The count and his men were put up in the lodge for the night, and in the morning, the four-hundred thirty-five men I had been able to muster were lined up in somewhat orderly rows in the large field that stood beside the estate. I had been up the entire night, working protective runes and binding wards into my flesh and into the armor I would wear; it would not do to be cut down in battle when there was so much left to be done. I wanted the war to be over as quickly as possible, so I could return here and resume my work. In fact, even to that end, I had arranged for a learned Jew, a rabbi from Lodz, to visit the lodge in a matter of some weeks, to discuss with him the science behind the phylactery. But, that would have to wait until the bloody work of men had been accomplished.

In the rising warmth of the morning, I rode at the head of my men, Hrothgar riding just behind me, holding my banners. From all sides, the sound of horses clomping and neighing, of men's voices, of the clatter of armor, of the snapping cloth of the pennon in the breeze, filled all our ears, and it seemed that the very sound of our coming could end the war, that a great wave of noise would roll out before us and sweep away whatever enemy was foolish enough to stand before that tide of sound.

Eventually, after perhaps three days, we reached the Elbow-High's camp at Inowrocław. The town was overwhelmed by the sheer vastness of the collected army. The little wooden buildings had been swallowed up by a constantly-moving mass of men, and from a distance it had all the appearance to me of watching the writhing of maggots swarming upon a rotted piece of meat. There must have been five-thousand men there.

As a senior noble, I was taken directly to the Elbow-High's campaign tent, an ostentatiously large structure seemingly designed to recall the glories of Alexander the Great himself. Its dimensions were sufficient to contain a living area, a fireplace, a dining table that could seat twelve men, a large map table, and much more. Upon entering, I counted seventeen men milling about inside. Inwardly, I was disgusted by his display of kingship and quelled my seething with the thought that perhaps his arrogant showplace would present itself an irresistible target to the enemy forces.

Choking back my bile, I bowed before the little king and made report of my levy. Without so much as a hint of the distaste that I knew simmered between us, he assigned me and my troops to the right flank of his army, under the direct command of his son, the Prince Casimir. I returned to my men and awaited further orders. None were forthcoming, and it was nearly a week before we were on the march again, a week I spent in a low-boiling rage that I could have been back at Wiskitki, tending to my various projects.

Luckily, though, I was surrounded by my own men, young and strong for the most part, and indeed some of whom I had bred into my guard. I knew them well, knew their limits, and had even enhanced a good number of them over the years with potions and tonics and even, in some cases, with binding. I was confident in the utter decimation and destruction my men could deal out. There were some dozen or so upon whom I had conducted pain eradication experiments, and even there in the battlefield, I kept my scientist's eye on them, to see how they fared when they were struck. I had given orders before we had left to the porters and stewards who marched with us that none of our company was to be left dead or wounded upon the field, and for that purpose several empty wagons had been brought along as well. Loathe as I was to fight it, there was the real possibility that this battle would offer a trove of research subjects for me when it was done.

The day of the battle dawned, and it grew hotter and hotter as the sun climbed the sky. We had marched to the city of Płowce, where a contingent of the Knights had barricaded themselves. All day we stood arrayed and ready for the battle but nothing happened. And then, finally, late in the afternoon, the Knights burst through their own barricades and onto the field, and it was begun.

My men surged forward like an ocean wave, crashing into the metal and horseflesh of the Knights with all the mindless fury of the moon-driven seas. They churned over each other, roiling and colliding in an explosion of sound and blood. Horses and men fell on all sides, banners clattered to the ground, sword rang upon shield or upon armor, and everywhere were the cries of pain or fatherland.

The day wore on into evening, and inside my armor I was sweating and felt I was roasting alive. All about me I swung with my sword, striking down man after man. I confess that I had had no desire to fight before the battle began but once it was underway, my own bloodlust was kindled and I lay about me as deadly as any born and bred soldier. I do not know the number of men I cut down at Płowce, but it was more than my share. The red haze seemed to descend over my eyes the moment the Knights burst from their pen, and coalesced into a fog of mindlessness and violence that thickened and saturated my limbs, my body, my brain.

I muttered curses and traced runes and sigils in the air at my approaching enemies, and each one was slowed and constricted by the time he reached me, practically impaling themselves on my sword to spare me the effort. I drove men to suicidal delirium, or made their eyeballs melt from their skulls, or made their very skin burst into boils as they rode at me. I did not fight fair, in the conventional sense of the word; I instead fought using science.

The Knights were valiant and foolhardy. The struck upon us in wave after wave, ignoring that they rode and trod over the corpses of their own number who had gone before and fallen. All at once, though, we were beaten back, and the Prince Casimir rushed from the field in retreat. Our line began to falter, but it was the strength and power of my own men who inspired the remaining Polish armies to rally and form up again and launch what would be the final onslaught against the Knights. In the low-light of the late evening, the banners of the red cross scattered from the battlefield and into the gathering night. We had won, and there were dead men as far as I could see.

Yet only one was them was really to matter.

After Płowce, the Elbow-High released me from my service for the time being and I was allowed to return to Wiskitki with whatever of my men remained. Hauled behind us, of course, were three wagons filled with the wounded and the dead whom I had personally selected from the corpse-field. As we made our way back toward home, a lone rider appeared racing toward us across the lowland, waving above his head a flag of truce.

The rider neared, and I could see a dead man strapped across the rear of the horse, the man in the saddle awkwardly reaching behind him to aid in holding it steady with one hand while trying the direct the horse with the reins in the other. There was no surprise in my heart when I noticed the rider was the Fleming. He reared up before me and dismounted, breathless. From his belt he drew a hunting knife and began to slice the lashes that held the corpse to his horse; the horse stamped and whined and chomped its teeth, obviously wary of carrying a dead body. I ordered Hrothgar and several other riders to go on, then turned my attention back to the new arrival.

The Fleming hauled the corpse down and laid it almost tenderly upon the ground. I now dismounted and went to him, looking at the body he had delivered me. It was exactly what I had been searching for for years. Tall and broad, his strength could be glimpsed even from a distance, and the power of that strength was not arguable but manifest. He had been a Knight; his tunic was torn, revealing a muscular chest so crossed with scars and wounds it reminded me of a map of Venice.

He lives, the Fleming told me, when he had recovered himself. Perhaps, I thought somewhere in the back of my mind, his horse was afraid of me instead. The Fleming knelt at the Knight's head, brushing the thick blond hair from the bloodied face. The eyes were closed, one was swollen shut and the other had a deep cut that ran from its corner down the side of the face. The neck was red and raw, one hand was sheathed in a greave while the other was naked, and when the Fleming pulled off his boots, we saw they were filled with blood.

But there was no doubt as to why the Fleming had brought him to me. Even in his wounds, even in his weakness and the dimming of his life's light, I could see he was perfect in all ways. He was the New Man I had been awaiting for years. I was suddenly overcome, as though my own child had found its way back to me after decades, and I sank to the earth and took the body of the Knight up and held him against me, near to sobbing. I cannot imagine what any of the soldiers or generals thought when they saw this, and even in aftertimes, when the Knight was a presence in my home and a known quantity, no one ever asked about him, the nature of his relation to me, his connection.

I directed the Knight to be wrapped in a cloak and placed in one of the wagons. The Fleming aided in pulling the man up and arranging him, and all the while I could hear the soldiers making mock of him, saying it was fitting that a Knight should wallow in the blood of his own dead, that he was a coward seeking to save his own skin by aiding me. More and more vicious the taunts became, but I ignored them as the logical expression of victor's anger. But I was foolish to do so.

As the Fleming jumped down from the corpse wagon, I heard the low but insistently fast whir of an arrow, followed immediately by the crush of impact, the strangled cry. I turned and stared agape at the body of the Fleming, lying on his back, an arrow sticking up from his chest. I rushed to him even as a low cheer erupted from the massed soldiers.

The Fleming's chest heaved, blood gurgled from the wound, from his mouth. His eyes fluttered, swimming, searching for anything to fasten onto, and finally he found my face and looked at me, wonderingly, confused.

When he was dead, the fire that I had ignored in my heart, kindled by the smallness of men's minds, erupted into an inferno and I whirled to face the smirking men who had formed around the Fleming's body. Pure rage and loss coursed through me as I raised my hand, palm outward, and began to chant and sing my curses. I called upon all the demons I had bound inside myself to aid me, called upon every dark and sinister thing I had ever portioned away for future use. A wave spread out from me, I was the epicenter, and all the men around me began to burn, their flesh and their armor melting together into a ghastly amalgam, dripping into pools of bloody molten metal on the ground. A great clatter, like hail falling onto stone, filled the air as hundreds of bones fell against each other and piled up in the scorched grass, men and horse together, some vast indiscriminate burial ground that surely would confound the future scholars of the world. In a matter of seconds, it was over. They were gone, all of them, transformed into the foul sludge that I trudged through, near shin-deep, spitting and cursing and kicking at the goulash-like slop.

I felt strangely alive, as though the entire universe had, for one moment, collected itself within the frame of my own body. But just as suddenly, I was overcome with a tiredness that pulled me downward. I wandered back to the corpse wagon; as I was the spoke of the wheel of carnage that had erupted outward, it seemed the wagon and the Fleming's body were unscathed. I took up his body and tossed it onto the heap in the wagon. His horse had wandered off and eventually I succeeded in harnessing it to the wagon.

Everything else was dead, the men and horses, the trees and grass; even birds had fallen from the sky, blackened and melting. I was alone now, going back home, with the greatest treasure I could want. I climbed up onto the Fleming's horse and spurred it on. It drove slowly, unaccustomed to dragging behind it such weight, but I called to it in soothing tones, whispering over it spells to give it endurance and strength to reach where we needed to go.

Never had I unleashed such a terror before, and as I drove away from the place, I turned and looked back. It appeared to me as though a vast lightning bolt had struck the earth, and in doing so had opened the very face of the land and caused to issue forth the foul and stinking bile of the world. I could not suppress the smile that spread across my face as I looked upon my work. Science was marvelous, and the proof was there for all to see, if not understand. The place vanished from view, but never from my memory.[80]

Through the gates of the lodge I rode alone, pulling a wagon of dead men behind me. The stable-boys rushed out and unhitched the wagon and led the Fleming's horse to hay. I ordered servants to unload the wagon, to pile all the dead aside from the New Man and the Fleming in the courtyard and burn them. All the others were superfluous, I knew, now that I had the New Man. His body and the Fleming's were taken to my laboratory.

From the high window of my quarters, I watched the grisly bonfire as the pile of corpses was lit. Behind me, on two large stone tables, were the bodies of the New Man and the Fleming, cleaned as best as could be and prepared. The New Man's breaths were shallow and far-spaced. I had closed what wounds I could and poured into him all the

---

80 In 1956, the municipal authority in the small village of Więźnigów began an excavation to build a grain silo for the local collective farm. This work uncovered the skeletal remains of some two-hundred seventy-seven men and nearly three-hundred horses, all of whom showed signs of being burned. At the time, the find was theorized to have been the location of a mass burning of enemy corpses after the Battle of Płowce, as many of the bones showed signs of battle wounds.

invigorating tonics and potions I had had available. I had done no true science upon him yet. I wanted to wait, for I felt I owed the Fleming his own finale.

Few things in life I regret, but even now, as I write this, I can still hear in my ears the vile taunts and insults my soldiers hurled at the Fleming as he worked to settle the New Man atop the wagon. At the time, I was too excited, too enamored of the possibilities before me, presented by the near-dead Knight now being wrangled atop a pile of his dead comrades, to take any note of the low current of hatred, the slow building of violence going on around me.

Or perhaps I did note it, and ignored it, for really, had not the Fleming served his purpose? In the event, I cannot confess to having been completely shocked by the sound of the arrow, and even in the moment, it sounded as though it had been flying in the air just beside my ear for years, as though launched from some impossible distance by some godlike arm, traveling at my side for an immeasurable time, merely waiting for the deadly moment to present itself.

I turned from the acrid smoke of the courtyard and faced the Fleming's body. What good was the body to me, though? It was the Fleming's mind that I had always used. He was thin and pale, all his strength resided in his mind. I took up the bone saw and took the cap of his skull off, then dug out the brain and placed it into a vessel filled with alkahest.

His blood I drained and stored in phials, his kidneys I ground into paste, his fingernails I burned for their ash, his teeth I pried from the jaw and his heart I placed in an iron box. In short, I made as much use of him dead as I had alive.

The New Man awaited. But I did not have all the tools I needed for my task. I sent for Alexander, and eventually the creature presented itself to me. It was docile at all times now, for my work upon it was complete and total. I told it to look upon the body of the Knight, to hold the man's visage in its mind. I saw the creature contemplate the New Man, watching his chest slowly and slightly rise and fall, the near-imperceptible flutter behind the closed eyelids, saw it flare its nostrils, taking in the faint scent of the New Man's sweat and blood. This is why you were brought here, I told the creature Alexander. For this and no other reason.

The creature finally, at length, nodded, as though satisfied in its own animal heart that it could not know the New Man any better at such a remove. The Fleming's body had been removed and the table washed clean, and so I instructed the creature Alexander to lay down. It did so, and was still and unresisting as I shackled its wrists and ankles to the chains in the floor. Even as I opened its veins and inserted the tubing that snaked from its arm into the New Man's, it did not resist me, as thought it had truly accepted its role in life, in science, unhesitatingly, willingly.

For days without rest, without stopping, I worked to create the New Man. Over the Knight's body, I said hundreds of spells and drew countless wards; on his skin I etched dozens of runes and sigils and bindings. I drained all his blood, constantly replacing it with an admixture of the creature Alexander's blood, the blood of the dragon, spirit water, molten gold, numerous potions and tinctures. All the years of research I had done into the elimination of pain I poured into him, pushing into his veins and nerves every heightening and overpowering impulse I could imagine, sending his brain and nerves soaring into the apex of pain and torture, to the point of breaking, the point of near-obliterating annihilation, only to bring back again to a merely slightly less intense level, and yet the relief of it was such like cold on a burn. Over and over again, I did this, sending the structures of his brain that had been built over the years by exposure to pain and suffering and horror spiraling ever upward, only to crash them into nothingness, then built then up higher than before, over and over, again and again, so that eventually, after perhaps a hundred such forays, the ascent into the pinnacles of pain were no longer felt, did not register in the mind as pain at all, but rather as simply the constant state of existence, a new architecture of pain and coexistence, such that pain and the attendant fear that went with it were dulled, were even perhaps dead, and the New Man finally awoke, purified, seared in the creating fire of all I had ever attempted, more perfect, more true, more human than any that had gone before.

14

[pages missing][81]

The Jew from Lodz arrived in the early autumn. He was called Solomon Wieckz, a renowned rabbi in his town, but more importantly, an invaluable source, I had been assured, of knowledge regarding the power over life and death, the bridging of the two worlds, or rather planes, as I had come to view them. I had gone as far as I could go on my own into my research on the phylactery; now I needed the assistance of a master. In some few things, it was humbling to realize, I was still but an apprentice.

The days prior to his arrival, I confess to being atwitter with anticipation. I went over and over my laboratory, making certain that everything was in order, that I had all the tools and ingredients I needed. Hrothgar and Marek I made as presentable as possible. I was intent on using them as showpieces, to prove my ability to this rabbi, to show him I was not some amateur warlock or hedge-sorcerer. Eduard, the gift given me by the Fleming just before his death, and the creature Alexander, Lukasz and the remnants of my other experiments I, of course, kept from his eyes; it would not do to have this man know just how powerful I really was.

To speak of Eduard and the creature Alexander as they were at this time, in the full bloom of their concert, the dawn of their cooperation, is a melancholy task, but perhaps to brighten the shadows that surround future events, some

---

81   The Duke's manuscript resumes some weeks later. Prior to the following entries there are seven pages of small, intricate script in a fine hand. It appears to be some kind of cipher or code, but the symbols are unknown, and numerous attempts by independent scholars and cryptologists have determined them to be indecipherable. At the request of the publisher, the Institute for Language Research at Rutgers University conducted an exhaustive and ultimately inconclusive study of the pages.

small digression here will be forgiven.[82] And as truly as I had attempted to shed as much of my humanity as practicable in favor of the armor of the New Man, I admit to the maudlin weakness akin to the father of the prodigal son: I wish Eduard back, that all that has gone between us be erased and we could go forward as we were.

But he is gone, for good, and here I must content myself with recollection, a word that stings in its own right, as I collect again in my mind the memories of those eye-opening days, when I first saw what could be wrought by a pure science wielded in strength and vision of purpose. It was the blood of the creature Alexander that truly made Eduard what he was, and so the two of them shared a bond that was closer than that of brothers, of fathers and sons. Perhaps it was more akin to that of twins to some degree, although even that bond is known as the strongest in nature.

The morning he awoke for the first time as the New Man, after the prolonged agony of his emancipation, I remember the day dawned clear and bright, the sky itself seemed washed clean of its imperfections and the light of the sun passed through the spectrum of the upper airs to shine down upon him and I with untainted and pure heavenly illumination, and though I certainly take no stock in the conventions of superstition, I cannot be totally honest if I do not confess some small feeling of satisfaction that even the heavens had smiled down on what I had done.

I saw his eyes flutter open, and a thrill coursed through my entire core. Long had he lain motionless, but for the shallow rise and fall of his powerful chest, that I had begun to wonder if the rigors of the ordeal had rendered him insensate or simple. But when I first saw the trill of his

---

82   Later records indicate that some years after these currently documented events, Eduard encountered the scholar Vermundr Karl, who somehow managed to break the mystical bonds that connected Eduard's will to the duke. Eduard remained loosely in Karl's employ for many years afterwards, but that is a story for another time.

eyelashes, like the some breeze written upon the body, I knew all was not lost; rather the opposite, that all was just about to begin.

The eyes opened and it seemed to me they shone with radiance like starlight freed from the deepest vault of night. He was instantly alert; there was none of the grasping confusion that afflicts the normal human upon waking, the briefest of horrors as the mind tries to ascertain where it is, and in what condition it finds itself. At once, he knew who and what he was, and who had made him. I gazed upon him, as the sunlight of the new dawn cascaded in through the embrasure and picked out the runes and sigils carven onto his flesh, making him look like some finely-wrought tapestry, filigreed and lined in gold. I confess again that the myth of Adam came fully into my mind then, and had even the slightest doubt been allowed to enter me, it would have been utterly consumed in the obliterating fire of my own creative will.

He sat up, breaking his shackles and restraints as though they were ribbons of tulle. He stood, marveling at himself, rightly so, and then looked up at me, full knowledge in his eyes. At that moment, he was radiant as an angel, and I saw suddenly the generations of him that would come after, legions of the New Man, one succeeding another, overpowering the weak and taking dominion over the whole earth. I let him look upon me, confirmed in my greatness, near overcome with pride. And then he spoke, his voice clear and strong, powerful, a voice born to command. Where is my brother, he asked, where is Alexander?

I had not expected this to be his first concern, but I was resolved to be honest with him, and so I told him that the creature Alexander was safe, in another part of the lodge. He wished to see the creature, and though I was loathe to allow them the comfort of each other's company so soon after his emergence from the transformation, I could not deny him his first wish, and so I led him to the chamber where I kept the creature Alexander. I left them alone together, and I do not know what transpired between them.

Some hours later, I summoned Eduard to attend me, and over the course of the evening, I tested his new-made abilities. I made him lift and carry huge boulders, which he did with ease. I bade him climb the highest tower of the lodge with but his bare hands and no ropes to assist him, and he did so like the mountain lions that I have heard leap from crag to crag in the mighty Alps with a fearlessness that is nearly demonic. I subjected him to fires upon his flesh, and attempted to pierce him with blades, but it were as though the pricking of the knives was the merest tickle of a feather to him, for even as I sank the blade near a half-hand's span deep into him, he stirred not nor showed the least discomfort, let alone sign of pain. And even before my eyes, the wound I had just made slowly closed itself, the flesh knitted itself back together, and in a matter of some few moments, the skin was clean and unblemished as it had been before. I had wrought the greatest miracle in history.

Gradually, in the course of some weeks, I allowed Eduard the freedom of the estate. He would accompany me as I rode into the village to meet with the elders about their rents or crops, and always, though he stood well behind me and kept silent during these meetings, his presence was palpable, and I could feel the sense of apprehension and wonder in the small minds of the folk with whom I was dealing. On one or two occasions, I believe it was his domineering presence that persuaded a farmer to sell us his daughter or son.

The creature Alexander I had also allowed more freedom. Keeping it confined, I grew to see, was hindering its natural abilities as a hunter, and there was a slight but noticeable improvement in the quality of the extractions I was able to take from him when he had been unfettered than from when I had kept him in bondage. Soon, I granted it the privilege of hunting with Eduard in the forests of the estate, and whatever trepidation I had that first time I let them go was soon erased when some hours later; they both returned, the creature Alexander naked and slathered in the blood of some other beast, Eduard himself stripped to the waist and begrimed, his sword encrusted with dripping gore.

And so for months, they were my emissaries to the dark underworld of science. I sent them out countless times, into the villages and solitary farms of the surrounding area, either for their own sport, but more and more often to procure for me another subject, for I never ceased in my effort to perfect my science. There were times I even sent them into the larger towns and even into Warsaw once, to obtain for me sets of twins, because I was still convinced the insuperable tension therein was the key to unlocking the mysteries of control.

In the end, five pairs of twins came to the lodge by the end of that season. Hrothgar and several of my enhanced guards had built and expanded several of the quarters to accommodate this and future influx, and it was not long before I had each pair in my laboratory, probing and delving them, attempting to see how far that tension could be stretched, and then extracting from them the humors of their fear and basest emotion that boiled up in them during the process.

By this time, the Jew from Lodz, Solomon Wieckz, had arrived and was somewhat a fixture at the lodge.[83] He had arrived on his Sabbath, riding in a wagon driven by a gentile, who also unloaded and carted the many boxes the rabbi had brought with him. Standing upon the ceremony of his religion, he excused himself to the quarters I had allotted him, and I did not see him again until the following evening, when we made a proper welcome of each other.

---

83   Lodz at this time was barely more than a village, a far cry from the great city of learning and culture which it would become.

Immediately, the impression he made upon me was one of deep and profound learning, that he was a man for whom the scientific world was more home than the mundane one. In another phrase, a kindred spirit. In aspect, he was not as aged as may be supposed, although he was surely my elder. His hair was short and black, dusted with white, and the sidelocks that hung down his temples reminded me of gossamer. His beard was short, by the standards of his kind, and likewise streaked with white; it was apparent that he kept it combed. His eyes were a bright blue, and they were set in a face that, without the beard, I daresay would be most boyish, were he to have none of the lines of worry and care that come with age. Indeed, his very skin seemed to glow with life and health, as opposed to most of the elders I had seen in the villages, whose skin had the appearance to me of onion skin or brittle paper.

We sat across from each other before the fire, he breaking his fast on apples and bread and wine, while I made show of taking some little broth, as my need for sustenance had grown less and less as the years had gone by, some strange and welcome side-effect from my endless experiments upon my person. He had no stomach for the small talk and inane chatter that so characterize initial meetings, and so happily we set about discussing the subject to hand. I sketched for him some small portion of my accomplishments, less the creation of the New Man and the creature Alexander, of course. He was most interested, upon its mention, of the Diacodus, and I assured him I would give a demonstration of its powers.

He listened, seemingly riveted, as I recounted my many adventures throughout Europe and the Russian lands. I hinted at the political intrigues involving John of Luxembourg, but I sensed his mind was not schooled in contemporary affairs. At last, my inventory concluded and I sat back, content in myself, and I saw on this rabbi's face a settled expression of regard and respect. Then his eyes crinkled and a smile broke the lower half of his face, and he began to chuckle, a warm and delightful sound that seemed to swirl about the room like smoke and settle into the very fabric of my cloak.

He assured me that he was happy in his soul to be at Wiskitki with me, that he had hoped for many a long year to find such a place and such a man. He sighed and poured himself another draught of wine and drank it down, staring into the fire for a moment before he resumed. He told me then the story of his work and his learning, as captivating tale as any in the annals of science.

As a boy, he and his folk had lived in Gniezno, his father being the Court Jew to the Voivode of Gniezno. The Voivode was a small-minded Baltic called Szandomir who had been bought his position from the Polish King. Szandomir was profligate and wanton in his spending, being lavish to his cronies and intent upon setting up Gniezno as the great city of the Kingdom. Speaking as one who had visited that place, I can assure any who wonder that his efforts did not succeed. In any event, as Court Jew, the rabbi's father was master of the coin and therefore responsible for keeping the coffers full. Taxes were piled upon the populace, rents were driven up, all manner of quota were increased, with predictable results: the people grew furious and foment boiled in the streets.

The rabbi told me he vividly remembered the autumn of his seventh year, when the shop-folk and farmers of Gniezno took to the streets with torches and pitchforks, yelling and screaming in anger at the excess of the Voivode and his decadent administration. Szandomir had constructed for himself a stout keep in the heart of town, displacing as it happened in its building a large market, and it was in this keep that the boy and his family lived, as part of the Voivode's coterie. From the high casement in the family rooms, he recalled seeing the mass of thronging people below, roiling and battering themselves against the stone walls to no avail.

The Voivode at first was dismissive of the plight of his taxpayers, but as the protests grew more and more fierce and violent, he quickly grew fearful, for he was a man of little will and vision and knew only the harsh ways of control and none of the subtle. One evening, the raging mob managed to break through the heavy wooden gate of the keep and some small number of them stormed into the courtyard, setting fire to one of the stables before they were cut down by the guards. This was enough to send the Voivode into fits. The rabbi's father was summoned, and the entire family supposed he was to be sacrificed to appease the mod. They tearfully parted from him, never expecting to see him again. The rabbi's mother began to pack up their household and ready them to leave in the night.

But the father returned an hour later, his face ashen. He refused to divulge to the family what the Voivode had commanded him, but immediately locked himself in his office and did not come out for several days. Eventually, on the dawn of the fourth day, the boy was wakened roughly but his father's hand upon his shoulder; the man looked awful and strained, and he beckoned the boy to follow him with an almost-predatory gleam in his eye.

Into his father's office the boy went, and his father quickly bolted the door shut behind them. The boy looked around and saw the room, where he had never been allowed before, not to be filled with account books and ledgers as he had always supposed, but rather with retorts and phials and ancient bound tomes written in various mysterious alphabets. A strange furnace glowed in the corner of the room and a large cupboard stood with its doors open, exposing its contents like some immodest whore; it was filled to overflowing with what appeared to be pungent spices and hunks of oddly-glimmering stone.

The rabbi's father began to mutter, speaking quickly and insensibly, and for the first time the boy saw his father's eyes were wild and darting, rimmed in red and flecked with purple, his fingertips black. There were patches of dried and dead skin on the backs of his hands and on his cheeks. The boy grew suddenly terrified, and the father noticed the boy's fear and a smile spread wickedly across the weary face and he reached out and placed a hand on the boy's shoulder, a gesture meant to be reassuring but instead which only served to redouble the terror in the boy's heart.

The father retreated to his writing table, still muttering incoherently, searching for something in a pile of yellowed vellums. While his father was searching, the boy's mind turned to thoughts of escape, and although his heart pounded in his chest, pulsing with fear and confusion, he found he was rooted to where he stood, immobile as a statue. After a moment, the father found what he was looking for, and with a look of triumph on his ghoulish face, looked up at his son, the trembling boy transfixed before him.

Quicker than the blink of an eye, the father was there beside the son, grasping the boy's suddenly pliant hand in his own, turning it over palm-upward. Before the boy could even look down to see what was happening, he felt the hot sear of a knife across his palm. He flinched and tried to draw his hand back, but still he could not move, still had no control over his own system. He felt the warm flow of blood on his hand, felt the warm trickle of tears down his cheeks. His eyes sought out his father's, wonderingly, beseechingly, but the father's face was intently looking downward at the boy's hand. The boy suddenly began to tremble, and the father glanced up into the boy's eyes, and if the sight of his son's tears moved him at all, it was only toward more cold disregard.

Finally, the father let go the boy's hand, and a sudden coldness washed over the boy, as though a pail of ice water had been thrown upon him. He could move again, he could feel the throbbing hot pain in his hand. He looked down and saw the deep gash still weeping blood. He looked up again and saw his father wringing a blood-soaked linen over a crystal dish, his back to the boy. There was a sudden flash of light and then a horrible stink filled the room and his father let out a scream of anguish that broke the boy's heart, because somehow he knew it not as a scream of pain but of failure, and even at that age the boy knew there was no pain so visceral as that of not succeeding.

The boy turned and fled, unbolting the door with his bloody hand, sending another spasm of pain up his arm. Just as he flung the door open, his father grabbed him by the collar and dragged him back inside, slamming the door shut again. The boy fearfully looked into his father's face, but now gone was the mad glint of the eye and the sinister bend of the mouth. The father was his father again, and his eyes, red-rimmed still they were, now boiled with tears of sadness.

Pure blood, the father said softly. I needed pure, untainted blood. The father then explained, in defeated tone, how years ago he had promised the Voivode that he could transmute base metals into gold. He had spent years collecting the needed ingredients, constructing his furnace, consulting the most learned of men and conducting all manner of experiments, all so that he could fulfill his foolish promise to that decadent gentile. The final ingredient, he had been sure, was the blood of a virgin boy, and at this they both looked down at the gaping lips of the boy's wound. The father stood up, still speaking, and began to wrap the slash in strips of linen.

So I have failed, the father concluded. He went to the crystal dish, and picked from it a smoking hunk of what for all the world looked to the boy like shining gold. The father held it out to him, and although it smoked like a coal, when the father dropped it into his hand, it was cool like a mountain stream.

But surely this is gold, Father, the boy said. It shines and gleams just like it. The father shook his head. It cannot be melted down. It is impure. Somewhere, my method was wrong.

The boy, however, was seized by a vision of the fate which awaited his father, and by extension himself. Surely, he said aloud, it could fool the Voivode?

The father shook his head. I have failed.

In short, the father's failure was confessed and the Voivode, now desperate and maniacal in the face of ever-greater and more vociferous popular anger, unleashed a fury of punishment upon his Court Jew. The boy's mother had the foresight to escape the keep with the help of a guardsman in the night, and so the family was spared the sight of seeing their father flayed and burned alive. They fled across the Interior, the boy's sister dying en route of some illness the boy was sure his father could have cured with his science. Eventually, the mother and the boy came to Lodz, where they settled under a new name. The boy's mother soon married the local rabbi and the boy was schooled in the lore and knowledge of his people in a way that his own father had neglected. He became a rabbi in his own right and a scientist of profound ability, taking up the mantle of his father and carrying it vastly further than that unfortunate man ever been able.

As he grew older, he traveled Europe and the Palestine, seeking out ever-rarer and more esoteric tomes and secluded, isolated scientists in their hidden places. He had even traveled to far Hibernia to seek out the mystic who had written the fabled *An long a sheol na nealtai*.[84] His mind was voluminous, and he filled it with a vast knowledge of the hidden world, writing his own treatises and conducting his own experiments on his travels. But eventually, he returned home to Lodz, and devoted himself to the study of the *victoria vitae*, the victory of life; that is, the conquest of death, everlasting life—not in the abstract, philosophical sense of the Catholics, but in the true scientific sense.

He had brought with him crates and boxes filled with bound vellums of his own work and others. Decades of work and study were now available to me, as was the brilliant mind of this great scientist. Eagerly, I listened to his tale, but also with equal measure of expectation, wishing him to be done so that we could retire to the laboratory together and begin this final work.

It was some days before the rabbi and I finally set to work, and in that time, I devoted myself to the further study of the insuperable tension and to the furtherance to Eduard and the creature Alexander's abilities. They were now nearly inseparable. Every day they were out into the world roundabout, either as my emissaries to the village hetman, or on their own grisly business. Upon their return, they would dutifully present themselves to me and tell me of their exploits, what of note they had seen or encountered, and surrender to me anything they had procured. While they spoke, I subjected them to various inspections and withdrawings, ever seeking to perfect the formula I hoped would allow me to strengthen the bonds between them and myself, and perhaps also serve as some gateway toward the victory of life.

---

84 *An long a sheol na nealtai*, or The Ship That Sailed The Stars, is a mathematical and alchemical treatise written in the late 1280s by the Irish monk known to contemporary scholars as Brendan Saltbeard. According to legend, he was thrown into the sea as a heretic by the Archbishop of Dublin himself, only to wash ashore in Spain the next day where he lived for the next fifty-three years.

In the early autumn, I received word from Istvan that the creature Alexander's twin, called Petr, had been sighted in Venice during the summer, making inquiries regarding its brother. I began to wonder if there was a way to draw this other creature to me by using its connection to its twin. I developed over the course of several days an idea, and taking the creature Alexander alone into the laboratory, I probed its mind on the subject of its twin. I could see and sense the agony the mere mention of the brother's name caused the creature Alexander, and a thrill of power rushed through me, that I had now another sure way of controlling this beast.

Taking up a fine needle and setting it into a cold-wrought fire, the creature Alexander willingly let me etch onto its tongue the name of its twin; it was my suspicion that in this manner, I could draw the attention of the creature called Petr, using the mysterious bondship existing between twins, and even perhaps use this creature Alexander to control the twin, subjecting the creature Petr to my will over a long distance using its twin Alexander as the conduit.

In the nights, while the others were asleep, I pored over the volumes the rabbi had brought. Ancient learning was coupled with his own experiments and theories, and it were as though a candle had been suddenly lit in a dark room, for as I read, the more clear the grand concept became to me, and the more sure I was of how to accomplish this final victory.

Immediately I took up vellum and quill and began to sketch out the rudiments of my first steps of the phylactery. I was surprised to find that I had most of what could be termed the base ingredients, or the Foundation, for invariably in the works the phylactery was likened to a pyramid or pinnacle, where the overtopping layer could not be completed if the level below it were weak or incomplete.

One morning, the rabbi found me at my writing desk

and peered over my shoulder. He pointed to one of my calculations and pronounced it a different, yet also correct, version of the Elean Contrast.[85] Together, we worked out several equations and I discussed with him the Foundation I was contemplating. He offered some suggestions, although overall he thought my plan to be sound.

As promised, I showed him a demonstration of the Diacodus, which he was greatly amazed by. I watched him as he was transfixed by the dancing forms called up by the stone, watched him quail slightly as one of them exerted its will more powerfully than the others to raise itself up and present itself to him. It was not one of the spirits I knew from my many consultations, but it had the aspect of a beautiful girl in the flower of her maidenhood. The other spirits tried to claw their way up into clarity but this one's will was strong and the others remained as a swirling mass of blackish purple smoke at its feet. I wondered at what manner of question this rabbi would ask of the spirit, what possible answer he could be seeking, and although I tried to maintain a discretion that was seemly, I was alert to any sound that escaped his lips; I began to ponder on what methods I could develop that would allow me to see a man's thoughts, to open his mind as a book, as it were, and to read within, but I soon gave this up for truly I had enough to do.

The rabbi and the spirit stared at each other, the old man rapt, with something akin to lust in his eyes, the spirit merely pulsing and fluttering like a moth from its pedestal of writhing smoke. Then, amazingly, the rabbi turned away and the spirits blinked out of form into nothingness. I could see he was shaken by the experience, and so I fortified him with a strong draught of wine and to distract his mind, I turned the conversation to more technical matters

---

85 Elean Contrast, also known as Zeno's Arrow, is a now well-known experiment involving the subjectivity of time: the distance of the flight of an arrow can be continually halved to the point where the arrow seems to travel infinitely. Today, it is considered simple mathematics.

regarding the phylactery.

I had already decided upon the vessel, which contrary to what may be thought, is merely the first stone of the Foundation. And though all else is built upon or beside that first stone, it is not the first stone that is the strongest or more important part of the structure. Though it need not be so, the vessel I had chosen was a thing dear to me, a thing which I had poured much of myself into already. It seemed to me the perfect choice to carry my eternal being ever forward into the endless cycle of years, a perfect ship, if you will, to sail the stars.

For days and weeks, I devoted myself to preparing and perfecting the vessel, even to the point of neglecting my guest and even Eduard. Day and night, I was in the laboratory, the retorts percolating, smokes and steams rising from six different small furnaces, the Athanor itself stoked and fiery hot, a vast cornucopia of granules and salts and herbs and phials spread over nearly every surface of the room. With minute detail, I etched into the vessel the preparatory runes and sigils, even into its inmost heart, its hidden places.

I placed curses and wards upon it, calling down the ruin of fate upon any who attempted to destroy the vessel. I burned a mare's heart and ground the ash into the backbone of it to keep a constant strength to the protections. Into its tissues and onto its skin I worked oils of wormwood and tinctures of isinglass.[86] From a mud made from menstrual blood and ground lime, I painted its thin edges, thus imbuing it with the powers of the moon and the earth.

Eventually, and with heavy labor, the vessel was completed and ready to be built upon. Even by my own superhuman standards, I was exhausted, but I knew there

---

86 Oil of wormwood and tincture of isinglass are alchemical substances often used to seal or confine whatever spells have been placed upon an inanimate object.

was much more and harder work to be done in the future if I wanted the vessel to hold my eternal spirit. I was glad to have the assistance of the rabbi during this time.

While I worked upon the vessel and its subsequent layers in the next weeks and months, Eduard and the creature Alexander continued their works on my behalf. I was not as able to devote my full attentions to them as I had in the past, and so in consequence, they perhaps allowed themselves a greater degree of freedom in their wanderings and actions. From far and wide in the land, reports came to me of petty outrages against persons and property, and always the descriptions matched those of Eduard and the creature Alexander. Pride welled in me each time I heard one of these accounts of theft, abduction, and worse; Eduard, it seemed, had been totally purged of his former allegiance to the Catholic way of life.

At the lodge, I encouraged Eduard to breed as he saw fit with whichever of the female stock I had available. I longed to create from Eduard's seed a whole race of powerful humans, each a step above the current generation, that much closer to perfection. The temptation to create a New Woman to accompany Eduard through life was overwhelming at times, but none of the female subjects I had thus far attempted to uplift had survived even the basest levels of pain eradication. I despaired of ever breeding a true New Human, from New parents, but having Eduard's seed spread amongst my breeding stock of females was the only viable option, until such a worthy female could be found.

Additionally, the boy Lukasz was now of breeding age, and several attempts had been made to beget from him another and more impervious version of himself, scaled over like a dragon or with skin like iron. The females I entrusted to the task were not eager, for the boy was fearsome to behold, but after several attempts went awry and no babe was kindled, I began to wonder if the fault lay deep in the boy Lukasz's own being. At one point in my life, I would have devoted much energy and research to this problem, and delved into him deeply to ascertain the truth and solution of his malady, but I must confess I had little interest in doing so now, and I neglected the boy Lukasz after his final attempt at procreation. I left him to his devices, employing him mainly in the smithy, for his scaled skin insulated him from the fierce heat of the place.

Weeks stretched on into months; the year drew towards its close. There was peace in the land, thanks to the Elbow-High's victories. I threw myself into the work of the phylactery with all effort. Never had I focused so much energy on one task, not even the creation of the New Man. From all over Europe, reports reached me of various matters of interest, like twangs upon the tendrils of a spider's web, and I the spider in the center disregarded them all in favor of the greatest and last of all works. Letters came from Istvan, from Vermundr Karl, from other scholars and scientists I corresponded with. None of it mattered, nothing they could be telling me could possibly have any bearing on the future, at least my future, for their concerns were the mundane, the earthly, and I was now focused on but one thing: the conquering of time itself, the continuation of existence past its allotment.

I consulted various of the rabbi's texts, seeing in them the truth and where they had faltered. I had a focus and drive I had not possessed since I was a boy. I felt, more clearly than ever before, that I was embarked upon the sole work which I had been placed upon this earth to accomplish. For hours on end, I strove in the laboratory to create and blend the right admixtures, write and develop the strongest and most powerful spells and discern the greatest runes.

Every piece of matter I had collected over the years seemed to go into the process, even the rarities I had spent fortunes and blood upon. My fragment of the True Cross was consumed in a flash of green fire, merely one simple piece of a larger requirement. The pages of an illuminated Bible I had procured from a Lithuanian monastery solely because the shade of red the monks had used was derived from a now-extinct flower that grew on the hillside of Calvary was transformed into ashes which were then used to coat a silver thread which was used to close up the wound made in the neck of a cockerel following his first crow of the new moon, his blood collected and admixed with dozens of other, equally obscure and rare ingredients and then set into a copper basin and boiled down until the scrapings could then themselves be admixed with imperial jelly and then made into an ink whereupon a single rune would be inscribed upon the lower left quadrant of my right eyelid.[87]

It may be supposed by whomever may find themselves reading this in the future that my person presented a gruesome aspect, covered as it was near from crown to sole with runes and bindings, but perhaps I may be allowed here a small digression to say that such carvings and writings are invisible to the untrained eye. True, the rabbi and possibly Vermundr Karl would have been able to see some of them, but surely not all; to the layman, I would present an absolutely normal person, untainted and unblemished, a fine specimen in all ways.

The same could be said for Eduard, who generated looks of wonder and exclamations of marvel almost everywhere we went. He won men over with his solemn steadiness and willingness to help, his powers of endurance and his inhuman strength. He was the handsomest man I had ever beheld, and it was the rare woman who did not swoon in his presence. Power radiated from him like the light of a halo, and most who met him knew better than to show him

---

87 Imperial jelly is an archaic, even in the Duke's time, name for the secretions of the honeybee that contribute to the making of honey. Incredibly difficult to harvest, it was highly prized by alchemists due to the persistent belief that honeybees were immortal.

anything but respect.

Eduard and I, during this time, saw each other less and less frequently. I had, whenever I was not occupied with the phylactery, spent more of my attentions upon the creature Alexander, trying to ascertain the level of control I could exert over it via the use and manipulation of the memory of its twin. The problem was that I could only observe the creature Alexander's reaction to these manipulations; I had no idea whether they were affecting the creature Petr in any way, if at all, or if the creature Alexander's reactions were to something completely unrelated to its twin.

Now and then, though, Eduard and I ventured out on our own. On one such occasion, he left before dawn one November morning, for we had much distance to travel. Our intent was to reach the village of Wladsiasz, for I had heard from one of my informants that residing in that place was a young woman who had borne seven children in one labor. In retrospect, I realize that concerning myself with such a thing, little more than a curiosity and surely of little if any scientific value, was a waste of my valuable time, but in the moment, there seemed something so vital and necessary about seeing this girl that it overtook my mind and I became obsessed with the idea of breeding her and Eduard.

The journey was begun mostly in silence, for it seemed that whatever bond connected us was fraying by the day. I knew, of course, that Eduard was bound to me for eternity, but there was still between us a seeming gulf, a yawning emptiness that I did not know how to fill. The break the quiet, I asked him what he and the creature Alexander did of their own leisure, when they were not fulfilling the tasks I set them.

At first, he was cryptic in his answers, saying merely that they hunted or scouted. I pressed him, and eventually his conditioning overcame him and he told me all they had done. The creature Alexander, he told me, was growing restless. Often, it talked of spending more time out in the forests and away from the lodge. Always, Eduard assured me, he dissuaded the creature from spending any more time away from me and my ministrations than it already did, and always it seemed to calm and soothe the creature to hear such things. But, near every time they were out alone, on their own business, the creature Alexander assumed a far-off mien and would often become distracted, as though ready to spring into a bloody fury at the least sign of prey.

For the entire journey, we talked of the creature Alexander. Eduard expressed his worries that the creature was reverting to its former self, and I began to wonder what each of them had told the other of their former lives, how much each of them actually remembered. It is good of you, Master, Eduard told me, that you take the care of Alexander that you do. I cannot imagine what manner of monster he would be were he not in your control.

Eventually, we came to the village and a local boy led us to the home where the fecund mother lived with her brood. She was a girl, perhaps sixteen, slight of frame to the point that it seemed that carrying seven babes, much less birthing them, would have been far too much strain for her. Her husband was there too, a boy of her own age, and obviously proud of his prowess. She showed off her babes, each a hale and healthy bundle of arms and legs and bellies and eyes and mouths and grasping fists. With adoration, she listed off their names one by one, which I promptly discarded from the vault of my mind. They were awkward country folk, doubly so in the presence of a noble, but they carried themselves appreciably and even managed to offer what hospitality they could muster.

My mind half-wandered, and it was all I could do to keep from ordering Eduard to throw the girl onto the table and take her, but I knew his method would kill or damage her for future use. I wondered why I was there, what purpose was being served by my being surrounded by mewling mouths and the scent of at least three foul sets of smallclothes. Suddenly, in the midst the boy-father's recounting of some tale relating to the birthing, I stood and set upon the table a small sack of gold coins, congratulating them and taking my leave. A great constriction had come upon me and I was seized by a sudden need to be quit of that place.

Eduard followed, asking after me. I waved him off and suddenly vomited onto the ground. A panic struck me, and I lashed out at Eduard, striking him hard across the face in my anger and confusion. He was caught off-guard and stumbled slightly sideways. I stalked to my horse, mounted and rode off back to the lodge.

He rode behind me for many miles, finally coming abreast of me about halfway home. We did not speak for the entire journey; I was still shocked by what had happened and why. I had not been gripped by such panic and fear in ages. At the lodge, I bathed in scalding water, for a chill had come over me as I rode through the gates that set my teeth chattering to break from my jaw. Pageboys poured bucket after bucket of boiling water over me, and still I shivered. My skin turned a deep red.

I wallowed in the hot water for a very long time; I must have gone into a trance, for I suddenly looked about me and it seemed that some long hours had past. The candles had burned down quite low and the water no longer steamed and bubbled. Wearily I stood, gazing down at myself. I looked no different, but now felt a stiffness in my joints as I walked to my quarters. I summoned the rabbi and he came and queried me.

Slowly, a smile spread over his face. I knew then what had happened, and a smile came to my lips as well, for like the moth whose time has come, the cocoon has outlived its usefulness. The shell was ready to be discarded. In a moment I was on my feet, calling for Eduard and rushing up to the laboratory.

The rabbi and Eduard stood watching as I flew about the large room, unlocking hidden drawers, pulling up flagstones, digging out the most treasured and secret tools I had acquired or built over the decades. On a sheet of silver, I lay them all out, gleaming in their virginity, for none of them had been used before. I took up the vessel and lay it down on the slab, bidding Eduard to wrap my left hand with an iron chain, my left ankle with a silver chain, my right ankle with a gold chain, and to leave my right hand unadorned. The rabbi stood to one side, watching on wide-eyed in amazement as this great task began.

No doubt had lodged itself in my heart once the process had begun. The confidence I had was unmatched as I settled my fingertips upon the vessel and felt the cool tingle move up my arms and spread from my shoulders inward to meet over my heart. My voice was uttering the beginnings of the incant, but my mind was already elsewhere, already ensconced in the far-future that I would now exist to see, to experience, and possibly to control.

All around me swirled clouds of light and sound; distantly I heard glass breaking, the waves of the sea and the cries of seabirds, a crashing of thunder. I shut my eyes tightly and it were as though they remained wide open, for I looked about me and saw that I stood upon the ivory face of the moon, starry heaven over me, and far below the planets. At my feet I saw a flower opening into bloom and I bent to pick it up, and as my fingers closed around the stem, I found myself back in the laboratory, Eduard behind me, his arms wrapped tightly around me, a long silver knife in my right hand, molten gold dripping from its blade and a gash down my body from throat to navel.

Eduard pulled backward upon my arms, and my body seemed to open. A rush of cold air entered me and I was instantly more alert and alive than I had ever felt before.

I felt Eduard's strength, inhuman and vast as an ocean. I could hear his heart pounding, or perhaps it was my own, and it filled the room and made the glasswares jump off the tables onto the floor. Suddenly, I felt surrounded, as though by thick fabric or even earth. My eyes swam with color and tears poured down my face. I could hear my own voice, as though from miles away, calling out in strange languages. Lightning crashed far off, or perhaps right overhead.

Again Eduard gave a great heave and, further open, my body tore, and then from deep within I felt a stirring, as though some small fire had been built of my animalcules, or that they had coalesced into a fist-sized, rapidly-revolving sphere that burned hot and then cold and then suddenly I felt a hand reach inside me and grip this sphere and begin to pull it out. I began to protest, but from deep within me a silence boiled up and drowned out my thought, and whatever was now moving through me like some inexorable comet continued on its orbit and exploded out of me and I made no sound and had no thought other than, Eternity.

And suddenly, my eyes came open and I saw myself in Eduard's arms, strain on his face, holding me up as my body bent over the slab and the vessel, light and tendrils of energy spewing from my mouth and my chest onto the slab, being soaked up into the vessel. Everything moved very, very slowly, but I, outside of my body, was able to move at normal speed and so I went about the room and viewed the scene from every angle, as though examining some long-frozen insect slowly thawed to life. As I neared Eduard, I could hear his thoughts in my head, his pleas to me and to his old god, his own self-confidence which I knew I had created within him.

Everything was alive in the moment; I saw the animalcules of the stone and the glass and the knife swirling and dancing, compressed into their forms, and understood the patterns they made in their movements. I saw in the air the countless infinity of atoms and particles, heard the music they made as they traveled and caromed off each other, the beautiful and inimitable music of creation which no man had ever heard. I looked down and saw my own constituent atoms and particles, their interplay and reaction, and saw etched in the air the intricate paths they made in their miniscule revolutions. I was fully aware of all creation in that moment, a moment which stretched forever and was yet over before I could blink my eye.

I was aware of the rabbi and instantly I was within his mind, his body. I could control him if I desired. I saw myself through his eyes, experienced the wonder and fear that he did as he watched my soul, my spirit being drawn from my body into the vessel. His years of theory and experimentation had come to this, and I knew as I rested inside his brain, inside his own soul, that he would never experience the like of this again, that his life was now a failure, that he could not be allowed to exist further and let others know this secret, and so with a thought I ended him.

Instantly, I was into Eduard's mind. I loved him in that instant, as a son and a self. I knew I could not exceed him in my creations, that he was the perfect man, the ultimate. And so fear of him consumed me in the flash of a moment. He was an invincible man and I hated the fear that he had inspired. The tendrils of my own self dug down into the caverns of his mind and strangled the passageways that led to memories of this moment, of his actions here in this room, of his part in this transformation of me from man into the transcendent. I longed to devour more of his mind, to consume all of him that existed before me, but a sensation crashed into me like an arrow as I tried to wrap my tendrils around more of his memory, and it threw me back into a solitude of sight and sound and weightlessness.

And finally, after a fraction of a second that lasted a century, I was back within my own self. I gasped, feeling the strong grip of Eduard around me. Cold racked me, but I felt utterly cleansed, pure as the thought of Science itself.

Behind me, Eduard collapsed. I remained standing, my body slicked with sweat, sheening gold. I gazed down at the vessel, which looked no different to me than it had before; if anything it looked more unremarkable than ever, a simple thing that could be overlooked by anyone. I took it up in my hands and instantly felt a warmth against me, an intimacy that I can only assume would be called love.

The rabbi was dead, slumped in the corner of the room. Eduard was unconscious at my feet. I felt both alive and expansive, as though my whole being could encompass the globe. I hid the vessel under the flagstone beneath the casement and with ease hefted Eduard in my arms and carried him to his quarters. A sense of unreality, or rather, dis-reality, settled over me. I seemed to hear the very seams of the world straining against the untrammeled power beneath it. Every moment seemed to stretch out vastly, an Ancient Day for every minute.

As time went on, I felt I was in two or more places at the same time, a sensation I found thrilling and powerful. I often had the feeling, when I closed my eyes, of soaring high over the land, seeing even my own lodge beneath me and all the patchwork farms spread out at its foot, the spires of far-off cities reaching up to me and the immense plain of continents stretching forever onward. But each time I came back to myself, and each time I was more and more sure of my victory.

Gradually, I settled myself to the lowly tasks of my earthly works. Eduard seemed disgruntled and weary now, and nothing I could do would lighten his spirit. The creature Alexander I ordered chained up again, recalling Eduard's confession. Whereas before, an anger would have taken me over, instead now a clinical detachment lay upon me as I drove the creature Alexander into new depths of pain and torment to extract from him the needed fluids which would keep Eduard compliant and vigorous.

At length, however, the creature Alexander proved an imperfect subject. The creature's capacity for withstanding such depredations was not as impressive as had been previously assumed. For years, I had taken the creature to heights of agony and mental anguish, seeking ever higher thresholds that could then be shattered, in order to milk it, as it were, of its precious humors. But there was, in fact, a breaking point, and when it was reached, I grew disgusted with the creature. It howled for my mercy before it died, and I had its corpse burned in the courtyard forthwith, hoping against hope that there was still some small life left in it that could suffer through those final flames.

I believe it was this that caused the next calamity of my life. Eduard disappeared. He and the creature Alexander had been parted for some small time, the creature being re-imprisoned and Eduard forbidden to have contact with it. I do not know if my valiant Knight knew of the creature's death, but it was only a matter of days afterward that he disappeared.

I had sent for him one evening, for I wished a report from him; he was training many of the lodge-bred young men to be soldiers in my enhanced army. I waited for over an hour, growing more and more irate at his delay. Finally, I sent a pageboy to hunt him down, and when the boy returned some time later to say that Eduard was gone, I flew into a rage that sent the pageboy's skull and several pewter flagons crashing into the wall.

All night I stormed and raged. With a flick of my wrist, the east tower of the lodge collapsed into a pile of bloody rubble. A few screamed words and the river erupted into fire. I traced in the air powerful sigils and thrust them out and away, a wake of leveling destruction that felled giant timbers and uprooted boulders.

I spent myself in anger, collapsing finally onto my knees, feeling an emptiness that surprised and enraged me even further, but I had no desire left in my heart for ruin. At least, not then.

Months past. I wrote desperate letters to my informers all over Europe, describing Eduard, demanding to know if they had seen him. For long hours, I would close my eyes, and that sensation of flight would overtake me, and I would will myself to fly over all Europe, hunting for him, but always it was the same: the sky over Wiskitki, the rest of the world spreading outward.

Many times, I tried to re-create the New Man, with subjects taken from my enhanced guard or from the breeding stables. All were failures, none had the capacity Eduard had had for the eradication of pain. Soon, I grew to inflict pain for its own sake, rather than for any scientific purpose, and it was in this way that I proceeded to winnow the population of Wiskitki to a fraction of what it had been at its height. I felt no remorse at this waste of life, whereas before I would have attempted some scientific justification for what I was doing.

I burned the rabbi's books and most of my own experimental notes. More and more, I indulged in fantasies of burning Wiskitki to the ground. But one morning, I happened to look out and see Lukasz crossing the courtyard. It was a cold winter day, but he was working in the smithy and so was bare to the waist. I saw his scales, grey and magisterial to me in that winter light. He was a strong young man now, from his work, and as he had grown, so had his scales grown to cover some portions of his body where they had not been at birth. He seemed to me in that moment a victory. I had laid aside all that I had accomplished when Eduard left me, to wallow in a pit of presumed failures. But as I looked out on Lukasz, walking across the courtyard, a light seemed to kindle in my heart again, and I pushed forever out of mind the notion of leaving Wiskitki, of losing another moment to doubt and hopelessness.

I took Lukasz into a sort of apprenticeship, teaching him some of the rudiments of science; he was a slow learner and exceptionally frustrating to instruct, and finally I had to let myself be content with allowing him control of the breeding program.

Time went on, and my work took on a new importance. I renewed my work on the treatise that would etch my name in the annals of history, and perfected my theories on the Planes of Anima, that made up our existence. From time to time, I would go to the laboratory and pull up the flagstone and take the vessel out, gaze at it for some moments before opening it up again and adding just a bit more of myself to it, then close it reverently and place it back under its stone where it would never be found.

Rumors began to come to me, from Bavaria, Vienna, Zurich. I discounted them at first, seeing in them more attempts by the agents of my damned cousin John to draw me out into assassination. But they came and more frequently, and each time they told of a powerful man in the remnants of a Knight's robes, hiding in the shadows of Munich, of Regensburg, of Linz, the clink of a money purse following him into the dark.

He was broken. Well, no matter. I could fix him, if only he would come home. More letters I sent, couching my terms. I wanted him back, I told them. He was ill and I could cure him, I wrote. Send him back to me, I urged.

I waited, and I still wait. What part of me is it that seems to feel him coming closer? Not the soul, surely, for that is locked away beneath the flagstones of my laboratory. What, then? What part of the human mind, or the heart for that matter, is it that senses the approach of another to whom one is bound? Perhaps, in all my years of experimentation and all my mastery of science, I had unwittingly created some new organ of the self, an invisible tendon that links two beings through all space and time, that no matter the sundering influences of circumstance, always will they be tied together, always will they find one another, always will the emptiness in the one call out to the emptiness in the other so that in some small way, the echo of that emptiness can fill the void of the other and so lessen the emptiness therein.

After all, what is science but the impetus that can set a thing in motion, a thing that cannot be stopped?

[pages unavailable][88]

---

88 While it is impossible to be certain of order, by our estimation, there appear to be at least five or six additional entries attached to the journal after this point (though these are omitted in the Latin copy). However, our translator, upon sending this last chapter, stopped all communications with us without explanation, and efforts to locate him have proven difficult. At this time it is not known where the originals are, or even if they still exist. Our contact with the Belgian police described the translator's apartment when they entered it as foul smelling, filled with low-slung furniture and disturbing objects, and every surface scrawled over with strange runes and patterns. Efforts to find another translator have proven fruitless as well, as of the few out there who have a competency in medieval Polish, all who have looked over our scanned copies of the remaining chapters have told us they contain nothing but gibberish. – Publisher's Note

Jeffrey Welker is a carbon-based life form who hates most things and lives begrudgingly in Seattle. This is his first novel in print, and definitely not his last.